STEPHANIE BURKE

KEEPER OF THE Flame

ELLORA'S CAVE
ROMANTICA PUBLISHING

What the critics are saying...

❧

"KEEPER OF THE FLAME is a neat book. Though we don't see the culture he comes from, Flame is a refreshing hero[...] The heroine is black and hero white, so KEEPER OF THE FLAME is an interracial romance, but it's never a problem or issue, just a fact. KEEPER is a fun story that promises at least two equally enjoyable sequels." ~ *The Best Reviews*

An Ellora's Cave Romantica Publication

www.ellorascave.com

Keeper of the Flame

ISBN 9781419955204
ALL RIGHTS RESERVED.
Keeper of the Flame Copyright © 2001 Stephanie Burke
Cover art by Syneca.

This book printed in the U.S.A. by Jasmine–Jade Enterprises, LLC

Trade paperback Publication June 2007

Content Advisory:

S – ENSUOUS
E – ROTIC
X – TREME

Ellora's Cave Publishing offers three levels of Romantica™ reading entertainment: S (S-ensuous), E (E-rotic), and X (X-treme).

The following material contains graphic sexual content meant for mature readers. This story has been rated E–rotic.

S-*ensuous* love scenes are explicit and leave nothing to the imagination.

E-*rotic* love scenes are explicit, leave nothing to the imagination, and are high in volume per the overall word count. E-rated titles might contain material that some readers find objectionable — in other words, almost anything goes, sexually. E-rated titles are the most graphic titles we carry in terms of both sexual language and descriptiveness in these works of literature.

X-*treme* titles differ from E-rated titles only in plot premise and storyline execution. Stories designated with the letter X tend to contain difficult or controversial subject matter not for the faint of heart.

Also by Stephanie Burke

ॐ

About the Author

ജ

Stephanie is married to the most wonderfully maddening Irish Viking ever created and has given birth to two children, affectionately known as The Viking kittens. Stephanie's main support in her writing career has been her wonderful parents who are always willing to take her spawns, uh, children for a weekend so that she can work, her older sister Teresa, the stuffed chicken, and of course, her Irish Viking, Dennis. Stephanie loves to write paranormal and fantasy characters with a lot of humor, because there is no such thing as enough laughter in the world. She also loves to write erotica, just to shock people, but in her heart she is a romance fanatic...

Stephanie welcomes comments from readers. You can find her website and email address on her author bio page at www.ellorascave.com.

Tell Us What You Think

We appreciate hearing reader opinions about our books. You can email us at Comments@EllorasCave.com.

KEEPER OF THE FLAME

Flickering, sensuously dancing, weaving it's mystery,
The candle flame grows higher, the light expands.
But the fire grows, writes it's own history.
Makes the tormented soul into a blaze, clear demands.

It seeks to conquer the frigid ice, the fragile crystal.
But cannot overcome, only co-exist.
The glow of the light reflects, ever mystical,
How can one soul, one heart, resist.

The frozen tundra, the glacial floes,
Desperate to eat away at the land.
Just as doubt, hate, suspicion grows,
Before love makes it's final, ultimate stand.

Fire and Ice, heat and freeze the blood in their veins,
Love will vanquish them, make their energies merge.
Within the heart, true love forever reigns,
Between two souls, one spirit will emerge.

On the edge of forever, what choice will they make,
They burn for each other, yet what is the price?
But winter comes forth, their spirits to take.
Together, though, the love will suffice.

Bound together in the eternal dance,
The frost quenches, the passionate inferno subsides.
But the torch of lust will capture romance,
The heat of love is where the dream resides.

- *Katherine Schlem*

Chapter One

ഇ

"Damn that man anyway!" Kendall muttered as she walked out of the swinging doors of Johns Hopkins Hospital. At this hour the parking lot was empty, but the sound of the nearby traffic told her the drive home would be difficult. The wet asphalt gleamed in the glow cast by the streetlights. The square empty black parking pads looked as dead as she felt inside.

The treacherous Dr. Richard Tanner was absent, thank God. That, at least, made her day a little brighter. She had tried so hard to keep a smile on her face, but it had been difficult when all she wanted was to go home and hide. As far as she was concerned, she had no family left to help her grieve. Her sister was probably catting around with the good doctor right at this minute.

"Damn him! Damn them, and damn me!" Kendall slammed open the door to her silver minivan and threw herself into the driver's seat. She sat there looking out at the bright yellow lines on the parking spaces as tears slowly tracked down her face.

"Damn me for caring." She wiped her eyes with the heels of her hands, then pushed the key into the ignition. After pulling an eighteen-hour shift on what was supposed to have been the eve of her honeymoon all she wanted was a little peace.

The radio began to croon nauseatingly sweet lyrics of undying love. "Damn love songs, too," Kendall muttered as she reached out to switch the station, but changed her mind. The irony was too good to pass up, even if it was at her expense. Maneuvering her car on to her street, Kendall sang along.

She threw up a her middle finger in an uncommon fit of bad temper when she looked up and noticed lights flickering on the waters of the lake behind her house. Late night boaters, no doubt, out having a good time, while Kendall's life crumbled around her. They were probably drinking and dancing, enjoying a nighttime cruise filled with all kinds of joy and laughter.

"Damn them for being happy!" Kendall whipped her van into her driveway. Her irrational anger faded into a deep aching sadness when she remembered the plans that she'd had for many a romantic tryst on that very lake. How different her current reality was when compared to her fantasies.

"A shower," Kendall murmured to herself. "No, a long hot bath for this old girl." Absently rubbing the tension from the back of her neck, Kendall popped open the mini-van's door and wearily headed for the house.

Thanks to last winter's blizzard, she'd been kept running all day. The combination of four-foot high snowdrifts and stranded couples always made for crowded delivery rooms nine months later. It was just a quirk of fate that the nine-month span ended around the time her wedding was to have taken place.

The most difficult part of the day had been dealing with the pitying looks and uncertain comments from her friends. What could you say to someone whose heart had been ripped out and tossed away like so many used rubber gloves in an ER?

She had smiled at all of her well-wishers and reminded them that at least she was getting an all-expenses-paid-for vacation this week, courtesy of the good doctor.

She had tried to laugh and joke, but the pain had gotten harder and harder to hide. And now it was almost unbearable. Tomorrow was the start of her vacation and new life, but the night was still her demon, her monster to face and to fist into submission.

"I'll deal with the world tomorrow!" she decided, a little spark of the old Go-get-'em-Kendall shining through her misery. "Tonight I get loaded!" She did have rum in the house, right? Maybe a bottle left over from when her sister flew in to help her celebrate her engagement. She would have to overlook the irony of drinking her sister's liquor to help her revel in the joy of her single state. Yeah.

With new determination, she hopped to the ground and gave a small nod to her property. All these double shifts were worth it as long as she could still afford to keep her own house.

The brick-faced split-level was barely within her price range. With careful budgeting, though, she would be able to keep up the mortgage payments alone. As an added bonus, Richard had no claim on it! She had bought it just after finding out the truth about her fiancée and was proud to say that no memories of him tainted her beloved sanctuary.

Her front yard always made her smile and tonight was no exception. In the warm, humid air of the late summer night she could smell the roses that grew in abundance around the perimeter of her yard. She had painstakingly planted and nurtured each one like a child and all of her efforts were paying off. Her flowerbeds were fully stocked. Gladiolas, Impatiens and colorful decorative grass surrounded the house like a vibrant, living welcome mat. The garden glowed softly in the illumination provided by her porch lights. Even the delicate white MoonFlowers she had planted beside her front door gave off an enticing aroma that teased and pleased her senses.

She paused in the perusal of her organic masterpiece of a front yard when she spied a pile of garbage near her front porch. Her eyes flared in sudden anger before narrowing into small brown slits. "Damn the person who left that there!" she declared. She gave a small snort of laughter. At the rate she was damning people, the word would soon lose all meaning. "I need to find some better swears!"

Muttering under her breath about overpriced community association fees and cheap, ineffective security, she stalked over to the pile of refuse. After all her hard work creating a horticulture showcase, she would be damned before she let a litterbug destroy her near perfect view.

She never expected the garbage to move.

With a shriek, Kendall fumbled for the pepper spray in her pocket. Hands trembling, she held her weapon before her. When the pile showed no other signs of life, her heart rate returned to normal. She inched closer to the dark pile and carefully nudged it over with the toe of her nursing shoe. Again she jumped back, barely controlling another shriek of fright.

It was a man.

A big man in obvious pain.

He groaned as a wave of pain flashed over his features. "Help me!" he managed, desperation washing over his face.

In the face of his unmistakable distress, Kendall's medical training kicked in. In a flash, the pepper spray was replaced with her house keys and she was squatting to help the man struggle to his feet. It wasn't easy. He was lying in a fetal position, his back to her as he strained to hold his head up and speak. Kendall placed her hands on his quivering shoulders only to pull back at the cold wetness. He moaned and she rushed to brush the wet hair from his face in an effort to calm him down. Dropping to her knees, she to eased her hands beneath his arms.

Muscles straining and screaming in protest, Kendall managed to pull the man the few feet to her porch, grunting and breathing heavily with the effort.

"Come on! Help me here!"

He must've been dumped by one of those boats, she reasoned. Maybe there had been an accident and he had managed to make it this far for help. Many scenarios quickly flashed through her brain as she helped support the man. Maybe after he'd been dumped he had managed to swim to safety.

The man's slow nod brought her back to the situation at hand. He braced himself and tried to force his body upwards. Working together, they managed to get him upright. Then they attempted a few shaky steps towards the front door. Struggling for each step, they made their way to the front door.

Once there, he released a tortured moan when his body tightened and began to spasm in her arms. "Come on," she urged, "you can do this!" She added a bit of command in her voice as she tried desperately to hold him upright long enough to get the key in the lock. His legs tightened, taking some of the burden of his weight, freeing up her arm for more movement.

"Shh," she crooned while searching for the right key, sighing in relief as it slid into the lock.

The key turned slowly and the tumblers clicked loudly, but finally the door slammed open under the weight of the man. Kendall ignored the noise and urged him into her hallway. They both let out a sigh of relief.

But there were still more obstacles ahead of them, mainly the couch. It seemed a million miles away across the room. And the man's wet clothes would have to come off. He was starting to shiver in the air-conditioned hall.

"To the couch!" was her war cry and together they nearly ran the last few feet before his legs collapsed beneath him. Like a doll, he lay there, as if it were too much of an effort to right himself.

"Are you okay?" she questioned in her best nurse's voice, dropping to her knees in front of him.

"My babies…"

Babies? She hadn't seen anyone else out there. Had there been an accident? Were there other people hurt? "Where?" she demanded. "Where are they?"

He groaned, closing his eyes in pain. "I am in labor."

"Labor?" Oh, no! He's escaped from a loony bin, she thought. Why do I get all of the nut jobs?

Before she could say anything else or check for a bump on the head, he pulled aside a long coat to reveal his extended abdominal cavity.

Shocked by what had to be an extreme case of peritonitis or some type of internal hemorrhaging, Kendall jumped to her feet and eased his legs up on the couch. Before she could run to call 911, he gripped her hand, his face twisted in agony. His back arched almost off of the couch and he sucked in and held his breath.

In front of her disbelieving eyes, his stomach tightened in what appeared to be an actual contraction. It lasted nearly a full minute before he began to relax and start to breathe again.

"Please, Mistress, help me!" he panted. "I am about to deliver!"

Kendall looked into the grayest eyes that she had ever seen — eyes that were now filled with anxiety and pain. Her rich brown coffee-au-lait skin paled as she read both truth and sincerity there, and not a drop of madness.

Swallowing hard, Kendall nodded. She believed him. She actually believed him. She was going to help deliver this man's child.

"There are some things I need first." She managed to force the words past her suddenly tight throat as she stared bug-eyed at the miracle man before her. "Just remember to breathe with the pain and try not to fight against it."

He closed his eyes and seemed to relax a bit as he ran a trembling hand through his long wet hair.

She turned and raced to the second floor, mentally reciting the list of things needed for a home birth. Breathing hard, she grabbed sheets from her linen closet along with a few clean, white towels fresh from the laundry. From the bathroom, she pulled her first-aid kit from beneath the sink before rushing back downstairs to the man lying on her couch.

"My name is Kendall Moore. I'll try to make you a bit more comfortable." She repeated her litany in her best bedside voice. Never before had she delivered this speech to a man, but there was a first time for everything. This was certainly the first time that she had seen a man in this condition.

She began to strip the man of his clothing. "Remember to rest during the contractions and pant when the pain gets bad." First came a sopping wet pair of black leather-like ankle boots. Then, with his help, she removed the long, many-pocketed black trench coat. It made a thumping sound as she dropped it to the floor.

After a pause to help him breath through another contraction, she slid his shirt, also in black, over his head, carefully untangling it from the long rope of his wet hair. She reached for the fasteners at his waist, but stopped short.

"How do I get these things off?" Kendall had to wait as another contraction stiffened his body. The pants were made of some long, flowing material, but seemed to have no visible zippers or buttons.

Finally the painful grip of the contraction passed. "The zip cords are on the sides." This contraction had lasted longer and now his body was covered in a thin film of sweat.

Sure enough, there were two tabs at the waist of his pants. With a few pulls, they separated down the sides to his ankles and she rolled the material away.

Kendall covered him with a sheet. She took no time to be embarrassed, she really didn't want to see just what he had been hiding beneath his clothes, did she? He was handsome enough, and he looked like he had a great body, but... Really, how could a man conceive a child without a little—odd—equipment?

She had no time to follow that line of thought. A small opening began to appear just beneath his navel. "Holy…" Her eyes widened as the opening grew. He moaned in pain, but he followed her directions and panted as best he could.

"This won't hurt." Kendall opened a bottle of peroxide and dumped it over his stomach, blotting the excess with a towel. The shock caused the man to jerk his head back in her direction, eyes wide in a near-panic at this liquid cold, though he voiced no complaint.

She knelt beside him when he was disinfected to her satisfaction, wiping his damp forehead with one of the towels. The rules had to be different when a man gave birth. "What am I supposed to do now?" There was no birth canal, for starters.

"Just catch them." He groaned as another contraction shook him. He was pale with pain and damp with sweat.

"Catch them. Right." He must mean from that tiny opening on his stomach. Now how would that work? Kendall stared in shocked silence as his abdomen spread open and a small head crowned. The man bit back a cry of pain.

"My God!" she cried excitedly. "Push or do what you just did again!" He raised his knees slightly and grunted with effort. They were rewarded when a small heap of humanity pushed its head through the abdominal opening. Quickly Kendall moved in to clean the child's airway, gratified to hear a small wail.

"Do it again!" she cheered as the sound of new life filled the room.

"What the hell do you think I am trying to do!" he growled at her. But then he seemed to gather control over himself as he began to strain again. With his hands clutching the arm of the couch above, tendons straining in his neck, he prepared to deliver his baby into her hands.

Eyes closed tight and jaw clenched, he threw back his head and groaned like a wounded animal. The growl exploded into a cry of both pain and relief as the opening widened and the baby was expelled from its warm cocoon.

Kendall ignored his outburst as the small child slowly slid from his body.

"It's a boy!" she cried as she laid the small body on his father's chest. She turned to her first aid kit, retrieved a package of surgical thread, and tied off the cord in two places. With a grin, she cut in the center of her bindings, freeing the child to breathe on his own.

She flushed brightly with success. Bringing a new life into the world always touched a place within her. Her smile faded as another spasm of pain crossed the man's face.

"What's wrong? Don't you dare die and leave me with this child!"

"It is the other child, Mistress," he gasped.

The pouch was opening again and another dark head was crowning. Pushing the first child higher on his chest, Kendall made ready to catch the next one. Within moments, the second child emerged from his body, crying in complaint at being thrust into its cold new world.

"It's a girl." Kendall spoke softly as the man closed his eyes in exhaustion. He seemed to sigh with relief.

For the first time, Kendall actually looked at the man. Even while in pain, his accent had sounded almost similar to a Russian doctor she had once had the pleasure of working with. His voice sounded Russian with a French lilt and the slow delivery of an Italian playboy.

The features of his face were strong—high cheekbones, a straight nose, and a stubborn chin seemed to scream that he was a mixture of cultures, but it was his crowning glory that caught and held her attention. His hair, even wet, was a most startling and unusual shade of red.

Kendall let her eyes roam from his exhausted face to the crying children he held lovingly on his chest. "What's your name?"

"Flame. My name is Flame."

Kendall let her hand linger on the baby boy. "Get some sleep now, Flame. You're going to need your strength. Your children are safe here for now."

"Yes Mistress." The lines bracketing his lips fading as the tension eased slowly from around his bruised-looking eyes. His face eased into a peaceful countenance as sleep overcame him.

* * * * *

The afterbirth came out in a neat little ball under Kendall's expert manipulation. With gentle fingers she massaged where his fundis would be if he had been a woman. The tiny placenta was expelled through the birth...slit.

Kendall tossed it and the sheet that covered him into a red hazardous waste bag that she had brought home from the hospital. They were the perfect size and color for her guest bathroom. That bag she hid in a thick dark contractor bag that she used to clean up garden waste, then the whole bundle went neatly into the garbage can out back. As bloodstained as it was, the sheet was a total loss, and as for the rest, well, it had served its purpose. No need to have any messy reminders around the house. If his doctor wanted a peek at it, he could go out back and dig it out himself.

Since the children had grown quiet, Kendall washed them and placed them in dresser drawers she had lined with pillows and a few sheets. She even sacrificed a few more of her sheets so that she could diaper the tired, red-faced babies. Then she did what she could for the new *mom*.

He had begun to shake uncontrollably, his teeth chattering as his body was wracked with chills. Kendall placed a hand upon his brow, noting with some relief that there was no developing fever. It just wouldn't do to have him come down with childbirth-fever after this miraculous delivery. Most women did this after giving birth though no one knew just exactly why. Kendall noted his condition and vowed to keep an eye on him. There was nothing else that she could do. Using warm water and a mild soap, she began to clean him up as best as she could.

He was made like any other man—a trifle on the large side, but normal. The slit that opened in his belly, his birthing pouch, had closed up tight, and the seam line was lost in the line of red hair that arrowed down from his navel. She couldn't tell that it had ever existed. His stomach was flat as a board. Women should be so lucky!

Shaking her head in awe, Kendall covered the sleeping man and went to make herself a pot of coffee. Her mind still struggled to accept the fact that she had just acted the part of midwife for a man.

* * * * *

As Flame drifted in a light but exhausted sleep, his frightened mind urged him to rise and flee from the house of this strange woman and take his children to safety. But his body refused to cooperate.

And then too, he had felt almost safe as soon as Kendall had decided to aid him. He had never thought to feel this way, especially the presence of a woman.

But that was dangerous. Kendall could behave like the very women he was running from. The best thing for all would be for him to gather his strength and depart at once. Unfortunately, his body was failing him.

The warm water that she used to cleanse his sore body combined with the natural fatigue of child birth all helped cause his thoughts to spin chaotically before the relief of deep sleep finally overrode all else.

* * * * *

Flame jumped, sucking in a deep breath as Kendall shook his shoulder. "Hey, wake up!" a soft voice commanded.

Flame fought to open his eyes and was almost frightened by the strange hazy vision before him. He blinked several times. Slowly his sleep clouded vision cleared to see the woman, Kendall, rocking his daughter in her arms.

The woman's skin was the golden brown color of the finest Tarcas stones on his planet and her eyes were of a color to match—very expressive, very beautiful, and very rare.

"What am I supposed to feed these babies?" she asked. "They have to eat."

"How am I supposed to know?" What did a man know of the care and feeding of a child? His duty was to bear them. His mind reeled in a shock so strong that it erased every ounce of sleep in his body. He was so very ill-prepared for this aspect of fatherhood. Would his children suffer for his ignorance? What was he to do? "What do you feed your children?"

"I don't have any children and if I did, I would breast-feed."

Surprised, he struggled to sit up, despite his sore stomach. "Breast-feed? Breasts do that?" He eyed her bust with avid curiosity and quite a bit of wonder.

Kendall stared at the man. She tried to reason through his responses, only winding up more confused. "Okay. Where do you come from? Who can I call to get you some help?"

Panic shot through him. "Call no one. I will leave you shortly. I thank you for your assistance, but I must go."

"I don't think so!" Her stomach clenched into a knot of anxiety as she pictured him with these newborn babies, collapsing in the street. And even worse, what if he planned on abandoning the children here, with her? "You are going to give me some answers, mister!"

Flame froze and dropped his gaze to the floor. "As you wish, Mistress Kendall Moore."

Kendall blinked at his quick change from worried, harried father to almost subservience. Had she done that? Who was he, and what was going on here? "Look, Flame. I only want to help you. Where are you from? Why were you pregnant? Where is the fathe…uh, mother of these children?"

While there had been incredible advances in medicine and her hospital had always been a leader in research and development, nothing about a pregnant man had ever popped up on the gossip mill. Maybe a government experiment? But then, the government would have killed him before letting a prized specimen like this escape and possibly end up in the hands of an enemy.

Victim of radiation? Nope, no loss of hair, glowing blood, missing teeth or any lesions that might tell if he was radioactive.

Then it hit her. The lights on the water, a pregnant man, a pouch that had disappeared as if it had never existed moments after giving birth! There could only be one explanation. She gaped at him. "You're an alien, aren't you?"

He raised his head and she saw defiant silver sparkles flashing in his eyes. He wouldn't melt the woman who had delivered his kids, would he?

Then the defiance was gone, and the sparkles faded from his eyes, leaving her wondering if she had imagined them there. "I seem to have need of your assistance once again, Mistress."

"Kendall. Call me Kendall." She gathered her courage again as she looked at the child she cradled in her arms. "Where in the universe are you from?"

"Two-hundred light years from your sun. I left my world looking for a safe haven, but I fear they have found me."

"Who?" Was this man some type of intergalactic space criminal?

"The Execution Squad. With my mistress dead, there is no longer a use for her children."

"What?" Kendall shrieked, the outburst startling his daughter in that shocking, jerky way that all newborns have.

"I will explain." He raised his arms for his crying daughter. Looking her over with liquid swimming in his gray eyes, he placed the infant on his shoulder where she instantly quieted.

Kendall was speechless. Execution Squads were way out of her jurisdiction, but then so were pregnant men. She shook her head ruefully. All of those "damns" she'd spat like gunfire had finally come back to haunt her. She looked up and saw that he was waiting for her attention. Once he saw he had it, he began to speak.

"On my world, Testrious, the women rule. The men had been captured and forced to labor for the women long before I came to be. Our role is worker, child-bearer and protector. We have no control over our lives. We work because our bodies are built for it. We bear children because the Matriarch decided that men would bear up better under the strain. Some of us were herded up and given the *honor* of being altered. They said that we should be proud of this because we were special." He snorted derisively at this reasoning.

"I was chosen because of my hair. It is considered special on my world. Usually, I would have served as a member of the Brotherhood, but the woman who wanted me was head of one of the five ruling houses. My *family*"—the word sounded ugly on his lips—"decided to make an alliance. So, I was sold to increase my mother's power. I was taken to my new life-mate and impregnated." He paused for a moment and a tortured expression crossed his face.

"In the beginning, there were five original ruling houses, and then my Mistress died. After scanning revealed that I carried a boy child, my mother claimed my Mistress's house and then there were four ruling houses on Testrious. Later I discovered the girl hiding behind her brother." He smiled at the irony of a male protecting a female even before birth. "I knew I had to escape. By their own laws, the laws of the Matriarch, my daughter would be my Mistress' heir. My family did not want to give up the properties and power that came with my mating."

"I discovered their plans shortly after someone, a spy no doubt, told of my secret. So I ran. The Execution Squad will kill me and my children when they find me. They managed to track me to this planet and this area. I evaded them for now, but they will find me. They are ruthless."

He turned to her, his voice urgent. "I must leave soon or they will find me here and then you also will be in danger. I tell you this, Mistress, because you have ordered me to do so. You must be on guard at all times. Tell no one you have seen me. I will disappear from your life."

Stunned, Kendall stared at the picture the father and child made sitting wrapped in sheets on her floral print couch. "Where will you go?"

"I do not know."

Before Kendall could gather her wits enough to respond to him, the second baby began to cry. Reacting to the distressed cry, Kendall reached for the child. "Before we do anything, they ought to be fed and named." Her voice was rather shaky, and she cleared her throat several times before turning to Flame.

"Ember. Her name is Ember. And his is Spark."

"I detect a theme here," Kendall mused, though inside, her mind was blown away by his words.

He looked up as he answered. "My family are known as Keepers of the Flame. It is a talent that we of the red hair possess."

Shrugging, Kendall rose to her feet and made her way to her immaculate country-style kitchen. What did little fire-keeping babies eat anyway? Ever practical, she decided it was easier to cope with the children's needs than to try and deal with his story, especially when the proof was wailing in her arms.

"Ah, Flame?" she called over her shoulder. "We need to feed these children. What do the women at home use? Think!"

"I do not know," he replied with a worried frown. Spark had now joined Ember and together they continued to wail, almost in harmony.

Kendall eyed her counters full of useful gadgets, but found none to aid in her quest. Finally, she opened a cabinet and spotted salvation. It came in the form of a few starter soy formula kits that she had gotten from work for a friend. At the last minute, her friend had decided to nurse, so Kendall had no use for the kits, yet was reluctant to throw out food that was still good. She had never had to prepare formula for her work, but after quickly reading the instructions, Kendall soon had two bottles ready for the children. She made her way back to the living room and handed Flame one of the little four-ounce bottles before seating herself on a chair.

"Food goes in here," she instructed as she carefully placed the square tip of the bottle into Spark's mouth. Instantly, his cries stopped as he latched on to the latex nipple.

"It's feeding time, Papa." She nodded to Ember's open mouth. "Remember to support her head, neck, and back."

Flame quickly caught on to this method of feeding his daughter. She immediately quieted down to the serious business of eating. Flame looked amazed as his daughter savaged the latex nipple the kit had provided. "And your women voluntarily do this to their breasts?" he asked as if only a fool would put themselves through this torture.

Unable to help it, Kendall burst out laughing. It did seem a little masochistic but nature had intended the ultimate usage of breasts as feedbags. She motioned Flame to hold Ember's head a bit higher while Spark just as violently consumed his first meal. Soon both babies were full, content and blessedly asleep.

Kendall rose from where she had placed a sleeping Spark in his makeshift bed, then sat beside Flame. "I want you to come with me on my trip, Flame." When he started to protest, she cut him off. She couldn't in all good conscience send them off to die in a strange place, all alone.

"You have no idea what you are going to do next. You're very weak and your children are too young for you to start wandering around lost and alone. If the Execution Squad is still after you, you need a guide. I had planned to leave the area anyway. I was going off to the mountains tomorrow for a vacation."

There was so much at stake here. She paused for a minute and stared into his eyes trying to convey her feelings to him. She needed him to understand the importance of her decision. "I want you to come with me. It'll be much safer than hiding here and you can have some time to decide your next move. But you need to get away if they can track you to here."

Flame considered her words. She was a woman, but still, she had delivered his babies, his new reasons for existence. He looked at his children, safe, fed and content. He would sacrifice anything to keep them that way. He had never loved anything more than the two babies sleeping in their makeshift beds. If the woman would help him he would give her his very soul. "I would be grateful to you for any help, Mistress."

"Kendall. Call me Kendall."

All too soon he would have to face the dawn and the problems that it brought with the new day. Flame closed his eyes and let sleep overtake him. For now, at least, he and his children were safe.

* * * * *

Kendall stood by her bedroom window and contemplated the stars. There were people living out there! Real people with real problems and real lives. People so similar to mankind here on Earth, yet so different.

She turned slowly, making her way to the canopied bed, thinking about the joys and sorrows experienced by this other culture. It was almost too farfetched to believe, but it was true. She looked around the sanctuary of her bedroom and wondered what Flame's people would make of it. Her bedroom, a contrast to her dogmatic nature, was an Arabian paradise. The sheer white canopy that draped her black iron bed was reminiscent of the tents used by great Bedouin warriors as they wandered the mysterious deserts of their homeland. The walls were painted a pale peach color that picked up the sun's rays in the early morning and transformed the room into a glowing desert landscape.

Other than the bed, the only pieces of furniture were a cedar chest at its end and a full-sized standing mirror draped with dozens of colorful scarves. As she lay there in the midst of all that was feminine, she thought on everything that Flame had revealed.

A whole planet ruled by women. Men giving birth. The power to soar through time and space. *What marvels they could teach my people,* she thought with excitement, estimating the possibilities.

As she drifted off into a deep slumber, the soft sound of her door opening caused her eyes to pop open.

"Flame?" she asked as she struggled to sit up. "Is something wrong? Is it one of the children?"

"No Mistress." His wonderfully deep voice almost purred as he stepped into the room.

"What's wrong? You shouldn't be out of bed!"

"I have yet to thank you properly, Mistress. This is a grave offense."

"You thanked me once, Flame. That is enough." Kendall sighed as she relaxed back into her bedsheets. "You really scared me."

"I wish only to please you." He stepped further into the room, leaving the shadows that hid his form and Kendall caught her breath at his beauty.

"Oh my!"

Flame was totally naked.

The moonlight toyed with the shadows, all that alternately covered and revealed him as he walked towards her.

His bright red hair draped across his shoulders and framed the massive chest that heaved with his deep even breaths.

His eyes glittered, the bright red sparks growing in intensity as he approached the edge of the bed. His stiff cock glistened in the darkness, clear drops of pre-cum on its tip shining as it brushed against his navel.

"For you pleasure, Mistress," he purred as he ran his large hands over his well defined chest to his thighs, then jerked the covers away from her nude body. "All for your pleasure."

Before she could protest, Flame was between her legs, forcing them open so that he could explore her suddenly wet womanhood.

"Wait!"

But before she could protest further, one large rough finger was running across her rapidly swelling clit as his face tilted up to hers, an expression of extreme pleasure crossed his handsome face.

"Flame!" She gasped as she tossed her head back, groaning out her passion as she fought to stay somewhat upright. She wanted to watch what was going on.

"I thank thee, Mistress," he breathed as his fingers parted her wet slick folds to expose her engorged pink opening. "And I take thee."

"Flame!" she groaned as she shuddered with need.

She was one to enjoy sexual contact, but this was amazing. The man but touched her and she was wet and ready to go. Fire coursed through her body, teasing her nerves as she peaked up and saw him lower that fiery red head towards her.

First his breath touched her, hot and damp, grazed against the moisture that was pouring from her body. Then there was the lightest brush of his tongue, as if he were testing for flavor.

Finally, with a sigh of pleasure, Flame settled his mouth against her and began to feast in earnest. Kendall shrieked as he lashed at her, invaded her feminine space, exciting her senses as her back arched off of the bed. With a skill that she had never thought passable, Flame inserted his tongue into her, laving at her inner walls.

Kendall's hands reached down to grab at his head, to hold his hair, to find a center in the vortex of swirling heat and desire that he sent her plummeting through, but the touch of his hair almost seared her with its power.

She reached another level of lust as this new sensation poured over her, though her, inside of her. She wailed as he began to nibble tenderly on the petals of her feminine lips, lapping up her moisture as if she were spun candy and growling his pleasure as he went back for more.

One stiff finger began to penetrate as his lips latched onto her clit, gently but firmly holding it captive in the hot cave of his mouth. His finger speared her, filling an emptiness that had begun to grow within her, making her long for more.

"Yes!" she breathed as he writhed on the bed, lost in total ecstasy. "More!"

Another finger joined the first, stretching her, preparing her for his possession, the lubrication her body gushed with easing his way. Just as she thought she could take no more, be begun to hum as he pressed his tongue against her captive clitoris.

It flowed upon her! Her muscles clenched, her body strained and began to quiver from deep within. She felt her emotions spiral out of control, fighting for release. Her inner walls tightened as the tension increased until it snapped.

"Yes! Flame, yes!" she roared, her inner walls clenched rhythmically, her release poured over her in waves....

Then she jerked up in bed.

Breathing harshly, she ran a shaky hand through her tangled hair as she eased out of the dream state, her muscles still quivering from the primal release that her dream forced upon her.

"Oh Lord," she panted as she eased back to the bed, struggling to regulate her breathing and return to the sleep state.

Still wondering about her mysterious visitor, she realized that it had been a long time since she reacted that way with any man, let alone the stranger who had just given birth on her new couch!

"I need to sleep!"

That said, her mind filed that fantasy away for future personal use and closed her eyes, forcing herself to calm. Having Flame around might be a good thing!

She fell asleep with visions of stars and rockets planted in her head. She scarcely remembered that tomorrow should have been her wedding day, or that the man with whom she'd be sharing the day or her fantasies with was not Richard.

Chapter Two

ဢ

Dressing in a pair of her favorite jeans and a pastel-colored T-shirt, Kendall drew her hair back into a bun and raced downstairs barefoot. She thought of all the wonderful things she could introduce Flame to as soon as the house was clean.

Said house was empty, though, and the mystery man had disappeared. Even the dresser drawers that had provided temporary cribs for the babies were out of sight. There was absolutely no evidence that someone had given birth or taken up residence in her home.

"Did I dream it all?"

She stood in the doorway of her living room. It looked just as she had left it before leaving for work yesterday. Even her couch was spotless, the flowers reminding her of her beautiful garden out front.

There was a knock at her door. Thinking it was Flame, Kendall raced to open it, only to slam it closed again. A large shoe stopped the door from closing, but the loud curse uttered as the door crushed on that foot made her smirk.

Her curses had indeed doubled back on her. The good doctor, the bane of her existence and the bringer of pain, was standing trapped by one foot on her doorstep.

"Open up, Kendall!" his low voice growled from the opposite side of the door.

"What do you want, Dick?" she fairly screamed at him, knowing he hated the dreaded nickname. With renewed effort, she put her back into her foot-breaking efforts.

"To talk. You owe me that."

What did that fool just open his mouth and say? Infuriated, she stopped trying to smash his foot and let the door swing open.

"I owe you? I owe you, you bastard! After what you did?"

"I thought that...that I could handle your little problem Kendall, but I was wrong," he stammered. "I still want to be your friend."

Kendall eyed him from the tip of his hand-made loafers to the top of his perfectly-styled head and fought to hold back her tears. "My little problem didn't seem to matter when you were climbing into my bed at every opportunity, *friend*," she growled. "In fact, my little problem seemed to make you hotter than a dog in heat in the middle of July, if I recall correctly."

He blushed to the roots of his blond hair. "That was rather crudely put," he managed, looking down at the sleeve of his blue suit. He couldn't meet her direct gaze.

"And how was I supposed to put it, Doctor?" she asked, fighting to keep her voice from cracking. "It was rather crude, what you did to me."

Raking his hands through his hair, he turned away, muttering under his breath.

"Do you want absolution, Doctor?" she asked quietly, her eyes filled with menace and her voice strained to keep her anger from boiling over. "Okay. I absolve you of all guilt. Go! You're free! Do as you please!" She made shooing motions with her hands before trying once again to slam the door.

"Damn it, Kendall!" he roared, turning and grabbing her by the arms. "Let me try and explain!"

"You would do well to release her," a new voice interrupted. "Now!"

They turned to see Flame standing behind them with his burnt auburn hair flowing around his stern visage. Richard was so startled, he dropped his hold on Kendall and took an involuntary step back.

Flame stalked towards Kendall, the force of his anger a physical thing. Tension fairly crackled in the air as his anger manifested itself in the piercing gaze of his eyes.

"Who is this?" Richard demanded trying to gather his wits about himself. "What's he doing in your house?"

"Has he caused you any harm, Mistress?" Flame's piercing gray eyes took in the measure of the good doctor and obviously found him wanting.

Shocked by Richard's outburst, Kendall was even more stupefied by Flame's appearance. He was dressed in all black, from the form-fitting leather pants to the long trench coat that fell to his booted feet. Flame looked intimidatingly male at about six feet seven. He managed to make Doctor Richard Tanner look small, washed-out, and insignificant. The brilliance of Flame's person appeared to dim the bright sun shining through her open door.

"No," Kendall managed after a deep breath. "Richard was just leaving." She owed Doctor Dick no explanations.

"Kendall," Richard started only to be abruptly cut off.

"Go tell it to my sister. She's probably waiting for you now." Kendall closed the door on his stricken face and turned toward Flame.

"So, we need to get car seats for the babies and some necessities before we leave. The trip takes about six hours and we need to head out soon." Kendall brushed back a bit of hair that had come lose from the bun at her nape and began to make mental lists as if nothing had happened. In true Kendall fashion, she plowed straight ahead when confronted with a problem she refused to face.

Flame looked at the door she'd slammed shut behind her. "Who was he, Mistress?"

"He was nothing. A mistake from my past."

"On Testrios, no man would ever shout in anger at a woman or dare to touch her without her permission."

34

But Kendall wasn't listening. She had begun to shake in earnest. Her mind needed an outlet, a way to reduce the tension that was eating her alive. Her release came, but it shook her whole body with its discharge.

"May I hold you, Mistress? You need comforting."

Kendall looked into his deep gray eyes and lost all control.

Flame's mind flashed back to his childhood lessons on the proper way to hold and comfort the woman to whom he was given. "A touch is a powerful thing, my son," his father intoned, pointing to the spectacle taking place before them.

On a pedestal bed, a man and a woman, both naked, lay in the aftermath of erotic splendor. The woman, breath still sobbing in relief, sprawled against her male. But Flame noticed the man's hands, caressing her back, easing her breathing, soothing her in a way that a father would soothe his son after punishment or injury.

As he recalled these memories, he found his hands making the same gentling gestures that he had seen after almost every lesson in sexual propriety.

After a few moments of wild sobbing, Kendall realized she was sitting on the floor of her hallway with Flame. He was holding her in his strong embrace and humming in a soothing monotone. The brightly lit hallway showed where her tears had dampened his black shirt.

"I'm sorry," she gasped, pulling back from the warm comfort of his arms. She ground the heels of her palms into her eyes and whispered, "I didn't mean to do that."

"Tension must be released, Mistress. Were you on Testrios, I would be required to take you to Vaporbath and work the tension from your muscles. You should never be allowed to redden your eyes with tears."

Kendall smiled at this wonderfully sensitive man. How many guys would sit on a hard floor in a cramped hall while a virtual stranger sobbed out her problems on his chest? Then she remembered the word he'd used. *Required.*

Sitting up she looked at him closely. "You said required. You didn't have a choice?"

The sun highlighted features suddenly cast in sadness and another indefinable emotion as he answered. "I am but a man, Mistress." The tenderness left his eyes.

"But you could say no? Right?"

"I had a choice." He released her, rising with amazing grace considering his sheer size and bulk of muscle. "But then I would suffer the consequences for making of the wrong choice."

Kendall was horrified. Never would she have believed that type of blackmail would exist on such an advanced world. When she thought of a planet ruled by women, she thought of a peaceful place where freedom would be encouraged. Then she recalled the Execution Squad and the implication that his own family would murder his children.

"We have to get you out of here," she declared, springing to her feet. She would deal with her own problems later. Right now, she had to help these people. "Can they track your ship?" Kendall peered cautiously through one of the windows designed into her front door.

Flame looked puzzled for a moment, then gave a negative shake of his head. "I sank my ship in your lake. They can only estimate my trajectory from the course I programmed into my navigational program. I knew they'd located me when their computer downloaded the information. I compromised that information before they could determine my exact location, but they have a general idea of where I am hiding. They cannot scan under water for my ship. I was salvaging necessary equipment when the man, your past mistake, arrived and began to treat you disrespectfully."

He'd sunk his ship. That explained the lights she'd seen while driving home. "Where are the children?" Now that she knew they had some time, she calmed a little. She had yet to hear the children and with all that yelling, the noise would have awakened anyone.

"They are safe," he replied warmly as he led her to the kitchen.

In there, two small clear boxes floated about three feet in the air, emitting a low humming sound. Inside were the children, safe and content. Sunlight lent a warm glow to the room, its reflections cast through a bank of windows that overlooked the lake behind her house.

"What are those?" Kendall gasped in awe at the devices that cradled the sleeping children.

"Education cubes. They soothe and teach." He looked proud of himself standing in her kitchen overlooking Spark and Ember. Both children sported bright fuzzy red hair and strongly resembled their father, or at least they looked like he did when he slept.

"Teach?" She walked over to touch one and smiled at the low vibration she felt under her hand. The children seemed content, each dressed in an odd sac-like gown and lying on their sides with their knees drawn up to their chests.

"They are learning Testrios as well as Earth languages subliminally."

"Testrios?" Her tongue stumbled over the unusual word as she turned to face him.

"My home world. It's the only spoken language."

"The only language?" She felt a bit like a parrot, repeating everything he said. "There is only one language spoken on your whole planet?"

Smiling, he nodded, his loose hair sliding over his shoulders and catching fire where it was kissed by the sun.

"The Founding Mothers felt that it would breed harmony if everyone spoke the same language. The five ruling houses met and decided on the universal language. All others were outlawed and soon forgotten."

"All five continents agreed to this?" She was incredulous. All of that history lost! She sat at her small wooden table and gestured for him to do the same.

"Tell me more." Then she added, "Wait! Five continents, five houses. Is each continent ruled by a single house?"

"It is so." He smiled at her grasp of the rules that governed his home planet. "The House of Sky, The House of Land, The House of Wind, The House of Ice, and The House of Fire. The Five Supreme Matriarchs rule the planet, though, officially there are only four houses left. My mother now controls the House Of Fire and The House Of Ice."

"You're a flippin' prince!" Kendall realized with some awe as she looked at the humble man who sat in her kitchen. He was royalty, yet he obviously loved his children enough to give it all up to save them. Then again, on his planet he was still little more than a slave.

"Yes, Mistress. On your world I would be considered thus." He lowered his eyes in humble acceptance of the title that was so hollow on his planet.

Eyes rounded in wonder, Kendall murmured absently, "Call me Kendall. Your Highness."

* * * * *

People stopped to stare at the spectacle making its way through the Baby Boutique. Not often did the eclectic group of women see a man, let alone a man wearing a double harness, dragging a reluctant woman through the baby powder-scented aisles with the enthusiasm of a three-year-old.

Kendall groaned as Flame spotted yet another baby innovation in the next aisle. They should have been on the road an hour ago, but big daddy of the year had to see what new wonders this Earth had produced in the field of childcare.

"What is cir-cum-cis-ion?" he questioned as he quickly scanned the latest pop baby-how-to manual he picked up from a nearby display. On the cover was a photo of the newest guru to hit the baby circuit. He probably didn't even have children, she thought as she watched Flame quickly scan through the book.

"They remove the foreskin from the penis of a newborn."

A pregnant woman who paused in desperately scanning the book section turned to stare at his odd question. "English is his second language?" Kendall offered as an explanation.

"Ahh. We have a similar procedure, but it is done before the chosen male is given to life-mate with his mistress. It assures pureness in the male, to keep the skin in place until then. The women of Testrios find an uncut manhood repugnant."

Kendall blanched. "This was done to you?"

Flame nodded, unconcerned, as if adult circumcisions were an everyday occurrence.

"I hope they gave you a good anesthesia," Kendall grimaced.

"No. It is a test of strength to assure proper masculinity in the man. He is not to cry out. It only hurts for a brief time," Flame added when he saw the shock on her face.

"Are you planning on...you know...with Spark?" In the short time since she delivered the babies she, well, had become attached to the little guys. She didn't want her solemn-faced little Spark to have to endure that. She peered over Flame's shoulder as if to reassure herself that Spark was okay.

"Oh no. He is legal citizen now. I read in your laws that once a child is born here, he is allowed to stay here. He is an American now like his sister and will be like other Americans. He will be cir-cum-cized," Flame pronounced the word slowly, "when he is ready."

Kendall shook her head at yet another Testrios oddity and they were legion. Flame had to dress in black as befits a mated man and he had to wear the long coat to hide his form. It wouldn't do to have a lady ogle another's property. He had to wear his hair loose to proclaim him altered and fertile. He had to carry both babies to show his reverence for life and his willingness to die in the protecting of them. The list went on and on.

All of the women in the store thought that she was the luckiest of wives. They assumed that he carried both children, one on each side of his broad chest, to give the new mommy a rest. One woman went as far to say that not all men would take such an interest in newborn babies. Flame just beamed like the proud papa he was.

"What wondrous things are these?" Flame asked as they rounded another corner and he spotted a display of children's clothing. Kendall could only smile as Flame's gray eyes lit up at a sight of tiny sailor suits and dresses.

"Kendall!" he cried in awe at the vibrant colors and intricate embroidery. "We must have one of each color for each of them."

She pushed their already overflowing cart beside him. "Take it easy on the old charge card, daddy. I only have so much money in the bank to spend."

"American currency?" he asked with one raised eyebrow. At her nod, he opened a small pocket on his coat to reveal a wad of hundred dollar bills. Her mouth dropped open as he added, "I also have a bank account, a driver's license and a social security card."

"Put it away!" she hissed at him as she glanced around to see if anyone was listening. "How did you manage to get all of that!"

He gave her a small frown. "People of your planet are not considered very intelligent."

Her face immediately bloomed with color.

"It was a simple matter for me to manipulate your computers to my advantage. I have the technology to do so at any given time. To make up for the loss, I deposited a significant amount of gold into your depository. Gold is a useless metal on my planet and we have great quantities of it strewn across the landscape, but the people here place great value upon it. I have dumped a load of it in your reserves."

"Well." She got out through her gritted teeth; "Thanks for explaining that to an idiot like me!"

"I did not mean you, Mistress." He smiled widely. "You seem to be most intelligent. You are a credit to you planet."

"Well thank you very much, Mister Supreme Being!" she said with a saccharine sweetness. "Now let's get a move on before your advanced race of executioners catch up with you!

"They will search in a hundred mile radius of where they will assume I have landed," he acknowledged, becoming serious once again. "You are right, Mistress. We cannot tarry here longer. Let us finish and leave."

After a small argument in the check out aisle, Flame paid in cash all the while reminding her that he did not want to be a burden. She grumbled while she installed two-top-of-the-line car seats in the back seat of her minivan. These were designed with a stationary base that separated from the seats so that they could be used as carriers.

Flame had held both children in their harnesses when they began their shopping trip. Kendall had driven slowly and prayed that no cop would stop them. It was a five hundred dollar fine to be caught transporting children without a proper car seat and she didn't know what Flame's reaction would be to the flashing lights and sirens of a police car.

While Flame stored their purchases, Kendall placed both the children into their new safety seats. The babies quickly settled in their new conveyance and they were quickly on their way back to Kendall's place to pick-up the rest of their gear.

In addition to buying what seemed to be a year's supply of diapers and formula, Kendall had persuaded Flame to purchase some shirts for himself in something other than the somber black. He relented and bought a few "scandalously colored" T-shirts and jeans all the while insisting that bright colors were for younger men.

As they made their way back home, Flame seemed a little listless and pale. Kendall noted his pallor and made a mental note to keep tabs on him. Anyone going through the stress of labor should be resting, not out shopping as if nothing had happened to him or her. The body needed a recovery period in order to heal properly and Kendall decided that Flame was going to get all the rest that he needed.

Packing the van was easy once they made it back to Kendall's house. Kendall already had her luggage packed for her aborted honeymoon trip and Flame stuffed his new purchases in a black duffel bag he'd salvaged along with the learning cubes and his necessary equipment from the ship. He'd been soaking wet when she found him because he took no time to sink the ship from land. Her spaceman slammed the thing into the lake and swam to shore. He'd gone back early in the morning to retrieve the things he felt he needed.

Kendall took one last look at her beautifully landscaped yard and started the engine. She tried to shake off the feeling that her life would never be the same after this trip, but the premonition remained. "How long before they start to search this area, Flame?"

"I came into your airspace cloaked from your radar by slipping through a small time window your government left open. I can camouflage the ship from sight, but your government would pick up the fuel trails my ship left behind. It will be several days before that window opens again and those who follow me will want to wait for that time." His low voice was almost pained and he looked at her with tired eyes.

"No fraternizing with the lowly earth peons then?" Kendall tried to make a small joke to cover her concern about Flame's condition.

"I do not think your government would take kindly to an invasion, Mistress."

Remembering all those specials about alien dissection, Kendall tended to agree with him. They no sooner pulled to the end of her driveway, than a car screeched to a halt in front of them. "Oh for crying out loud!" Kendall got out before Richard slammed out of his car and raced to the driver side door.

"Kendall, I need to speak with you!" he cried, oblivious to her passengers.

"I've said all that I'm going to say to you Doctor Dick!" Kendall growled at the man. He had a flare for the dramatic. With his Nordic good looks, he should have pursued a career in acting instead of going to medical school. His ice-blue eyes pleaded with hers.

"Where are you going? We need to try and work something out. There are factors…"

"Do you wish him eliminated, Mistress Kendall?" this came calmly from the passenger side. "This I can easily accomplish."

"What?" Richard turned just as Flame sat forward and glared at him. His hair was starting to do that breezy thing again and his eyes were beginning to sparkle. All traces of weakness seemed to have been obliterated by the annoyance that seemed to radiate from him in waves.

"This has nothing to do with you, buddy!" Richard turned again to Kendall. "Who is this clown anyway?"

Torn between righteous anger and frustration, Kendall made a swift decision. "Doctor Dick, meet my new, ahh, boyfriend Flame. Flame…ah…MacIntire."

Both men turned incredulous looks on her.

"When exactly did this happen, Kendall?" Richard asked.

"Not that it's any of you business, but we met a few weeks ago."

Flame raised one red eyebrow, but his hair did seem to be settling down a bit. His expression seemed to say, "At your discretion, Mistress."

With a nod for emphasis, she added, "Now you are holding us up!"

"Where did you come from?" Richard growled at Flame, ignoring Kendall altogether. His face was set in a stern doctor's mask as he demanded answers.

Anger tightened Flame's face. How dare this low-caste male address him in such a manner? He might be a mere male, but he was royal born!

Flame did not mind the untruth that his guide told for he could sense that she wanted to help him and his children, but disrespect by a man to even the lowest woman was not to be tolerated. Even though he hated the society that spawned him, its rules were too ingrained to let such importance go without major repercussions.

"Where I come from is no concern for a past mistake such as you!" Flame spoke in a low controlled voice that was more frightening than the mightiest of roars. "You would do well to tender your responses respectfully when answering my mistress, small man, or you will have need of me to correct your unseemly behavior!"

With some shock, Kendall realized that Flame was about to do something…alien…to her ex if she didn't step in right away. "Let us go Richard!" she cried out. "You have no reason to be concerned with my life anymore! You made that abundantly clear when I caught you… Just let us go!"

"This isn't over." Richard stated as he backed away to his car. "We need to talk Kendall. I can't let it end like this. There are things that you need to know!"

With the slam of a car door and an angry squeal of tires, the good doctor once again left them.

Kendall turned to Flame. "We had better get out of here before anything else happens." With a tired sigh he nodded, hair once again in place. "Damn those curses!" Kendall muttered before starting up the engine again and easing out onto the small street.

Blissfully, the children remained asleep.

Chapter Three

❧

"Now I know why I don't work in the nursery!"

After about two hours on the road, the children began to get antsy. First Ember started with a light alto causing her brother to add his harmony and soon they were both wailing in time to the music playing on the radio. Appropriately enough, Pasty Cline was singing that she was crazy.

"I can relate!" Kendall muttered as she spotted salvation up ahead. A wonderful blue sign read *Rest Stop Ahead*. With an overwhelming sense of relief, Kendall pulled over at the nearby rest stop to feed and diaper the children.

Flame had been quiet thus far into the trip.

At first he gasped at every oncoming vehicle on the road, so much that Kendall had to question his offer to drive. She watched as his eyes grew larger. A semi sped past going in the opposite direction.

"Cars are not going to hit us, Flame. They are supposed to keep up with the flow of traffic. It's only going about sixty miles per hour."

Although his face remained expressionless and pale, he managed to nod politely before once again checking his safety belt.

"I know what I'm doing, Flame. I won't get us in get in an accident." She blew out an exasperated breath as she watched him tug at the belt.

"Do you think you can do any better?" she questioned. "You are so shaken by this light traffic that you would probably wrap us around a tree! Why is it that men automatically think that they are the better drivers?" Even this alien, who had never driven a car before, thought that he could do better. Men were the same universally!

"I do not think I could do better, Mistress. I only have a bit more experience in handling high speed maneuvers!" His voice rose a bit as Kendall executed a swift lane change and passed the car in front of her.

"You're frightened out of your gourd!" Kendall crowed with delight.

Flame clenched one hand to the headrest as the other hand braced him against the dashboard. "Not frightened, Mistress. Merely a bit nervous at traveling in this manner."

"If riding in a car makes you nervous, how do your people get around?"

"We walk, Mistress." Wide-eyed, he watched a passing tractor. "It is more energy efficient and healthy for our people. Of course, women have the option of riding in a solar power anti-gravity vehicle or a litter."

"I suppose there are groups of muscular men to carry the litter around?"

"Of course!"

"How healthy is that? I mean lugging around all of that dead weight all day? It must be murder on the back."

"I do not know, Mistress. I have never had that particular duty." He turned to face the window. After that his mouth closed up tight, leaving her to try and hold back her mirth as he flinched at each car that passed.

Then the children started crying.

Flame appeared almost as much at a loss as Kendall. He winced as the crying grew in unbelievable volume before reaching unattainable heights. He looked back at his red-faced, screaming children and paled a little more.

"We'll have you guys fixed up in no time," Kendall crooned in an uncertain voice as she swung into a parking space near a picnic table.

The moment the car pulled to a stop, Flame unfastened his trusty safety belt, hopped out, and raced to open the rear passenger door. "Why do they cry?" As panic widened his eyes, he eased Ember out of her seat, pulled her to his broad chest then grimaced at the wetness he felt on her bottom.

"I think they need changing, Mistress."

He gasped as he held the little girl at arm's distance. The odor that emanated from her small bottom was…unpleasant.

"Oh, boy, do they!" Kendall waved her hand in front of her nose when he extended the little girl in her direction.

"No way, buddy!" she cried out as he tried to hand off the smelly, uncomfortable baby. "I'm labor and delivery. I don't know nothin' 'bout changin' no babies!"

Flame looked a little panicked, the babies began to cry harder, and they began to draw strange stares from the people around them.

Kendall began to feel a little uncomfortable as guilt vied with impatience within her. Flame's eyes pleaded with her for help and it seemed that Ember too was begging for assistance. Her large gray eyes filled with a fresh flood of tears and her tiny pink lips trembled.

"Oh for goodness sake! Give her here before we get arrested for child abuse!" she cried finally reaching for the little girl. Funny, but Kendall swore she could read relief in Ember's little gray eyes. The force of her cries seemed to ease off. Resigned, Kendall grabbed the little pink diaper bag and stalked over to one of the wooden tables.

Patiently, she explained the convenience of disposal diapers as compared to the cloth that Flamed seemed to prefer. Kendall spread out a changing pad thankfully provided with the diaper bag.

"Cloth diapers are for protecting your shoulders from cheesing and moist baby belches," she explained. She laid Ember down, peeled the diaper tabs and then…"Oh my God! What has this child been eating?"

The aroma that waft up from the diaper could only be likened to a landfill. "Give me the wipes," Kendall ordered, while trying not to breath through her nose.

Even Ember seemed to laugh at her as she wiped the soiled little bottom. After powdering the little rear, Kendall replaced the soiled diaper with a fresh one and smiled at her accomplishment. Ember was no longer squalling or smelling like a miniature red-haired skunk. She turned to Flame so he could share in her newfound abilities, only to come face to face...well face to bottom with a soiled Spark.

"Oh, no, buddy. You're on your own with this one. I've done my tour of duty."

Flame looked at Kendall with pleading eyes, to no avail. Spark's little mess was all his. Flame paled a little more, but gamely laid out Spark's changing pad. Copying Kendall's actions, he soon had his son quiet and dry.

After a small debate over who would drop the offending diapers into a nearby garbage can, the decidedly wan-looking Flame took charge of his son while Kendall began to feed the laughing Ember.

"They've grown so much in just one day!" she gushed as the little girl, after the change of diaper, again savaged the latex nipple. She looked and smelled like a little angel again. "Is that normal?"

Now that the babies weren't squalling their little heads off, they again resembled little red-haired cherubs. She turned to the silent giant beside her, a smile on her lips.

"In ways of growth, yes. But my children are very small." He looked distracted, but not by the laughing children running in the play area or by the groups of adults eating, talking and generally enjoying the warm summer weather.

"Small?" she gaped, looking back and forth between the children. "They weigh at least seven pounds each!"

Flame managed to muster up a small grin. "A normal Testrios child is at least ten of your pounds at birth. Twins often weigh the same, if not a little more."

He looked down at his contented son who ate his meal with the same hunger, if not the same enthusiasm shown by his sister. "They are a little premature, Mistress."

"How premature?" Kendall knew the dangers that befell many premature babies. The thought of underdeveloped lungs alone in her little charges caused her to shudder. But they seemed to be all right, a perfect ten on the Apgar Scale, the scale for determining the health of a newborn, since birth.

"Three of your months, Mistress."

"Three months! Holy cow! How long do you guys carry a baby anyway?" These two seemed to be perfectly developed children, if not a trifle advanced for their ages. No newborn on Earth would be able to giggle, let alone give those little smiles that they seemed so fond of giving.

"We are altered to gestate over a twelve month period."

Ouch! Kendall winced in sympathy. It seemed hard enough for a woman to go nine months with a full load, let alone twelve months carrying that enormous weight.

"You said 'altered' once before. What exactly does that mean? If you guys aren't natural baby factories, how can your bodies be altered to enable you to carry a child?"

Flame stared down at his son, a tortured look on his face. "The pain I endured will not be repeated for Spark."

Kendall decided to change the subject. Flame didn't look good at all and she wanted no undo stress on her new...friend? Yes, friend. That was a good safe way to describe this man. He was her friend. Her extremely attractive and masculine friend, but friend never-the-less.

She didn't know when she had decided he was a friend, but it probably had something to do with the way he'd defended her against Richard. No one had ever stood up for her like that. In fact, she was always championing *other* people's causes. She was a regular White Knight. No one had to charge to her rescue because she was the one who did all the charging.

"It's a lovely day. I'm glad the weather is holding. Baltimore weather is so unpredictable, and that's one of our more endearing traits. One minute it's sunny, the next it's pouring rain." She continued, knowing that she was babbling, but didn't stop speaking. "Sunshine is always good for the babies, you know. You never know when it's going to get cloudy, so you had better enjoy it while it lasts." Kendall smiled as she breathed in fresh air and listened to the birds chirping in the trees, before looking back at Flame.

She rambled on, but she couldn't seem to help herself. Flame wasn't answering any of her questions and he was beginning to look worse than he did a moment ago. Maybe his adventures in driving weren't the real cause of his recent loss of color.

"The cabin where we are going to has every available comfort for us to enjoy while we're there, a fully stocked kitchen and a Jacuzzi bath in the bedroom. Plus with this weather, the flowers will be in full bloom outside in the forest. It's got to be a beautiful place with the leaves beginning to turn and the animals scurrying around."

Placing the now empty bottle on the table beside her, she positioned the sleepy girl on her shoulder and patted her back until she was rewarded with a tiny burp. Smiling, she inhaled the smell of new skin and baby powder. It was a combination that brought a yearning to her heart and almost a tear to her eye.

Blinking back the moisture, she turned to Flame just in time to see him pale and began to shake.

"What is it? What's wrong?" she demanded as she placed Ember in her portable car seat and reached for Spark. These sudden surprises had her nerves shot. She didn't know what to expect next.

Relinquishing the child without a fight, Flame lurched without his usual grace to the back of the minivan. Dragging out his duffel, he uttered a single gruff curse as he rooted around until he pulled out a small black case.

With shaky fingers he pulled out a tiny black pill and swallowed it down with a small sigh of relief.

By the time Kendall had refastened both children to their anchors in the back seat of the minivan and rushed to assess Flame, he was leaning against the side of the van panting with his hair tangled and hiding his face. Even in the waning light of the afternoon sun, his hair looked unusually dull and lifeless.

Grabbing his wrist, she quickly began taking his pulse, all the while scolding him in her best no-nonsense nurses voice. "I knew you were up too soon after giving birth! Your pulse is racing...I think. Is your body chemistry different than ours? Are you spotting? Wait a minute. You're a man. Of course you're not spotting! You have nothing to spot from! I've never had this conversation before with a man! What the hell is wrong with you?"

Kendall didn't like not knowing what to do. She decided right there that she was never going to place herself in a predicament like this again. On shaky legs, she guided the silent, grim-faced Flame to the passenger seat and helped him inside.

"My body is rejecting the alteration." He spoke as if he expected it to happen. Still ignoring his tangled mass of hair, he leaned back in the seat and bit back a moan of pain.

What more could happen? Would intergalactic tribes of plague-carrying mutants descend upon her next? Kendall sighed as operation Save the Alien Daddy took another unexpected turn.

"What can I do?" she asked at last as his body began to shudder and sweat.

"Nothing, Mistress. I apologize for your distress but my body will right itself soon."

"Why?" Kendall demanded. "Why is your body doing this and why can't I help? And don't you dare apologize to me again, Flame. You are in serious pain and your apologies aren't helping us now. I want to help you and I don't know how!"

Kendall tamped down her frustration in the face of his all too real pain. She looked on in concern at his stiff body.

"My body rejects it because it is unnatural, Mistress. Our physiology is much the same as yours. Anything unnatural placed in it will be rejected after a time. You can do nothing but drive us to safety."

"Cut out that mistress crap, Flame! Is there nothing I can do?"

Flame shook his head. "No, nothing. Just get my children as far away from the search zone as possible."

Like a wounded animal, Flame suffered in silence while Kendall strapped herself into her silver minivan, once again charging to the rescue. This knight business sure does stink, she thought as she eyed the man almost bent double with pain that he refused to acknowledge or accept. Yup, sometimes it stinks being a knight.

It was near full dark when they arrived at the small cabin. They had only made one other stop to care for the children because Flame was in considerable agony. Kendall knew his condition was serious when he didn't try to assist her with Ember and Spark. He remained quietly alert, but said nothing. The beauty of the day was lost.

After carrying in the sleeping children still in their seats and placing them in the relative safety of the living room floor, Kendall rushed to help Flame inside the thankfully stocked cabin.

Feverish and barely lucid, Flame allowed Kendall to guide him to the only bedroom in the four-room log cabin. They both collapsed onto the pale blue comforter on the bed in a tangle of arms, legs, and auburn hair. The heat from his body frightened her more than the feel of his hard body in such close proximity to hers.

"Flame!" she tried to rouse him after separating their bodies and half-dragging, half pulling him to the top of the bed. "What can I do?" Her voice broke with her fear. She hated to see people she cared about suffer and she did care about this man who was fighting so hard for his children.

"The alteration is dissolving." He repeated in a daze. "I took an enhancer to speed up the process, but it comes with pain. There is nothing you can do. A man must bear the pain in silence."

"You mean it didn't have to happen this fast? Flame, you could have spared yourself this pain." Kendall looked down at his feverish face and sought to calm her sudden anger at this man. If he could have spared himself the pain, they all would be spared a lot of trouble. What did she know about alien medicine anyway? Would a good dose of Tylenol help with the fever and pain?

"Mistress Kendall. We do not have a week for me to lie in seclusion while the alteration dissolves, nor do I wish to maintain the alteration for my next conception. I want that part of my life finished. It has to be finished for only then will my children be safe."

Kendall was horrified. What kind of people forced this abomination on their own? Testrios women, already on the low end of her opinions plummeted down to contaminated operating rooms and Richard. For Flame to willingly go through all of this to save his small family garnered more than her respect and admiration, he earned her unwavering loyalty. She would do what ever it took to assure him a new life on Earth!

Something cracked in her heart and she lay down beside the man and offered the only support she could. She took him in her arms and clutched his shivering body to hers. Crooning a wordless tune, she rocked him from side to side striving to ease his pain a little, giving the same comfort he had willingly given to her.

Flame stiffened at the contact, but gradually his body began to relax. He drifted off with the smell of her skin on his nose, the feel of her fingers softly stroking his hair and the sound of her voice lulling him to sweet oblivion. He had never before enjoyed a woman's fondlings, but now he puzzled at his body's easy acceptance of touch. His last thoughts were that he had to evaluate his reaction to her and proceed with extreme caution.

"Do it like this," the female voice hissed as she used his bound hair to yank his head up. "If you want to pleasure a woman, Flame, you need to remember that nipples are directly linked to a woman's clitoris! Now do it again!"

Again he turned his attention to the heaving bosom that lay spread out before him. In his mouth was the flavor of woman, the unmistakable feminine musk filled his senses and made his body crave something unknown. Already he had been suckling upon his instructor's breasts for over an hour, trying to get it right.

The brightly colored nub of flesh glistened with the moisture from his own mouth, and stood out, engorged with the desire he was bringing to her, but too slowly. He ran his hands across the warm firm flesh of her stomach, until his thumbs caressed the tip of her pubic bush.

"Better, young one," she purred. "You will be as good as your father. You want to make him proud, do you not? Can you see him there, watching you?"

Indeed his father was watching him, and that made him more aware of his lessons and less aware of his own body. Turning again to the woman who lay under him, he playfully lapped out at her right nipple before taking the hard button between his teeth and gently bit down.

"Yes!" she praised as she released his hair. "Now soothe the pain."

Running his fingers through her soft feminine curls, he grazed the top of her slit while he gently sucked on the fleshly treat that filled his mouth.

His trainer hummed in pleasure and he felt her moistness grow.

Taking a little initiative of his own, he let the pads of his searching fingers slide lower, through the slick moisture, to find the pulsing bead of her.

Now what would be the most sensitive side, the left or the right, he mused. His father had taught him that all women were created different. Some preferred direct stimulation while others abhorred it. Some held more sensitivity to the clit on the left than the right. Some preferred gentleness, while others liked it rough. The trick was in correctly reading the woman.

To make his task a bit easier, he bit gently on the nipple again and smiled as he felt her shudder in reaction. Taking a cue from her actions, he grasped her clit between two fingers while he captured her lonely nipple with his other hand.

Simultaneously, he began to pinch the throbbing women's flesh between her legs while he roughly stimulated her nipple. Her head jerked back and harsh grunts and groans exploded from her lips.

"Harder, damn you! Harder!" she shrieked, and like a good pleasure slave, his fingers drenched in her warm wetness, he complied.

* * * * *

The sound of her voice woke him. It was unnatural to hear a woman speak so softly, but then she was an unusual woman. Unusual women inhabited this whole planet, but Kendall seemed more unique than the rest.

To be brought to tears by a mere man showed a weakness that would not be tolerated by any house on his planet, yet she was amazingly strong. In the time that he had known her she had delivered his children, believed him and offered to aid in his escape, and had taken care of him in a situation where the strongest of men shied away from the pain they too must one day endure. He knew because he had helped countless others in the pain of alteration and had dreaded the same ever happening to him. Kendall was strong. She had helped him endure.

He had learned quickly about endurance.

If only his mother had not seen fit to pull him from the Brotherhood, he would not now be fighting for his life and those of his children's while tying to assimilate into a totally foreign society.

Tessela, his mother, in truth probably had no thought of providing an egg that would create one such as him. He was the only male to be born with the energies of his forebears coursing through his veins. His twin sibling was born with hair as black as night and not a spark of the energies that he possessed.

Rightfully, his sister should be the one next to rule. After all, what good was a man with the power? He could not be recognized as a voice in the Matriarch. He could not even argue with a woman without serious repercussions. To Tessela, he was a problem to be dealt with.

The only person who cared about his future was his sire. Alonzid sought to teach his ungainly son all he needed to survive. Pride and strength were fed to him along with each of the rules that men had to obey. When his father petitioned his mother for his placement with the Brothers, he thought he had found the one solution for his strange son.

His sire saw him struggle with his sibling and his peers for acceptance. He saw him fight to control the strange energies that had a tendency to show themselves when under extreme duress or when his temper flares, which was often. If an object burst into dust or exploded with heat, it was a safe bet that Flame was nearby. Escape to the Brotherhood was the only option for a man who often appeared less obedient than a man should with his flashing eyes and hair that waved with every strong emotion.

Flame liked the isolation among the Brothers because he no longer stood out. The Brothers, deemed unfit because their bodies could not accept the altering or were in difficult positions, welcomed the strange boy and helped him master his unique power. He learned control because he no longer had to deal with the other young boys of his house calling him names or the utter jealousy he saw in his sister's eyes.

Although not raised together, siblings were often left in each other's company during non-training hours, and his sister made no secret of the contempt she held for a useless man being born with her legacy. He was an oddity. He was bigger and stronger than the rest of the boys in the household and his hair bespoke of the power that should have passed him by. So it was a relief to leave his mother's house to go and train in safety with the Brothers.

After years of training in the healing arts and more importantly, training to disguise his emotions as well as harness his energies, his mother removed him from the only safe haven that he knew. It seemed Catla, the new head of the House Of Ice, liked to collect unusual things and he was the most unusual to come to her attention in a long while. He still remembered the look of horror on his sire's face as his mother brought him home. His father quickly explained the duty of a mated man to him with fear in his own gray eyes.

Everyone but him, it seemed, knew of the woman's cold evil heart, but no one saw fit to warn him about the nature of his new life-mate. He still remember the last words his father spoke to him before he was taken away for his manhood ceremony.

Endure.

"Flame?" her soft voice startled him from his dark musings. "Are you feeling better?"

"I feel no pain, Mistress." He could not bring himself to disrespect her by using her given name. He had not earned that right yet, though he was startled to think he might wish to.

Mistress Kendall again was dressed in those odd pantaloons called jeans and a brightly colored blouse called a T-shirt. Her hair was pulled back into a short tail with an equally colorful tie and her Tarcas brown eyes were alight with concern for him.

"I was worried about you. You've been asleep for two days now and I didn't know what I was supposed to do if you didn't wake up."

"Two days! The children. I must see to them!"

"Relax. They're taking a nap, Flame."

Flame leaped from the bed and stopped cold. He was naked as the day he was expelled from his father's womb!

A blush, amazingly the same shade of red as his hair, spread up from Flame's chest to his face. Kendall bit back a bark of laughter as he again dove for the bed and jerked the covers up to his chin.

"Ah, your clothes are on the trunk over there," she pointed to a cedar chest beneath the room's only window, "And your bag is at the foot of the bed."

She shrugged and sat on the edge of the bed. With that many rules to govern the men, nudity had to be a taboo. "I've seen naked men before, Flame. Your body is just the same as theirs."

Who was she kidding? She had only seen bodies like that in the magazines her friends snickered about on breaks. He had the body of an athlete. Not overblown like competitive body builders who were just skin and muscle, but firm, muscular flesh. He didn't even have stretch marks! And that sprinkling of auburn hair that arrowed down from his navel, well that was a treasure trail! Not that she was looking in anything but a clearly clinical way, she tried to convince herself.

He still looked horrified.

"What's wrong?" Had he figured out the turn her thoughts were taking?

"You saw me unclothed!"

"Yes. I saw you unclothed when I delivered your babies too. And let me tell you it was no easy task to undress you with all of those strange fasteners. Why do you wear so much?"

"To hide my largeness, Mistress. It is required that all men dress with decorum."

Yet another Testrois oddity. Most men she knew, Including Doctor Dick, would have worn as little as morally possible to show off that body. Kendall shook her head. "The shower is to the left and breakfast will be waiting for you when you're finished. Do you know how to operate the shower?"

At his nod, she eased out of the room to give him a little privacy and made her way to the kitchen where the twins were contentedly snoozing in their seats.

"Daddy will be here soon, guys," she whispered as she kissed each tiny cheek. "And we will figure out how to make you safe." She hoped they came up with some answers quickly before she became too attached to the adorable babies and their handsome father.

During the time that Flame was indisposed she and the children had come to an understanding. Changing diapers was not her idea of a good time, but then neither was screaming babies. Having never spent any great period of time around newborns, she decided to treat them like little people with incontinence.

"Listen up, guys," she commanded that first night as both babies sat in their seats, and damned if they didn't stop fussing and looked at her. It was unnerving at first, both sets of those little gray eyes following her every move, but she quickly got past it in the face of the lecture she was about to deliver.

"There will be no unnecessary crying. We will do a feeding every four hours as suggested by Doctor Know-it-all in his little book." She gestured to the book she waved in the air like a small shield.

"I'll change diapers as needed, but please take it easy on me. I'm a beginner." Both children seemed to glance at each other in silent communication before turning again to Kendall.

"Hugs and kisses will be unconditional, but I don't want any trouble out of you two. I will not tread the boards with you two just so you can get your kicks off of running me ragged. Until your father regains consciousness, I am in control."

Both little rose bud mouths seemed to pucker just then and Kendall was almost at a loss to explain why when her lecture was going so well. "Are you guys hungry?" she asked as she dropped the book on the kitchen table and cautiously approached the twins.

Their little faces began to screw up like two identical prunes. "Is it daddy? Do you want daddy?"

Their eyes slammed shut and in unison, almost like synchronized swimmers, they began to whimper and wave their arms and kick their legs.

"Oh daddy will be okay, little ones." Kendall dropped to her knees on the tile floor and began to pet and stroke their little faces. Soon she was sitting on the floor, bouncing a twin on each leg and she was damned to know how it happened.

Ember and Spark exchanged discreet glances as Kendall began to cater to their every whim. They had come to an understanding all right, and now it was clear who was the boss. The conspirators smiled and drifted off to a contented sleep. Kendall wondered again for the thousandth time, "Damned if I know how I get myself into these messes."

Chapter Four

ဩ

Kendall turned from the stove at the sound of his footsteps. Flame hadn't eaten in two days and he need food to stay healthy for his children. Still, she was amazed at his body's ability to heal itself. After almost two days of extremely high fever, the furnace abruptly cut off and he fell into what she would assume was a natural sleep.

Whatever enhancer he took to speed up the natural breakdown of the alien augmentation in his body could mean things for the medical world. The thought of what it could do for antibiotics alone left her staggered. It also took her mind off of his sinfully gorgeous body and deep masculine voice. And then the fodder for all of her recent fantasies walked in.

Looking extremely uncomfortable in his new thigh hugging blue denims and tight white T-shirt, Flame tentatively entered the kitchen. He almost timidly walked towards his children and nuzzled each little cheek. The children seemed to posses a sixth sense when it came to their father, for the moment he walked in the room, both pairs of gray eyes popped open and they seemed to crow with delight. Ember seemed to look as if she approved of dad's new duds, while Spark gave the interesting new clothing a cursory glance before looking back at his father's uncomfortable face.

"You look great!" Kendall cried as she appreciatively sized up the man in front of her.

Forget the enhancer. A picture of Flame in those form-fitting jeans was enough to motivate any female patient to make a jump towards an instant recovery!

He blushed! She could see the light red color climbing up his face before he turned stoically to her.

"What is it?" she asked.

"I feel naked, Mistress!" he gritted out rubbing his damp hands down the thighs of his jeans. His actions drew her attention to how muscular and perfectly formed his legs were. "How am I to function when every line of my body is exposed?"

Exposed and looking good, she thought to herself before realizing that he was perfectly serious. "You are properly covered, Flame." She held back a grin. "Lots of men wear even less than you are right now. You should see the beaches in Ocean City in the summer!"

His eyebrows shot up. "I do not think I could ever wear less than this, Mistress. That would be a flogging offense on my world. These clothes are almost indecent!"

"Look at me, Flame. I'm perfectly decent and comfortable without having to bundle up from head to foot. You'll adjust. Now let's get some food inside of you. Sit down and get ready to eat."

What was a beach and what kind of unsuitable man would wear less than what he was wearing now? It had taken him a few moments to dredge up the courage to go before his mistress like this! Certainly she would not expect him to venture forth out into populated areas wearing less.

When she turned to the stove, Flame discreetly examined her body in the strange and revealing Earth clothes. Her breasts seemed to be high and firm in her thin shirt, an admirable trait in any woman, if one cared about things like that. Her waist appeared, in the indecent jeans, small. Not small enough to span with his two large hands, but small enough to give her the perfect start on the hourglass figure that the women on his world craved. Her hips gently flared to those rounded thighs and long legs that he could imagine wrapped around his....

The room was getting warm. Flame felt a not wholly uncomfortable tingle start in his groin. He looked down just as a part he never gave any thought to began to stiffen and rise. He looked back at Kendall, this time in alarm. She was turning to him and all he could think about was the fact that she would see him this way. These Earth clothes left little room for concealment. Thinking fast, he leaped to a seat at the table and, for the first time in his twenty-nine years of life sat in the presence of a woman.

This physical reaction he was experiencing when in her presence required some deep thought on his part. Until he figured out what was happening to make his body…do that throbbing thing, he would have to hide his condition from her and hope to disguise any bulges that she might see.

Kendall turned to the man and smiled to see Flame dutifully sitting at the table with his perfect posture, waiting to eat as she instructed. He looked a little uncomfortable, but he had followed her orders to the letter. Too bad the table covered all the good parts exposed by his new wardrobe. He was enough eye candy to make her develop cavities.

"Eat," she commanded with some amusement. Yes, having him around the house was actually starting to make her feel pretty darn good.

* * * * *

"You need to own and operate your own business, Flame," Kendall stated with some certainty. "That's the only way that you will be able to supervise your children all the time without having to explain to someone why they need extra attention, or why you need the extra time off from work."

Soon after Flame had consumed the last bite of his first meal prepared by a woman, Kendall pulled out a book called 'The Yellow Pages', and began flipping thin papers. She spent a lot of time mumbling to her self and shaking her head as he and the children looked on in bafflement.

"I need a comfortable spot to think." She herded them all to the small living space provided by the cabin. The rest of the morning was passed by her asking him questions like, "Do you think that you can operate heavy machinery?" and "You definitely don't look like a white collar investor. Do you understand the stock market?"

Between feedings and diaper changes, Flame kept his attention on Kendall as she continued to ask in these inane questions.

His body's reaction was cooled in the face of his uncertain future, but the feelings were there, simmering beneath the surface, threatening to break free every time she glanced at him from under her long eyelashes while burying her nose in the thick book. But her words brought him back to the business at hand.

"My own business." That was said with a bit of wonder. He could own property on this planet, without having to get special permission from the Matriarch. He had never thought to do just that. He paused in his contemplation of the strange reactions of his body to pay attention to what his Mistress was saying.

As for Kendall, she couldn't help but wonder what part she played in his future plans as she voiced her opinions. Would she be a friend, a confidant, or a fond memory? Would he let her visit the children or would he disappear completely from her life?

"What does this flame-keeping business mean?" she questioned after dropping the book to the floor. "Both Spark and Ember have red hair, so does that mean that will have the same problems and energies that you do?" She pulled a nodding Spark from his seat and into her lap. She wanted both babies to live a normal as possible life under the given circumstances. "Does that make them special in some way too?"

They had moved the discussion to the couch in front of the massive wood-burning fireplace that dominated the living room. The large beige couch was made of some soft material and had wonderfully large cushions to would you up while sinking you in heavenly comfort. Sitting on it was almost like being in a warm embrace of a lover. Kendall rocked the sleeping Spark in her arms as she regarded his father. She was really becoming attached to the little guy and his sister.

"We have special energies, Mistress."

Kendall inhaled the smell she decided to name "new baby". She had discovered this wonderful new scent shortly after giving the twins a basin bath for the first time. It was a hypnotic smell that made her long to hold the infants more so that she could experience it. No wonder people loved having babies so much! The little buggers came with their own lure. Those thoughts saddened her a bit, but she pushed them aside for the moment to deal with the issue at hand.

"What do you mean by energies?"

If they changed form or floated in midair, they needed to be warned about society's views on the strange and supernatural. She remembered the strange exchange earlier between the children while she was laying the law down to them and added telepathy to her list. But then, even on Earth it was said that all twins held a special bond. She would not worry about their silent form of communication just yet. They had bigger concerns to fret over.

Flame began pacing the carpet in front of the large picture window.

Watching Kendall hold his son was causing an almost burning sensation deep within his heart. He glanced at his sleeping daughter lying in her cube and felt a surge of warmth so strong that it almost brought tears to his eyes. His children were just like him, different and surviving in a world where they might not be accepted and quite possibly harmed out of fear and misunderstanding.

He walked to Ember and squatted down to examine her sleeping form. What did those white stripes mean? He ran gentle fingers over her tiny head and watched the little streaks of silver glisten. Would she be even more different than her father and brother? Spark possessed a few of the telling stripes, but not as many as his sister.

"The energy passes usually to the female heads of the ruling houses ever few generations. I do not know why I was born with this," he absently tugged on a lock of hair as he looked up at Kendall.

Flame began to pace the length of the room again. "I will need isolation to teach them how to control their energies, Mistress. It may prove to be a complication to your plans for us." Especially if Ember had inherited some of her mother's energies, he added silently to himself. Could she be taught to control the fire within the same way he learned to, or would he have to seek and find a new method to help her control her two opposing energies?

"But what do they do? These energies, I mean." Kendall placed a small kiss on Spark's forehead.

Flame quit his pacing to stare Kendall straight in the eyes. It was time to expose another facet of his unusual life. Now she would have reason to fear and mistrust him and he would be able to put some needed distance between them. The things she did to his equilibrium were a bit freighting and wholly unexpected.

He had no doubts that she would continue to help him, but he was about to give her a reason to disappear from his life on a permanent basis. He found that possibility disheartening even though the prospect of distancing himself from her sounded reasonable. Watching her caress his son caused a tugging in his heart almost as sweetly painful as watching the daily changes in his children. He did not know how to deal with them, so he would do his best to avoid these unsettling emotions.

"We can manipulate fire, Mistress. Each Great House came to being because of their control over an essential element on our planet. Each element is vital for life and the ability to control is inherently passed on to women, the original bearers of life. This is why the women rule there. On Testrios I am an oddity, but not considered very dangerous. I am not allowed to venture far from my home and if I tried to cause problems for the Matriarch, I can be easily eliminated. On your world I sense that I could easily cause great harm and destruction, and no one would be able to stop me."

Kendall eyed Flame with more than her usual curiosity. Until she had met him she thought things like control over a destructive force, like fire, beyond the scope of human ability. But his very existence proved her thinking wrong and caused her to broaden her thoughts and open her mind to the unexplained. X-Files, eat your heart out! She was living with the real thing!

"What do you mean by manipulate fire?" She adjusted her hold on Spark to cross her legs on the couch and snuggle back. She had to be comfortable for this one. This explanation would have to be good.

"Fire holds no secret from me, Mistress." He spoke in a quietly assured voice. "It can not harm me. I can control it, harness it, use it for whatever purpose that I deem necessary."

His words were without a hint of boast or bravado, like he was braced for a blow and Kendall instantly believed him. Never had she been so close to such an extraordinary being. He was bigger stronger and more handsome than any man, than anyone she knew, yet he seemed to be waiting for her to pronounce him unsuitable and run in fear from him. She would have to work on his self-esteem. Modesty was sexy but pitiful was well...Richard.

After taking a moment to center his thoughts, Flame raised both hands to the level of his eyes and inhaled deeply. With a flash his gray eyes grew dark and began to sparkle. His gorgeous hair took on a life of it's own as it began to flow around his head. Tiny slivers of flame danced upon each fingertip as he began to move, to dance with his hands.

Twirling and spinning his hands in midair, he wove and shaped and melded the small tongues of fire until a perfect white rose glimmered before him. He extended his left hand the fire blossom floated in the air above Kendall.

Kendall's eyes opened wide and she unconsciously gripped the sleeping child in her arms closer. Her gasp of amazement filled the silent room. Fire danced and swayed above her head, yet she felt no heat and did not smell any smoke.

Again his hands moved and the rose floated back to him and melted in on its self only to emerge as a bird, a fiery phoenix that followed the fluttering movements of his hands as his arms moved in intricate gestures. The fiery red bird reared it's head and Kendall swore she could her it let out a cry of anguish before it circled the room leaving a rainbow colored wake to mark it's movements and it's passing.

Finally the phoenix sank on itself, as Flame pressed his palms together, not unlike the legends of the mystical bird, only to be explode in a flash of hot fire, reborn as a snarling scarlet dragon.

The dragon then split divided it's self into two as he separated his hands. Two beasts, one a deep red, the other an icy blue, followed the movements of his hands as they rose and begin to circle the magnificent man that had called them forth. His body began to turn and sway in a dance more seductive than any dancers, more compelling than any master sorcerer's controlling the beasts' movements as they lazily glided between his spread legs and around his moving wide spread arms.

In a silent clash of power, the two creatures of legend circled to pause in front of Flame, before they began to circle each other, as if waiting for each other to make the first move. With a silent zip, they circled to the sky as they began to fight a battle in the air above Kendall, each snapping and struggling for supremacy. The red circled almost lazily around Flames body while the blue weaved and darted through his arms and legs as if looking for an opening that would allow him to attack.

In a sudden burst of movement and flowing hair, Flame sent the two combatants swirling about the room. Kendall could see the pull of tendons and sinew as the flying monsters passes close to her face. Her head whipped around the room as she tried to keep progress with the savage battle taking place in this very room.

She felt a scream well up in her throat as the blue dragon, with an almost evil expression on its face, opened its mouth and a red ball of fire shot out to circle the red dragon. In retaliation, the red spit out a powerful burst of white flames that engulfed its intended victim.

Finally, in a death scene found only in the wildest of imaginations, both dragons flew above the puppet master controlling their movements and became engulfed by the flames that they themselves created. In a clash so realistic it was almost heard, they exploded together in a colorful display of light, destroyed by the might which had brought them to being, the man called Flame.

As each fiery ember softly floated to the ground around Flame, they disappeared without a trace of smoke or odor, before touching the furniture or the rugs covering the wooden floor.

In the midst of the fiery finale, Flame stood alone; hair whipping wildly as silver eyes reflected the blaze that lived within him. "Are you frightened, Mistress? I know that no one here on this planet possesses these abilities." He spoke softly as if he expected her to turn a bolt from the room.

"Call me Kendall," she replied automatically. She was still awed by what she had experienced because of this magnificent man before her. "I'm not frightened of you, Flame. If you wanted to French-fry me to a crisp, you would have done so by now. Don't expect me to turn my back on you and these children now."

She looked at the baby in her arms. He felt right in her arms—just where he belonged. "You need me."

And maybe, just maybe, she needed them.

She turned to grin up at Flame with a suddenly light heart. "Have you ever heard of pyrotechnics?"

Chapter Five

ᔕ

"This was a good idea, Flame." Kendall panted as she jogged along side him, trying her best to keep up. "I haven't felt this good in such a long time. I needed the exercise, although matching you is out of the question. Where did you learn to move so quickly through the terrain like this?"

"Men are required to learn these skills as young boys, Mistress. Much practice is necessary."

"I bet you never thought you'd be using them now." Her voice rasped as she fought to keep up with his vigorous movements.

"Indeed, Mistress. This is one skill I had not thought to use."

Eventually even Flame began to tire. Sweat beaded on his forehead and he began to fight for his breath. He had already stopped several times to help her along.

"I've got to stop!" Kendall cried, exhausted from trying to keep up with his grueling pace and long stride. "I need air! My legs are killing me! My back will never be the same!" The man was a machine while she was merely flesh and bone. "No more!"

"As you wish, Mistress." His voice was also a bit raspy.

"Call me Kendall. Under the circumstances, don't you think it would be wise?"

"Yes, Mistress."

Exasperated, Kendall plopped down on a large rock and refused to move another inch. Above her the red and gold leaves resembled a canopy of fire that offered cool shade instead of blistering heat. The grass on either side of the worn rocky trail was still lush and green.

As she earlier predicted, the small woodland animals scurried back and forth along the forest floor storing food for the upcoming winter season. A warm breeze softly rustles through the leaves, stirring memories of her youth: of skinned knees and bikes, drinking ice cold lemonade with friends, running through fields of tall grass, and just lazing about enjoying the last dog days of summer.

It was a glorious day in the woods and Kendall found herself drinking in all the sights that it had to offer, including the tall red-headed man standing before her.

"You can't go around calling me Mistress!" she finally sighed as she looked up at the tall man. "People will look at you funny! People will look at me funny! They'll think that I'm some kind of sexual predator bent on controlling your every movement!"

Oh Lordy! The thoughts that image conjured up! Shaking her head a bit to clear her mind, she strove onward. "Remember what we discussed yesterday? You are now a respected businessman in a lucrative field. You don't follow orders from anyone, you give them!"

Flame had to take a deep breath and shake his head to dispel the images that popped into his head—of ordering her to strip out of her clothes so he could examine the differences between them personally. Of ordering her to strip him of his garments and then do the same for herself.

It was certainly warm this time of the year on this small blue planet!

The whole idea of this nature hike was to help ease the tension that had shot up between them in the cramped confines of the small cabin. Exposing a small bit of his power to her back at the cabin had been a calculated way of putting some distance between them. If she feared him a little, he would have a reason to avoid being in her close company and limit the time they spent together.

But now she seemed to be drawn closer to him, as if they shared a secret only the two of them knew.

Flame had analyzed the feelings her presence caused in him and was amazed to discover that his body was sending a loud message to his brain. He wanted her in a most shockingly carnal way. He had thought such desires long dead inside him. Even his own body would not heed the orders he gave it. He did not know how to answer her properly. "Yes, Mistress," he managed, trying to decipher her feelings.

Kendall sighed. Time to change the subject. Flame was beginning to look uncomfortable again. "How does that little computer thingy of yours work? I can't believe how fast you changed those records and downloaded all that information."

Kendall recalled the little palm top computer that Flame had whipped from his black duffel bag the previous day. After speaking a few guttural-sounding words, the little black box began to vibrate. In a few moments it spit out a small disk, not unlike a miniature CD, with all the information Flame needed to start a new life in the fireworks business. It was amazing. She did want to know more about it, so it was the perfect topic to use to give the man some time to pull himself together.

Flamed leaned against a nearby tree as he observed Kendall. Both children were asleep, snuggled on his chest safely in the double harness and he smiled at the sweet noises they made.

The sudden image of his Mistress snuggled up against his chest and cooing made his body harden yet again. Quickly he sat on the ground to hide the change in his body that those blasted Earth clothes so easily revealed, using the harness as a little extra shielding.

"The computer is of the same design as the navigational computer on my ship. It is capable of picking up any signals broadcast from any satellite on this continent." His voice sounded rushed even to him. Surely she would know there was something he was trying to hide.

"So it's a mini receiver?"

"That is correct. It can also create subliminal files of any information I desire and replay them to me at any given time. The information is automatically accepted by my subconscious and I assimilate the skills as if I have had extensive training in the subject. It is really quite efficient."

"You don't have to be asleep?" Kendall smiled, looking speculative.

"No, Mistress, sleep is unnecessary, but it can be done that way also. The brain is a remarkable organ. It receives input from all around us, categorizes it in order of importance, stores what is needed and disregards the rest. You just need to be taught how to listen and your brain can absorb all kinds of data. I learned your language while flying to this planet and learned other useful information while sinking my ship in your lake."

The images that thought produced—his ship in her lake! There was something about the words that caused another instant rush of blood from his brain and into his nether region.

Even Kendall began to eye him mysteriously with those sparkling Tarcas brown eyes as she took in what he had said and shifted through his words, no doubt searching for a double meaning.

"Tell me about your past mistake."

He changed the subject out of desperation as again his lower anatomy began to painfully fight the restraints of his earth jeans. The look she was giving him was having a direct effect on his libidinous desires and he was in danger of acting like an untried youth struggling to serve his first Mistress properly.

"I guess it's time for a reality check." All through his short computer lesson, Kendall had been hungrily eyeing his magnificent body and trying to keep her mind focused on his words, but it wasn't easy. She had begun picturing a fantasy with him naked and wet in the sunshine, swimming to her in warm tropical waters of some South Pacific island, while she lay in wait on blush colored sand wearing a thick coat of oily sun block, a big smile, and little else.

He had made her forget that she could have been here devouring Richard with her eyes instead of an intergalactic fugitive who had probably never even seen a naked women outside of an altering room, let alone know what his body was trying to tell him.

She hadn't missed the flashes of desire in his eyes or the bulges filling out the front of his pants, nor had she misunderstood the reasons for this impromptu nature hike. Flame was a bit horny and the giant of a man didn't know what to do about it.

"Okay, I'll tell you about Richard," she finally sighed. "It might do me some good to get the whole sorry story out in the open."

Flame nodded encouragingly. This talk of another man was already making his blood return to its proper place. Funny, even though he was relieved to have his blood flowing in the right direction once more, the thought of Kendall in the arms of another man made him feel, well, odd.

"It's simple really, Flame. He betrayed me. We were supposed to be married, ah mated," she added at his confused look, "a few days ago. The day I first met you actually, but I had broke it off with the jerk some time ago."

Flame looked sympathetic but patiently waited for her to continue.

"It was going to be a big ceremony. I wanted to do it right. My marriage was going to last for lifetime and beyond," she explained as tears welled up in her eyes.

"I called in my older sister from Ohio. She's the only family I have left and I wanted her to share in the joy, in my joy." The last was said in a singsong voice that heralded the coming of some great irony or tragedy.

"My sister is a beautiful model and had the time off between jobs. Heck, she could afford to take a few days off anyway. She rushed right down to Baltimore, nothing but warm smiles and tearful hugs. She actually said that she wanted to help me in any way possible and do anything she could to aid me on my journey to wedded bliss. She helped me, all right, the prissy overgrown slut."

Kendall looked down in her lap and clenched her hands into a fist as if what she was about to say was so shocking that she actually felt ashamed about what she was going to reveal to him.

"A week after she got here, I got off work early and dropped in to surprise Richard. And I wanted to check my wedding gown. It was such a perfect gown! I felt like a fairy tale princess when I wore it. My veil was designed to look like a crown to prove to the world that I was princess of the day. He and my sister were to have picked it up from the bridal shop, you see? I didn't have the time to pick it up and they both said that they would be happy to do it. Because my sister didn't know her way around town yet, Richard offered to drive her. It was a perfect arrangement. Richard would get to know my sister, my only living relative, and she could find out why I wanted that man so much."

Flame nodded again. He saw that this last ditch effort to bring about some sibilance of sanity in his over-stressed mind had opened an emotional valve in his Mistress that needed to be released. He saw that this self-contained woman needed to talk about her experience, her pain, but had no one to help her vent these painful and destructive emotions. He found himself even more startled to find that he wanted to be her confidant; he wanted to be the one to help her. He was better equipped to understand humiliation and betrayal than anyone she knew.

"I came home and caught my sister wearing my wedding veil!" she wailed at last, covering her face with her hands.

"This veil is sacred?" he asked, confused but still encouraging her to continue. How could the donning of such a simple garment mean a great betrayal?

"No, but my fiancée was!" she cried. "She was wearing nothing but my veil and Richard! He was making love to her, right on top of my wedding gown!"

Flame winced, then frowned at the tears streaming down her face. That indeed was a true betrayal. On his world, a woman's mating gown was something sacred passed down for generations in even the lowest of houses. In the five ruling houses, the mating gowns were passed down from the five original Matriarchs and were considered valuable pieces of that family's history worthy of showing that power still ran through their blood, and worn only at the mating ceremony to reaffirm their family's position.

Thinking of the beautiful gowns from the original five houses brought to mind the picture of a gown so white it hurt the eyes to stare directly at it. Only in his mind the ice white gown was flawed, the hem of its great flowing skirt splattered red with blood.

Chapter Six

❧

"Richard's apartment was closer to our hospital than mine, so we thought that it would be a good idea for me to have a key."

Kendall stared off into space remembering the sound of the key turning in the lock and feeling a little bit naughty because she carried a bottle of Champagne and wore nothing beneath her light summer coat.

It was the soft music she had heard first. She slung open the door; picturing Richard reclined in his favorite chair listening to Pachobel, sipping a glass of his favorite Bordeaux. Instead she heard the odd rustling of tissue paper. Instinctively, she turned to the sound, thinking that Richard might be cheating and peeking at her dress before the wedding and that she might catch him in the act.

She pulled the bottle out of her bag with one hand as she let her coat slide open revealing her body in all it's natural glory, then stopped frozen. The sound of the bottle shattering like her dreams of the future caught the attention of the straining couple on the kitchen table, and brought her out of her shocked daze.

"Do you know the worst part?" she asked beginning to control her tears now that the first burst of emotion had past she began to pull herself together. "Besides the fact that they were doing it on the gown that I had hand picked from about two thousand dresses, he said that I drove him to it! He said that I was too independent and sexually aggressive for a woman who couldn't have children. He said that he screwed my sister because I scared him! He said that my sister was what a woman was supposed to be."

Flame stared at her, face frozen in amazement. Never had he heard such a ridiculous reason for breaking such an important vow.

Women on Testrios were proud of their sexual prowess. As a young man, he was drilled as much in the ways of physical pleasure for women as he was in basic rules for survival. Being able to feel the full range of sexual desire was an achievement to be proud of! Not every woman could.

And as for having children, what woman would want to? It was a painful and messy affair that could drag on for hours at a time. That was why The Matriarch decided that men were better-equipped to deal with dangers of childbearing.

Kendall was a perfect example of Testrios femininity, except she had a heart with a capacity for deep feelings for others. That alone set her apart from every other woman he had known and made his Mistress unique.

"Mistress, I can not fathom the thoughts of such a man, but know this. You should not waste emotion on such a man as he. On my world, it would fall to me as mate to a house leader to terminate this being, for one such as he is not a man. A man would consider it his life's duty to protect his Mistress from any harm, be it internal or external, and not to cause pain to fill the eyes of his life-mate. The fault is not yours, Mistress. The responsibility must rest on his shoulders, his and those of your sister."

"But Flame," she cried out with great anguish, "I am sterile! Unable to have children!"

"So am I, Mistress," he stated flatly, his gray eyes dull with the seriousness of his statement.

She stopped shaking her head in protest, shocked into silence. She had forgotten that on his world a man was only as good as his ability to reproduce and protect.

"I feel that I must reveal a little more of myself to you, Mistress. You do not seem to understand how unusual I really am. I ask you, what good is a man who possesses my energies if he cannot yield them? I was sent to the Society of Brothers at a young age and it could not have happened soon enough. My twin sibling had always hated me." He paused at her indrawn breath.

"Yes, I have a twin. I told you once before that twins were a common occurrence on my world. Until the scientists perfected the fertility drug administered, many men carried up to seven, even eight children successfully per pregnancy, but the strain on the male body was great. Later it was deemed too much of a population hazard to allow the practice to continue and twins became an acceptable amount for a man to bear during a single pregnancy."

Once again Kendall was speechless. There was another one of these hard-bodied space jockeys flying around somewhere? Would he pop in large with child and needing a place to hide too? The women on this planet would go wild for another one of her aliens if he in any way resembled her daring space man.

"My twin is female and the next ruler of the House of Fire but hates me because she possesses not the slightest of energies."

Kendall hid her shocked reaction and waited for him to continue with his tale. How could a sister hate a brother for something that was not on his doing? She cocked her head to one side and continued to await the conclusion of this strange story.

He smiled lost in thought for a moment, then continued. "My sire said that I was in anguish when he petitioned my mother for my placement with the healers. I was happy there until my mother returned for me. In truth, I thought that she had forgotten my existence. I was ten of your years when I was sent away and almost thirty years when she returned for me."

"After all that time, what could she possibly want with you?" Kendall asked, lost in his life's story.

"My mother wanted power and saw that she could increase hers if two great houses were combined. It has never happened before but there is no rule against it, probably because we all live on different continents. Only traders and the Ruling Matriarch, their life-mates and close assistants often meet each other. I did often wonder though, how my family's shame came to be heard in the House of Ice. No matter which paths the information traveled, it seems the uniqueness of my situation came to the attention of the Ruler of the House of Ice."

"Catla loved the unusual. She was the first daughter of the House of Ice to be born with hair the color of blinding snow in several generations. As a result, she was indulged her every whim and considered special. Her mother was killed in an accident when she was still quite young and that made her a young ruler easily swayed by the attention of others. In fact she craved much attention, needed it, and owning one such as I could only give her more of what she craved.

He pulled a lock of his deep red hair forward and eyed it thoughtfully before giving an un-Flame like snort and throwing the lock over his shoulder. Kendall almost giggled at the gesture that was so at odds with his normal controlled behavior. The gesture was almost human!

"It was determined through testing that my body could accept the alteration that would allow me to carry a child. The scientists were not sure if someone with these energies could be altered, but after the tests were performed, I was immediately taken away for my manhood ceremony."

"Isn't that where they remove...My God!" Kendall's mouth opened and shut without losing any sound, she was so shocked. Without even being trained for such a role in life, Flame was snatched away from all that was familiar and put literately and figuratively on the chopping block.

Flame watched the color leach from his Mistress' face and decided not to tell her of the jeering women of the Ice house who witnessed him being stripped and examined for approval like a choice animal at a breeding mart. Nor would he tell her how ill-prepared he was for pain of the actual circumcision, her word for the ceremony.

He could tell her that instead of his week of recovery, he was immediately forced to stand in attendance behind his Mistress that very evening for a council meeting.

"Even my mother seemed surprised to see me there. My sire hid the tears of sympathy as he watched me fetch for Catla, my new life-mate." Even when he felt that he would scream from the pain of his surgery, his sire's eyes commanded him to silence. Pride was the only legacy his sire could give him for he could do nothing to help his unique son now.

"After the meeting, I was immediately taken to the altering room. When I balked at such treatment, I was ordered to receive twenty lashes with the discipline whip," which he silently endured, "then I was taken and impregnated with Catla's egg."

"They didn't give you time to recover? That's barbaric! You could have died from shock or from blood loss!"

The nurse in Kendall was totally outraged. Any civilized people would see the needs of their own, not exploit them for their own behalf.

"The next night," he continued after Kendall had calmed herself somewhat, "was the celebration of out mating vows."

In extreme pain he had knelt before his mate and accepted the cutting of his hair ties, freeing his long hair so that he was then declared to the world a mated man. Then he was passed the Ring of Attendance, a small ring of metal keys that allowed him to oversee the day-to-day operations of Catla's great house. He was to be the perfect example of masculine behavior, someone the men of the House of Ice could emulate.

"You were a damned butler!" Kendall groused causing a startled yet quickly smothered laugh from Flame as he took in the meaning of her words.

"That is a perfect example of my role within the House of Ice, Mistress. A butler indeed!" But the smile quickly left his handsome face as he told her of the rest of the "blessed" event.

"Later I was forced to stand behind Catla at out mating feast, as she told me to fetch her food and refresh her drink. I can remember her sitting on her family's throne, tossing her blinding white hair that matched her blinding white gown. To her I was nothing more than fancy street laborer." Once she even threw her drink into his face as she declared to the humor of her excited friends that her drink was not hot enough for the cold conditions of the ice continent. She also added that she was helping her new life-mate to adjust quicker by giving him an example of what true heat was. Flame said nothing as the near scalding liquid burned his face and chest. He eyed the shocked expressions on his mother and sire's faces with silent accepting eyes before turning to fulfill the orders of the beautiful monster they had sold him to.

"I remember after that my mother approached me for the first time since my infancy and halted me in the performance of my duties to Catla. I remember that she grasped my chin and tilted my face to observe the burns there. Testrios women are as tall as most of the men, but she had to reach up to touch my face. Everyone in the room quieted as they awaited what she, the great leader of the House of Fire would do. She reacted because she probably wanted to save face, for it was a direct member of her bloodline being driven like an animal before her peers."

"What did she say, Flame?" Kendall was entranced by his skill in telling an obviously painful story. How could a person go through so much and still keep his pride and self esteem intact?

"She said 'Treat your life-mate with respect, Catla. People judge you on not how obedient a man is, but on how well he receives his bondage.' She then returned to her seat and raised her right hand so that my sire, Alonzid, could gently clasp it in his. That is the traditional pose for a mated couple and my parents, with grace and dignity, sought to correct Catla's behavior. Catla herself glared at me and I knew I would suffer for her slight public humiliation."

"Didn't your mother know that a spoiled child like that would place the blame solely on any convenient scapegoat around, mainly you?"

"I like to think that she was honestly trying to help. I would also like to believe that she did not know how vicious Catla would be in retribution."

"What did she do to you, Flame?" Kendall leaned forward, eyes filled full of compassion as she awaited his answer. Automatically she knew that she would not like what he had to say.

He would have preferred not to have to answer her question but his Mistress questioned him directly and no matter how personal, he had no choice but to answer.

"Twenty lashes with the whip and a light flogging with a staff. Catla enjoyed delivering each blow."

He spoke of it as if it had happened to someone else, cool and detached, but Kendall knew he was leaving out some important facts and decided not to pressure him into revealing more than he wanted to.

"On the final day of the two day ceremony, I again took my place behind my mate and carried out her orders."

Only his sire noticed that pain in his eyes and that he moved without his characteristic grace. No one noticed that he declined to eat for he knew that if he opened his mouth, the screams would escape. He soon found it hard to concentrate and flushed with embarrassment when Catla repeated a request for the third time. Only the strength of his sire's eyes held him upright.

It would be a day talked about for years to come, Flame totally lost his tenacious grip on consciousness, standing upright in his proper place behind his Mistress. His eyes just rolled to the back of his head and his head slumped forward.

"They didn't give you time to recover?" Kendall asked softly.

"Catla did not want her actions made known to my mother. The rest of the story, I cannot recall for my memories of it are scrambled."

What he did not see was his sire break away from his proper place behind his mother and race to catch his son. He didn't hear Catla's cry of shock or his mother's bellow of anger. He didn't feel his life's blood seeping through the back of his elaborate red tunic to pool at his feet, the result of several raw open wounds on his back. He did remember opening his eyes to see tiny splatters of his blood on the hem of Catla's white gown and thinking that how he would never be able to remove the stains.

He lost consciousness again soon after and didn't see his sister fighting to keep her meal down when his father tore open his tunic to discover the source of the bleeding.

At first accusations of assassins bandied about the room causing the guards to seal off all entrances and exits, until the bloody wounds that covered back and shoulders were exposed.

"I remember when I awoke my outraged father demanding to know how long ago I was impregnated. When I told him the night of my manhood ceremony, he told me that if I survived, my son would be proud to know that his sire was being spoken of as the strongest man on all of the continents."

"That is all? They didn't take you home? What kind of parents are they? What kind of love is that?"

At the same time she demanded answers from him, her heart was aching for him. She seemed to feel an awareness of how he had become the man she had come to know.

It took courage and strength to go through what he did and not blame his parents for his suffering. It also took a lot of self-control and pride not to shout to all the worlds what had befallen him. Pride was all that he had left and he had refused to lose that.

"My sibling visited me to inform me that Catla was to be severely reprimanded for her actions." His sister stood at the foot of his bed with regret shining in her gray eyes that so much resembled his own. "For a moment, I think she felt the time lost between the two of us and regretted it. She said that she was sorry for what had happened to me and that she had felt my pain."

"What did they do to that bitch, Catla?" Kendall demanded. Her blood screamed out at the injustice that was served upon him that he seemed to feel was normal. She wanted to hear that that spoiled brat got what she deserved. Catla was the one who delivered the near fatal blows to Flame and she deserved the same treatment.

"I do not remember, Mistress. I remember drifting in a deep sleep and resurfacing to hear that Catla was not happy with her choice of life-mate or with the son I carried. I do remember waking once and finding myself in an examining room with a scope on my stomach. I was happy to see my fellow Brother, Devo, standing beside me and smiling."

"Devo was from a lower ranked house and was sent to the Brotherhood when the woman who wanted to breed with him died. He had the most unusual eyes, more unusual than your beautiful eyes, Mistress. His held a rainbow and changed with his every mood. He had to fight to keep his feelings hidden as much as I had to fight to keep my emotions from showing. Being the two most unusual men in the Brotherhood, we became good friends. He was the perfect man to tell me that my son was healthy and was already doing his duty by protecting his sibling."

"They didn't know that you carried twins?" How could such advanced medical technology miss a little thing like that? "How far along were you into your pregnancy?"

"I was about a month into my gestation period when I found out about the twins. The original tests were performed at my mother's insistence when she suspected what Catla had done."

"They can tell the sex of a child that quickly?" Kendall eyes almost glazed at the thought. Imagine never having to return baby clothes because you bought the wrong color or having to argue over baby names, only to find out you picked the name for the wrong sex.

"Usually, but Spark hid his sister well. I believe he was able to cloak her with the energies that he possesses. But Catla never knew what her egg had produced for soon after a servant came to inform me of the death of my life-mate. Because there was no female heir, I was to return to the house of my mother until the time my son had reached maturity and a proper Ice Continent bride was found. My mother was to seize control of the House of Ice until such a time."

"But you carried a female; Ember, and by all rights, she should be the next leader."

"My life-mate was murdered, Mistress. I would not let my child face the same fate without doing all that I could to save her."

"You hid Ember's existence from them." Kendall's eyes filled with understanding. This man truly loved his children and would do anything to protect them. This was proven time and time again.

"Indeed, Mistress. I was planning on returning to the Brotherhood then traveling to some distant part of the Wind continent with my children. I was as much an outsider in my mother's house as I was when I was a child. I held the same rank as my father, but it differed because my power belonged only to the House of Ice. I was again a problem to be dealt with

87

and I did not want my daughter caught in a power struggle. It was better for all concerned if I disappeared with my children."

"So why did you come here to Earth. Wouldn't it have been safer for you to go to a lost sector on your planet than to a strange New World?"

"Someone, a spy sent by my mother no doubt, overheard the plans I was making with Devo. He was willing to travel with me because he found himself pregnant. With the woman who ordered him impregnated dead, his child would have no house to claim it and that is a serious dishonor among the women of my world. His child would never be anything but the lowest of servants."

"On the night before we were to start our journey, my father came to my room and explained that an Execution Squad had been dispatched to hunt me down. My sire knows all that happens in his domain and knew of the female child that I carried. He had made plans for me that I knew nothing about."

"You must hide, Flame." His sire told him as he led them through a complex labyrinth that ran beneath his mother's great house. "Go to this planet, Earth. I have programmed the coordinates in the flight computer. They are a primitive planet deemed unworthy to know of our existence, but in most places men are deemed equal to women." His sire winked at him. "Such a barbarous place is beneath our planet's notice. Go and protect your children, my son. Protect them better than I was able to protect you. I will aid Devo with his plans and you both will have a chance to live a peaceful existence."

"That was the last time that I saw my sire, Mistress. I am not even sure that he is still alive for protecting me and aiding in my escape. Now I am not a man to my people, Mistress. I can serve no purpose beyond training and protecting my children. I can understand your pain, Mistress, but I also know that you cannot blame yourself for the actions of others. Am I responsible for Catla's death or the whole system of government on Testrios? Maybe this Doctor Dick was not the right man for you. Ultimately, we are all responsible for our own happiness."

When put into that perspective, Kendall could not help but help agree with Flame. Maybe Richard wasn't man enough to accept her the way she was. The ability to bear children was not what being a woman was all about. Little girls became women then they accepted themselves for what they were and faced their responsibilities willingly. Kendall had always excelled at taking care of business as well as she could and she had long ago accepted not being able to have children.

It had been hard for her, who wanted a large family, to accept. After her parent's death, the victims of a drunk driver on a cold rainy night, she and her sister became a family of two. But having an older sister to share her sadness and triumphs with didn't lessen the pain of knowing that she would never be able to create a large family of her own. She could have adopted, but then she still would never know the joy of having a new life flutter inside her stomach for the first time. She would never know how it felt to carry and nourish a tiny life growing inside of her body, or feel herself swell with new life. She would never be able to swap first-hand tales of the horrors of labor and how it felt to see your creation, your child, take it's very first breath and make it's presence known to the world. But she had come to grips with that pain and she would survive Richard too.

"What happened to your sister? Was she made to answer for her crimes against you?" Flame asked. "Has she come to understand that she also had the right to refuse the use of your property?"

Kendall was just starting to coming to terms with her womanhood, when he brought up her sister. She thought back to all the time that she had stood beside the woman and watched her finesse and flirt her way out of trouble. Her sister got whatever she wanted whenever she wanted it and knew how to use her ultra feminine charm to help her get ahead in life.

After her parent's death, it was Kendall who made all the arrangements while her sister simpered at the family's attorney who fell all over himself to offer her condolences.

It was her sister who could, with a flash of her tear-filled eyes. Get them the best tables at restaurants or get out of speeding tickets.

No man had ever turned her sister down when she was after him, and amazingly enough, jilted women took her side when their boyfriends were caught in compromising positions with the beautiful gentlewoman with the heart-wrenching eyes.

Her sister had never taken responsibility for anything in her life and never regretted a decision she had made. Why would she break a streak now?

"No. I just threw my ring at Richard, ran out of the apartment and called the caterer from a pay phone on the way home to cancel everything. Maybe I should have faced them after that horrible scene and made my sister answer to me, but I felt too ashamed. In a matter of weeks, my sister managed to get the man I spent months chasing! You should have seen them, Flame. Richard was walking towards me, buck-naked and my sister started crying fake tears. She looked so ridiculous with that veil covering her face and trying to hide her bare butt behind the train of my gown! Now that I look back, it does seem a little funny." Kendall smiled at the memory of the staid and proper Dr. Richard Tanner naked and stammering as he chased after her and her sister doing shock and confusion with the talent and skill of an Oscar contender. Then she sobered.

"I'm such a coward. I should have shut the door and had it out right then and there." She shook her head at her own cowardice and hid her face in her hands.

The babies gurgling brought her back to the present. Flame gracefully rose to his feet and extended a hand to assist her.

Just then as she raised her head to look at him, the afternoon sun broke through the fiery cover of leaves above them and bathed golden light upon his face. She was struck by how absolutely beautiful his face was to her as he gave her a rare smile and patiently waited for her to accept his help. The sun transformed his hair into a fiery nimbus that highlighted his whole being as it flowed gently around him with the light summer breeze.

"He was not the man for you." But I am his expression seemed to say. "You are no coward, Mistress."

"But I ran away!" she began only to stop as she realized that her pulse was racing and her voice sounded breathless.

"It is never too late to right a wrong, My Mistress. Even my sire sought to right a wrong that was not his. You can face what you have to."

While she basked in the reassurance he was giving, he added, "You are more woman then I have ever known in my lifetime, Kendall."

Kendall flushed with pleasure at the sound of her name on his lips. She felt a tingling that flowed down her body and caused her nipples to tighten.

Here was a man who would not judge her or make her feel inferior because of what she lacked. He even thought her plain brown eyes beautiful. She felt a lightness that even the after-glow of sex with Richard, the man she thought she loved, could not make her achieve.

She took his hands and jumped at the electricity that seemed to flare up every time they touched. Her whole body quivered as he helped her to his feet.

As he turned to lead the way back to the cabin, she realized that she felt something for the big guy that she thought never to feel again, pure unadulterated lust. The beauty of the day was magically restored.

Chapter Seven

೫

As he hiked through the lush green grass of this planet towards their shared cabin, Flame reflected on what had taken place in the clearing. The discussion did not turn out the way it should have.

Flame didn't notice the setting sun or the hues of pink and gold painted across the evening sky. Each step he took reverberated with the sound of Kendall's name. With each breath he recalled her emotions running the gauntlet from astonishment to outright anger as she took in his story. He found it…stimulating to think she expressed such emotions for him.

He had told her the story of his life in an attempt to infuse her with some of the courage and self-confidence that she had displayed since they'd met. Her tale of woe seemed to expose the spots of vulnerability, and he could not stand to see her weakened by this Doctor Dick who was no real man, in his opinion.

He saw her confidence return, but with it came that speculative look in her eye. Devo had warned him about that special look a woman was wont to bestow on a man. The enticing smile, the smooth conversation, and the coy looks.

"They get you into their beds and take what they wanted." Flame could still hear the pain in Devo's voice. "Women never even check to see how you fared after the act. They just give you a pat on the head and then send you back to your room until they again had a need of you. They promise delights that turn your body into fire and your mind into mush. They always make sure that you want to be used again and again."

The worst part of the betrayal came later. "Women almost always say that they want to see what a child of yours would look like. Then it's off to the alteration room for you. Then during the next twelve months while your stomach swells big with the child you created together the woman starts eyeing the next man with a bigger chest, until you come to the realization that you have been used and discarded. The woman always moves on to her next conquest, forgetting your existence until the birth." Devo's voice had turned bitter. "Then if your child is female, she'll be taken away from you immediately to receive "proper" training. If you bear a male, the woman will not even give him the benefit of her House's name."

Flame refused to believe Kendall was the type to use him in such a manner, but she kept looking at him with that glassy-eyed expression Devo had warned him about. Even more disturbing was the fact that his own body betrayed him each time those brown orbs looked at him just so.

Could it be that he was—his breath caught with gasp and a shudder—facing the desire to lust after her as well? Devo had explained the symptoms and warned that a cold bath was best cure for returning your blood to its proper place. But could the mating lust be upon him? This required further thought.

Once they entered the cabin, Flame disappeared to care for the children while Kendall headed for the kitchen for a snack. Once there, she noticed the light on the forgotten answering machine blinking. A little afraid she had been tracked by some government type who would want to know about the sunken spaceship in the lake behind her house, she leaned against a nearby wall and with trembling fingers pressed the play button.

"Kendall, I know you're there. Pick up the phone."

It was none other than Doctor Dick himself. Her fear turned to frank curiosity and then to anger.

"Look, I know you are there and I really need to talk to you. Your sister and I are on our way there right now. Please Kendall, just hear us out. It's important."

"Damn! This is just what I need right now." Kendall groaned sarcastically, dropping her head back against the wall. Was it her dumb luck or was the old wives' tale about talking people up true?

"Exactly, Mistress." Flame watched her slide down the wall with a miserable groan. "You need to confront them and place your past behind you. It is the only way you will finally be free of the shadow that they cast on your life."

Kendall swore silently to herself. What she needed was a little self-affirming sex to put a new perspective on life and close the door to the past, not a confrontation with her ex.

"Now is the time to right that wrong, Mistress. You can face them now and on your own terms."

"What happened to calling me Kendall?" She glared up at him from her place on the floor. She did not want to face this particular past mistake.

"What will you do, Mistress?" he put emphasis on the title.

She winced. Perhaps he was right. The past had to be faced. "Will you help me, Flame?" She looked up at him, feeling a little lost.

"All you need do is ask, Kendall." But instead of moving toward her he turned to leave.

"Where are you going?" Kendall called after him as she struggled to her feet.

"To shower." He called the explanation over his shoulder as he raced for the bathroom.

Kendall eyed his escape with suspicion until she realized the reason for his retreat. It was kind of hard to ignore his reaction to her when her face was waist level with the evidence of his desire. She bit back a chuckle, realizing her red-haired mystery man wanted her just as much as she wanted him.

"Soon, Flame, soon." She promised as she walked into the living room. She would choose the place to have this showdown. She would maintain control.

* * * * *

Flame stood under the stinging spray of chill water in the shower.

This cold was not working; he thought as he closed his eyes, braced his hands against the cool tile wall.

His organ throbbed in time with the pounding of his heart. All he could think about was Kendall.

Kendall, in her tight pants, her rounded bottom swaying as she walked. Kendall, smiling at him as she walked, her breasts bobbing beneath the shirt she wore. Kendall, her full lips parted and her Tarcas stone eyes shining as she discovered something about her self, or flashing in anger as she raced to defend him against his past.

Kendall had filled his mind and was ruling his senses.

An unconscious moan escaped his lips, the sound echoing in the shower stall, resonating a deep needful cord from within his tense body.

Flame had never felt this, this arousal, to this level before.

He pulled one hand free of the wall, running its cool touch down his chest to his groin, hoping to massage away the ache.

But instead, as his hand touched his painfully erect cock, the sensation that shot through it caused his sack to tighten and his knees to buckle.

Shocking waves of heat and need rushed through his at first contact.

What was this?

Was this why the men were forbidden to touch themselves?

His eyes slowly closed and a deep rumbling groan escaped his throat as he slowly stroked himself again.

From the thick base of his golden shaft to the now angry purple heart shaped head, tingles of lighting followed his touch.

Tentatively, he touched his sac, feeling the hard roundness of his full testicles within, shuddering as he rolled them gently in his palm, sending a new sensation shooting up his back and around to his cock.

His whole body shuddered and despite the coolness of the water, he broke out into a sweat.

Fisting his hand around his shaft, his thumb gently caressing the small darker line of flesh that showed where his foreskin had been removed during this manhood ceremony, Flame tightened his hand and began to pump.

"Gods!" he gasped as something inside him shifted and his hips slammed into his touch.

His skin prickled and tingled, burned where he touched. He felt his testicles tighten and push up against the base of his cock as clear droplets of his pre-pleasure beaded to the tip of its head.

Steam began to rise off of his body as his hips sent a demand to brain, a command that could not be denied. Pump and pump hard! Now!

Giving in to this new need, his hand began to squeeze and slam down on his erection, the tip of his fisted fingers catching just under the head of his penis, sending extra fire shooting with each rough touch.

His eye squeezed shut, his face broke out into a grimace of pleasure, his hand flew faster than lighting, increasing the need, increasing the desire, increasing the pleasure.

Suddenly, he saw a clear picture of his Kendall in his mind. His Kendall, baring her brown flesh, offering him her nakedness, sharing her body with him. Her smile was open and engaging, her eyes slumberous with desire, her arms and legs spread in welcome.

"Kendall!" he gasped. "Love me, Kendall."

As his words circled around the steamy shower, Flame's eyes snapped open.

What was he doing? It was against the rules to self-pleasure!

Cursing himself a fool several times over, he jerked his hands away form his body, denying the shuddered of release that beckoned just over the horizon, ending the intense pleasure that had spread across his body, but leaving the need shimmering just below the surface.

Shuddering, he stepped into the cold spray, ignoring the sizzle as the water touched his heated flesh, ignoring the heat and humidity that now filled the room, ignoring the primal smell of sex that filled the air.

Even worse that the thought of breaking that rule, of losing his control, was the thought of experiencing such a great cataclysmic release alone.

If and when he ever earned such a pleasure, he wanted to have Kendall beside him, over him, under him, not just a phantom of her in his mind.

He closed his eyes and let the cold spray caress his face although the biting cold did nothing to assuage his desire.

But for his Mistress, his Kendall, he could wait. He obeyed the inner sense told him that the solo release would be a hollow one. His victory would come with Kendall. Even if it took him the rest of his life here on this planet, he would earn the right to prove himself worthy of her.

That, on all the energies that swirled through his body, he swore.

* * * * *

Richard and Caressa arrived later that evening soon after Flame and Kendall pulled both squirmy babies from their baths.

The scene had been so peaceful and domestic. The front of Kendall's shirt was soaked from the splashes made by the growing babies. The water carried the unforgettable smell of baby soap and new skin.

Sitting on the floor with Kendall, Flame felt a pull at his heart as he watched her struggle to place his son's kicking legs into the blue sleeper that she had picked out for him. It would be wonderful to stay here on this mountain with her and pretend to be a typical American family, but neither he nor his children were quite typical.

Already Spark's hair was a fiery red while Ember's red hair was streaked with slashes of an almost blinding white. He looked down at his daughter content in her baby seat wearing her pink sleeper while he contemplated the meaning of that phenomenon.

Before he could comment on her coloration, there was a knock at the door and all of the warm family feelings evaporated.

Kendall tensed at the sound, instantly alert. Flame automatically took up a defensive position in front of Kendall and the children as the door creaked opened and the two people entered.

"Well, it looks like the nuclear family in here." The female spoke softly while wringing her hands. She eyed Kendall with large slanted eyes and gave her a tentative smile.

This woman had to be the older sibling that Kendall had spoken of, her estranged sister. They looked very similar from their golden brown skin to their wavy black hair, although this woman let her flow free around her shoulders while Kendall kept hers in a neat and tidy bun.

The most startling differences between the two women were in their height—the older sister stood several inches taller than Kendall—and in their eyes. While the brown of the sister's eyes was mixed with a dark gold, only Kendall's eyes possessed the deep brown shade of the rare and prized Tarcas stones. It was a shade so deep it could mesmerize anyone who dared to linger and stare too long.

Also, unlike Kendall who preferred those dreaded revealing blue jeans, this woman was dressed in a soft flowing gown that looked to be made of wild flowers on a soft white field. It was feminine and delicate, but Flame decided he preferred the straight honesty in Kendall's style of dress. A woman could hide lots of things behind the abundant material of the sister's dress, weapons for instance, just as Catla hid her true nature behind a mask of innocent beauty and power.

"Hello, Caressa." Kendall spoke stiffly from the floor. She cradled Spark in an unconsciously protective embrace. "Richard." She nodded at the man who stood behind her sister dressed in a brown suite.

No one made any threatening moves toward Kendall or his children. Flame gracefully sank to the floor and began shoving baby paraphernalia back into the baby bags, but kept a wary eye on the visitors who had invaded their temporary home.

"You can call off your Irish wolfhound, Kendall. I promise not to touch you." Richard plucked an invisible piece of lint from his jacket sleeve and eyed Kendall expectantly.

Kendall raised an eyebrow at his commanding tone, but instead of calling Flame off, joined her steely eyes gaze to his. Richard ran a finger under his restricting collar as both cutting gazes focused in on him. He began to look a little like a deer caught in a set of oncoming headlights.

"Who are these adorable children, Dallie?" the sister, Caressa broke in. She eased a little closer to her little sister and turned her eyes to Flame. "And who is this handsome man?"

"They belong to Flame," Kendall answered, her voice sounding possessive. "And he belongs to me."

She turned to face him. "Flame, this is my sister Caressa. I've told you all about her."

"Jesus, Kendall! There is no reason to be so ruthless." Richard placed a protective arm around the jittery woman and eased her to his side.

"There is no reason for you to make such a noise in the presence of my children and my...girlfriend," Flame countered with a small grin at Kendall. He remembered the word that she had used to describe him earlier to the man, Richard. He should keep consistent with her story.

Richard's defensiveness did not bother Flame. It was clear to him through the man's actions where the man's heart now lay. A true man would remember where his loyalties lay.

Flame turned his attentions to his children who seemed a little startled by the loud outburst. They hadn't cry. Instead they both turned to Kendall in perfect accord, as if to say, "This is the man you wanted?"

"Have a seat." Kendall gestured to the couch situated in front of bathing party and ignored the look she was getting from her charges. "We will be with you all in a moment."

A tense silence filled the room while they finished with the children and in single file marched from the room. In the bedroom, they placed the children in their cubes and observed each other over the bodies of the squirming children who seemed to be shaking their heads in dismay about Kendall's choice of mate before closing their little eyes and beginning nodding off.

"Mothers all over the world would kill to have these cubes, Flame. Do they come in adult size?" Kendall sought to cover her unease in her usual way, by ignoring it, but Flame would not allow her to hide from herself.

"You are being very gracious, Mistress." The babies seemed to nod, once again in complete accord. "I will bring out the refreshments I have prepared in a moment."

"Thank you, Flame," she whispered. She knew she meant more than just the pastries he'd cooked. She walked around Spark's cube and threw her arms around Flame in a big hug. He stiffened as her arms moved around him.

"What's wrong?"

"I have never been touched like this before." Flame's voice noticeably deepened. "What is this ritual called?"

"You have never been hugged?" she looked up into his eyes with evident astonishment.

"No. But I think I like it." He wrapped his arms around Kendall in return, delivering an enveloping embrace. She watched his eyes close in evident enjoyment.

"Hugging," he mused. "I must do this with my children often so that they too might know of this warm feeling of comfort."

"Only you would make such a simple act seem so special, Flame!" Kendall declared. She eased out of his arms and turning to face the living room.

His words had touched a deep part of her and infused her with confidence. If a man like Flame could face his past and move on with the joy of discovery in his heart, so could she.

She tugged her damp shirt into place and walked into the living room to face her past, leaving Flame to stare in open-mouthed wonder at what a damp, nearly transparent shirt did to her breasts and her nipples.

This was going to be a long evening, he decided as he looked down at his swelling lower extremity.

By the time Flame had recovered his control, Kendall was gone and he had to rush to the kitchen to retrieve the refreshments that he had prepared earlier. The pastries were easy to make with her simple cooking devices; still he took pride in the fact that he was able to produce something beautiful out of the ingredients that he found in her kitchen.

He really did not know what whipped cream was exactly, but when combined with something called strawberry syrup, it made a light and delightful filling for the bread-like substance called pound cake. All he had to do was make a center pocket in a slice of the pound cake and add his makeshift filling. The few red berries he found fresh were sliced and decorated the top of his pastries and something sweet called "powdered sugar" was sprinkled on top. For a quickly thrown together snack, it was pretty and looked impressive.

When Flame arrived at the battlefield, everyone was staring at the floor or the ceiling, anywhere but at each other. Again tension fairly crackled in the air of the room.

"Refreshments?" He offered his tray first to Kendall, then to Caressa. He purposely said nothing to Richard, just shoved the platter in the other man's direction with great indifference.

Flame marveled at his actions. He did not understand the possessive feelings that had come over him while dealing with his Mistress, but he knew that he held an intense dislike for the man-child who sat primly on the couch beside the sister and now openly eyed Kendall.

"These are delicious." Caressa gushed after sampling one of the little pastries on the tray. She licked a bit of frosting off of her fingers before turning to her scowling sister, "When did you learn to cook, Dallie?"

"I didn't. Flame did the cooking." Kendall crossed her arms in front of her. Caressa's mannerisms and flirtatious nature obviously annoyed his Mistress.

Kendall had moved a kitchen chair into position in front of Richard and Caressa; a position no doubt calculated to give her the upper hand in the conflict as the chair lifted her higher than the couch cushion's lifted their guests. Hiding a grin, Flame placed the tray in the coffee table within easy reach of their guests before taking up a stance behind Kendall's chair.

Automatically he took up the position of life-mate. It felt right to support his Mistress in this small way. Confidently he reached for her right hand and clasped it into his.

Kendall was startled at Flame's gesture, knowing what it must cost him to take up such a position again, but she gladly accepted his help and support.

She turned her attention to the Doctor and her devoted sister. It was more difficult than she imagined, watching the two of them together. "Let's cut to the chase, shall we? What do you want."

"A chance to explain." Richard was obviously observing the easy way Flame and Kendall touched. "When did the two of you meet anyway? Where is the mother of those children?"

"Dead," Flame's answer was curt. "And when we met is none of your concern, for you had already forced this treasure from your life." She felt the energy it cost him to prevent the red sparks from filling his eye.

Richard blanched a little at the blunt answers, but dogmatically continued onward ignoring Flame's dark look and Caressa's startled glance.

"My condolences." He turned to Kendall. "I know what I did was wrong, Kendall. I should have told you how I was feeling but I didn't want to break your heart."

"So you screw my sister on top of my weeding gown instead? Thanks for sparing me all of that grief, Doc." Her cold brown eyes stared unforgivingly straight into his soul.

"Dallie, it wasn't supposed to be like that!" Caressa desperately tried to explain, breaking into the intense stare-down. "I didn't mean to hurt you. Richard and I started talking, and he told me that he really was intimidated by you, Dallie. You never need anyone. He needed to be needed. I needed to be needed too, Dallie. All our lives you never turned to me to help you with anything, you never needed me."

"And when I do want my sister beside me, this is what I get, Caressa. I needed your help and this is the help I get." Kendall waved her left hand towards Richard and tried to hold back the anger that was snaking through her blood. She was starting to lose control, but Flame's firm grip on her hand helped calm her a little.

"I am so sorry, Dallie, but when Richard and I picked up that gown, I wanted to be you. You know, totally confidant and always knowing what to do? Just like you. I told Richard what I was feeling and he told me that it was nice not being around a superwoman, that he liked having a woman around that he could actually be some use for other that a sexual toy."

Richard cursed under his breath as a blush suffused his face with color and even Caressa seemed to regret what she had said.

Flame's hand tightened around hers in a stay-strong gesture as she drew in a deep amazed breath.

"That never stopped him from wanting to play as I recall," Kendall was now looking in disbelief at the two of them. "As a mater of fact, he started more games than I care to remember."

She contemplated telling the story of how Richard liked to dress up like a little boy in shorts and knee socks, and get disciplined for his bad behavior. She'd bet money that dear needy Richard had never told her sister about that one!

"I know that Dallie, but you can be scary when you set your mind to do a task. Richard told me that you made him fell like less of a man sometimes and that he only felt confident about his work as a doctor when he was around you. Did you know he wanted to have children? You convinced him that children weren't necessary to his happiness. I told him that I always wanted children of my own and a special man to make my dreams come true. We didn't mean to Dallie, honest to God, but we started comforting each other and then…then things just sort of happened." She finished in a rush and looked down to clasp her hands in her lap, drawing Kendall's attention to a perfectly shaped set of hands that now wore a suspiciously familiar-looking ring.

"So, my sexual excesses aside, you both wanted to be needed and completely forgot about the person who brought such needy people together in the first place." That ring did look familiar. She leaned forward a bit to get a closer look.

"That was no excuse for what we did, Kendall," Richard ran his fingers through his hair, ruining his salon-perfect hairstyle. "We both know that we made a mistake. I know I should have talked to you about how I was feeling, but I didn't know how to tell you."

"You compound that mistake by using that ridiculous story," Flame added with his eyes narrowed in anger. "You have made Kendall feel that this whole affair was her fault, that she was lacking in some way, all because of your treacherous actions. You have made her feel half a woman and this is not so."

Kendall watched Flame take several deep breaths, slowly relaxing muscles that had gone tense with the heated exchange of words. He loosened the grip he held on her hand. Kendall noticed that he looked both surprised and perhaps a little liberated by having offered an opinion during their discussion.

"My God, Dallie, I never felt you were not a real woman. If anything, you are more woman than I!" Caressa turned her stricken gaze first to Richard and then to her sister, "You are more woman than I could ever be."

She spoke passionately as she pressed both hands to her heaving chest, the perfect picture of a distraught female, and turned to Richard to confirm her words.

"You were never half a woman, Kendall. I never felt that way. You just frightened me." Richard ruefully admitted as he patted and stroked Caressa's shoulder in a comforting manner. "I guess that I just thought that I wasn't man enough for you, Kendall. And when I ran into someone who needed me just a little, I guess I lost my head."

"I've got to tell you something else, Dallie." Caressa walked over to Kendall and knelt gracefully at her feet, spreading the skirt of her dress around so that none of her legs showed. That gesture alone made Kendall want to kick her sister, but her next words stopped her actions.

"I didn't mean for it to happen, Dallie, but I'm pregnant. I'm going to have a baby. Richard's baby."

Kendall's hand tightened convulsively around Flame's as she drew in a quick painful breath. All was silent in the room again.

For a moment, she flashed back to when her gynecologist told her that her painful cramps were being caused by endometreosis, back to when he told her that surgery was the answer, that she would never have children. She, for a moment, relieved the painful heartbreak, the mourning for all her children not yet born, and the agonizing pain in her suddenly motherless soul.

Gently, Flame cupped her hand between his, silently telling her that even in the face of this latest betrayal, she was not alone.

After a moment of quiet contemplation, Kendall gave a wry grin to her kneeling sister. She had finally got a clear look at the ring on her finger. It was the same one that she threw at Richard when she had stormed from his apartment. Despite the smile, she realized burning liquid filled her eyes. Kendall blinked them back to observe the people, the strangers, in front of her.

She had begun to distance herself from the situation the moment she had met Flame and begun to put it in its proper perspective. Jealousy pinched at her slightly, she could never have children, but she also felt a strange sense of relief.

It was time to set her mind at ease and her heart free. Her sister could have her seconds. What good were old leftovers anyway? She wanted a new meal on her plate, one that was piping hot and spicy and was melt-in-your-mouth delicious.

"You know what? I seem to be hurt more by the prospect of you two being the parents of my niece or nephew than by the thought of losing Doctor Dick over there."

Now that she had said it, Kendall realized that her words were perfectly true. She turned to face Richard. "I hope you kept the wedding dress as well as the old rock on Caressa's finger. It's much too late to try and find a new one before Caressa begins to show and my hand-me-downs can easily be lengthened. Remember, Richard, you have a reputation to uphold."

Strange as seemed, losing her fiancée didn't seem so tragic anymore. If anything, Richard now seemed to be a pathetic little boy to her. Then she came to another somewhat startling realization. The real betrayal was that she had blamed herself for their actions.

Flame was right. She could control her life but had no power on the actions of others. After she had gotten over the hurt and embarrassment, she felt nothing but apathy for them. She had finally settled her past mistakes where they belonged, in the past.

She released Flame's hand and slowly rose to her feet. She strode to the front door heal held high and swung it open with relish.

"I congratulate you both on finding each other in this mixed-up crazy world. I wish you joy and happiness. I wish you heaven. Call me when my niece or nephew is born and I'll send a gift. Finally, I'd like to thank you both for preventing me from making a terrible mistake by marrying you, Richard."

She then turned to her still kneeling and now somewhat shocked Caressa. "You are my sister and my only living relative; Caressa, but I don't want to see your face for a while. In fact, I don't want to see either of your faces for a long time." She turned to encompass Richard in her gaze. "Now get out."

Richard helped a stricken Caressa to her feet and the couple exited the cabin in silence.

Caressa must really be upset, Kendall thought to herself. Her sister gave no thought to the mascara running down her face nor did she move with her usual flirty walk. Kendall gently closed the door after them and mentally dusted off her hands.

Chapter Eight

𝕊𝕆

"I've just realized that I don't know those people, Flame."

Kendall wrapped her arms around his waist. "I can't believe that my sister is pregnant by my fiancée! And that she thought that I would be, I don't know, happy about it."

"I thought that he was your past mistake, Mistress? Do you regret not keeping him?" The thought that Kendall still had feelings for her previous lover made Flame just a touch angry. What did she find so appealing about the half-man, anyway? What feelings did she have for him? The thought of his hands on her soft curvy body in a fit of sexual excess made him...

Why should he care?

"Oh, he's in the past, Flame. I guess I'm feeling a little, well, insulted by the whole thing." She looked up inquiringly into his eyes. "Am I intimidating, Flame? Do I scare you?"

"Maybe he was not man enough for you, Mistress." There was something wrong with his voice. It voice sounded raspy and had dropped an octave. Flame hugged Kendall to his chest, becoming familiar with the new embrace and the longing to feel her arms wrapped around him. "Again I tell you that you are the most courageous woman that I have ever known. Any man would be insane not to welcome your advances. Your strength has great pull upon me, Mistress, as does your kind heart."

"Would you, Flame? Would you welcome my attentions knowing that I scared another man into the arms of another woman with my, ah, zeal?"

Her simple question and direct gaze caused a burning in his heart and a tightening in his manhood. It had happened a thousand times before since knowing her, when she stroked his hair or gifted him with a smile, but this time the feeling was more intense. What sexual act exactly did she perform that frightened the half-man?

"Before, you said that my eyes were beautiful, Flame. Did you mean it?" Her eyes had gone soft and misty and Flame felt his blood slam into his lower region.

"What is this feeling that I have around you, My Mistress?" he finally asked. His voice dropped deeper and took on a husky sound. "Why does my body react for you when it never has done so before?" He pushed her away in an attempt to put some space between the two of them. "What is it that you do to me?"

Without trying, she had shattered all of the warnings that Devo had planted in his mind. With a flash of those eyes, those Tarcas-brown eyes, he was ready to kneel at her feet and swear his loyalty. It was frustrating, it was pleasurable, and it was confusing and new. This had to be lust, for no other feeling would make him her willing slave and fill him with a desire to put into practice what he had learned as theory.

Kendal stared at Flame, picking up on his unspoken meaning at once. "You're a virgin?"

She should have known. All the clues were there, but she had ignored them, thinking that an actual sexual act was involved in his pregnancy somewhere. "You have given birth but never had sex?"

Color highlighted his face. "No, Mistress. I know all of the technical details, but I have never submitted my body for the pleasure of a woman. It is unnecessary to copulate in order to reproduce."

What was wrong with those women? The sex part was half the fun of having a baby—well at least that was what she had heard from many a woman in the throes of deep labor pains.

Then too, her hormones raced out of control as she came to full realization of what his little disclosure meant. She was the first to solicit a sexual response from this man. It made her feel powerful and powerfully...curious? What technical details was he taught and could they apply to an Earth female? Her curiosity was running wild.

Flame had understood that at sometime in his life, a woman might find him physically desirable and that he may be called upon to fulfill that duty. It had been explained to all the young men of the Brotherhood when they reached adolescence and by his father who was considered a master of the sensual arts.

But he, himself, had only felt repugnance for the emotionless act that had been described with such detail. Even Devo was at a loss when it came time to explain what could motivate a man to stroke and caress a woman with such ardor without a thought to his own satisfaction.

What Flame was feeling now was nothing like the emotions he had expected to feel. He knew that if he backed away from Kendall now, he would damage their relationship, for he recognized the lust in her eyes. But if he stayed near her, he was going to give into his baser instincts and take her on the floor like a wild animal, as his new emotions were demanding that he do. He was beginning to understand what had motivated Devo to place himself into a compromising position with a lady of a great house. He now felt a full understanding of his brother's choices, and indeed felt compelled to make some the same decisions.

"We have to do something about your virgin state, Flame. It's not fair that they denied you the pleasurable experience before knocking you up." She stepped closer to him, pleased to see that the curious sparkle was back in his eyes and his hair had began to wave around him.

Reaching up, she ran her fingers through his hair, wanting to know again the feel of its wonderful texture, but this time, when it was alive with his emotions. She gasped as she received a mild shock, more like a tingle, from his wonderfully electric hair.

It traveled down her arms and across her chest causing her nipples to tighten, before shooting down explode beneath her navel causing her eyes to open in pleasurable surprise.

"Did you feel that?" she whispered gazing up into his shining eyes.

"It is my excitement, Mistress." His voice was rueful but his gaze was steady. "It is sometimes hard for me to contain my emotions."

Kendall gave him a wicked grin before tangling both hands into his wonderful hair and pulling his head down to her level. She placed her lips against his and gasped as the same tingling touched every nerve ending in her face with a sharp pleasure before it flashed down her body awaking and arousing her every nerve-ending straight to her toes.

Flame moaned softly at the feeling of his very energy penetrating her body. It felt as if he was stepping inside her to experience every nuance of her pleasure and adding it to the feelings soaring through his body. The gentle touch of her lips twisted his insides and threatened to break his control.

Almost as if in a trance, his arms moved around her body and pulled her closer to the heat of his chest as he sought to deepen the contact between them. He sighed softly into her mouth as he closed his eyes and felt the soft press of her warm body.

"Like this," Kendall murmured against his mouth before she slowly traced his lips with her tongue.

His eyes flew open at the contact and his jaw dropped in surprise, giving her the perfect opportunity to press her advantage. She quickly gained access to the warmth of his mouth with her soft tongue and savored the unique flavor of him.

He closed his eyes with a groan of pleasure that rumbled from the center of his soul as her small warm tongue danced against his.

"This is not very sanitary," he felt compelled to point out as she pulled back from him a little to gage his reaction.

His mouth had set her tingling nerves on fire and her skin began to itch with the want of him. "Yes, I know, but kissing is so enjoyable," she pointed out before she tightened her grip on that glorious mass of auburn hair and pulled his mouth back to hers.

Flame groaned low in his throat before thrusting his tongue into her mouth, effectively taking over the kiss, proving that he was a fast learner. He crushed her small body into his larger harder one and delighted in the primitive thrill of dominating her in this small way. The soft mounds of her breasts contrasting with the feel of her pebble-hard nipples pressing against him made him want to rip off her shirt and squeeze them in his hands.

Kendall shuddered at the sensation of being crushed in his arms and moaned at the feeling of his arousal pressing full and hard against her stomach. His hands hungrily roamed up her back to pull her closer, leaving a trail of fire in their wake.

If the simple act of kissing this man inflamed her senses, what would physically making love to him do to her?

"This shirt, may I remove it, Mistress?" he rasped between knee weakening kisses and persuasive laps of his tongue.

He absently fingered the cloth that separated him from her bare flesh. He had a sudden urge to lick her skin all over and the shirt was in his way. If her body tasted as good as her mouth, no matter what she said, he was going to stay and feast for a while.

"Yes," she managed as she untangled her fingers from his hair. "If you remove yours too."

He stepped back from her and whipped her T-shirt over her head, all shyness forgotten in the face of his need to see and feel her bare skin.

He looked and all movement froze. In puzzled delight, he stared at the white lacy bra that cupped and lifter her breasts so invitingly. His mouth went dry at the sight of her nipples straining against the soft lace and his fingers began to long for the feel of the soft skin that this garment so temptingly offered.

"This garment, Mistress. I have never seen anything like this." Tentatively, he ran his fingers over the lace covering and yet exposing her nipple.

Kendall moaned at the contact and wished that the material would disappear so she could feel his rough fingers on her flesh, caressing her as she longed to be touched.

Taking matters into her own hands, she grabbed both his and pressed them to her aching breasts. Again her body shuddered as she forced his fingers to tighten ever so slightly around her aroused flesh.

Flame almost cried out in joy at the feeling of her soft breasts in his hands. In the back of his mind, he marveled at the many and varied uses of that particular part of the female anatomy.

After a moment of this torture, she began to demand, "Remove it, Flame. Take it off of me."

Never one to question her orders, Flame grasped the delicate lace between his fingers and granted her request by ripping it in two. His mouth dropped open as her full rounded breasts sprang free from the cups and were exposed to his sparkling eyes.

His eager hands cupped her softness and they both groaned at the jolt of sensation that shook their bodies. Her softness made the fire in his soul burn dangerously out of control while the power vibrating through his body almost scorched her turgid nipples into tiny points of pleasure.

"You are magnificent," he groaned before falling to his knees to take a berry-colored nipple into his mouth, gently laving its velvety surface with his tongue.

Kendall cried out at the sensation of his soft wet tongue stroking her nipple and the electric jolt that followed. She grasped handfuls of his hair and pulled him closer, savoring each hot caress. The feel of his electrified hair rippling against her naked chest finally caused her knees to give way.

"Fire!" she gasped as he caught her to him and carried her the few feet to the couch. The bedroom was just too far away.

"You feel like living fire." She shook at the touch of his soft cotton shirt against her sensitized nipples as he lowered her to the cushions.

"You make my control slip." Flame growled before standing in front of her, a hot quivering mass of tension, awaiting the next command that would bring so much pleasure to them both. His responsibility was to deliver to her the ultimate pleasure, a job which he now reveled and gloried in.

"What would you have of me?" His eyes glowed with impatience and he absently licked his dry lips, drawing her attention to their glistening surface and causing her to shudder in reaction.

Kendall ground her naked back into the soft/rough texture of the couch, enjoying the brush of the material against her skin. What she wanted was easily enough asked for, she decided as she looked hungrily up at him.

"Take off your shirt, please." Kendall all but moaned at the picture of this powerful man with sparkling eyes and electric hair looming above her, awaiting her pleasure. "I want to feel your naked skin against mine."

"As you wish, My Mistress." That slow deep voice brought another shiver of excitement to her nerve endings.

Instead of pulling off his T-shirt like any other man would do, Flame grasped the neck with both hands and slowly ripped the material from his body. The sounds of that slow, almost teasing, rend made her the back of her neck tingle and her mouth water almost as much as the sight of his bare chest. His eyes bored into hers, holding her captive within their heated gaze.

"May I taste of you again, My Mistress?" He asked as he slowly, hungrily raked his eyes over her body that lay frozen in a wanton sprawl before him.

Now she understood his comment about his slipping control. He would do nothing to her without first asking for permission and receiving her approval. With that knowledge came arousal so painfully delicious that it brought tears to her eyes.

"Please!" she moaned raising her open arms to him and looking into his eyes. "I need to feel you, Flame."

Filled with a ravenous hunger, Flame shoved the coffee table aside, mindless of the pastries that crashed to the floor as he dropped to his knees before her. He placed his hands on her shoulders in a gentling motion before slowly lowering himself to her.

His lips dropped to lay a soft tingling kiss on each eyelid, before moving on to the corner of her mouth as his hair tickled her hardened nipples. Once there he murmured onto her trembling lips, "You taste of delicate strength, My Mistress."

He pulled back slightly to raise her hand to his mouth and lightly kissed her palm. Her other hand came up to rest against his cheek. He nuzzled against her there for a moment with closed eyes before turning to kiss that palm too. Then he lightly clasped both her hands to his chest before again lowering his mouth to hers. His skin burned.

If their previous kisses were like Kendall, bold, brash and knowing, this kiss was all Flame, slightly seeking, curious, then bolder as he parted her lips with his questing tongue.

He tasted, found her flavor pleasing and dove for more. He began to devour her slowly with his hot mouth and tender lips.

Kendall moaned and pulled her lips from his. The room had started spinning and she could hardly breath. Never had desire struck her so hard before. She lifted her head, exposing her neck to his caresses as she looked up towards the heavens to regain some of her composure.

But Flame wanted her wild. He trailed his mouth to her neck where he added soft licks from his wet tongue and gentle nips from his teeth. Kendall moaned as her mind and body were assaulted with his white-hot desire, for he described in erotic detail what he was going to do to her in his raspy voice and how it would make him feel. His heated breath against her made her arch closer to his warmth and wish that these feelings would never end.

"May I lick your flesh with my wet tongue, Mistress?"

She nodded her head yes. She was too far gone to talk.

"May I run my thumbs beneath this wonderfully soft skin underneath your breasts, and watch you tremble?"

"Anything!" she near shouted and then hissed at the feel of his thumbs finding yet another erogenous zone on her body. Who knew that the skin beneath her breasts were so sensitive?

When he finally reached her breast with his giving lips, she sobbed out loud with relief and impatience. She grasped his head between her hands as she arched into him, greedy for what he could make her feel and demanding more.

His mouth devoured her. He nipped and suckled until the throbbing in her loins matched the pounding of her heart. His hands tortured and gently rolled the nipple of the opposite breast, lest it felt neglected, and caused her arms to wrap around his head, pulling and writhing against him.

"I can't stand it!" she sobbed throwing her head back as her lower body rose and fell against his hot bare skin of his chest with her need. "Please, Flame!"

"Let me worship at your altar, Mistress." He raised his head and deliberately shook his head to let the tendrils of his hair flow over her damp flesh. She shakily nodded her head instinctively knowing what he meant and shaking with anticipation of his possession.

The rasp of the zipper sounded loud in the silent room. Her jeans scraped against her sensitive skin as they were eased down her legs and cast aside. He looked at her tiny paisley panties for a moment before asking, "May I remove these as well, My Mistress. May I reveal your precious womanhood and revel in the riches that you would serve me?"

His voice, already gravely, dropped another octave in his excitement. His gray eyes were now shot with a rich red flame as his fingers tenderly stroked the damp material covering her.

Would she let this innocent yet suddenly sensuous creature have access to her throbbing body, to tease and explore at his will?

Kendall nodded her answer even though inside she was screaming, yes please, yes!

With shaking hands, he carefully eased the last barrier from her body, spread her legs, and was struck mute with the beauty that he beheld.

Like the most delicate of Testrios orchids, her petals were tightly furled, but a hint of deep rose glistened there with the dew of her excitement. Suddenly he wanted to make those petals open for him and reveal the stunning beauty that they would reveal to the man who knew how to nurture and pamper the blossom within.

So with awed reverence, he ran one finger over her quivering flesh and watched as she arched her hips towards him with abandon, held helpless in the grip of madness brought on by the one called Flame.

He noticed her scent first. Fresh and clean, she smelled slightly floral, wholly enticing, and definitely woman. Suddenly he wanted to be bathed in her juices and surrounded by her scent. It was more compelling than anything he had ever come across. He wanted her smell in him, on him, to mix with his essence and create a wonderfully unique smell that they only could make together.

He lowered his head to drink at her fount and lost himself in the special taste of her. With a sigh he burrowed closer, all inhibitions forgotten, as he gave into his needs, needing badly for her to release more of herself to him.

Flame buried his hot mouth into her womanhood. A sharp cry of pleasure escaped through her lips as his tongue shot electric shivers though her as. Hungrily he lapped the rich nectar of her with ever increasing urgency. With lips and tongue, he bathed the seat of her woman's pleasure while a finger gently inserted itself inside her quivering walls.

"Will you grip my manhood with such ferocity, Kendall?" his rasping breath sent another spasm thorough her cleft as it wafted over her wet skin and caused her to whip her head from side to side on the couch. "Will you allow me to plummet your depths and put an end to your torment?"

He again buried his face between her tights and wrapped his tongue around the pearled bud of her desire, before beginning to gently suck and nip at it. He had never thought to perform this rite for any woman, but now that he had tasted dewy sweetness of Kendall, he found it difficult to stop. He added another finger to the first, delighting at the moist slippery feel of her.

"Flame! Please now! Oh, I need you in me!" she cried as her whole body began to tingle and twitch beyond her control.

Her hands alternately tugged at his hair and massaged his scalp, the feeling of his hair sliding through her fingers taking her to another level. She had enough of waiting and wanted satisfaction now.

"As you wish, My Mistress." Flame tore himself away from her to undo the fasteners on his jeans, all the while keeping an eye on her vibrating body. With his face wet with her juices, he gave her a wicked smile that caused her stomach to drop and her passions to elevate even higher. And then he eased down his jeans.

"My God!" she gasped as his jeans fell to the floor and she took in the full scope of his magnificence. His member was built in proportion with the rest of his oversized body, long, hard, and thick.

"Do I disappoint you?" he asked.

She responded, but not in words. From the moment she pulled his mouth to hers, a fire he had never before felt had exploded in him. He'd felt the pleasurable sensation of his manhood filling within the bounds of the cursed clothing, but now that he was set free, he felt his manhood swell to new heights and throb with a life all it's own.

"There is just so much of you!" she choked out as she eyed his tumescence warily.

"You need not fear that I will harm you, My Mistress. Only pleasure awaits you from my body. I have been trained thus."

He ran his hands down his stomach to caress the part of him that had grabbed her attention and caused him so much grief, as if to show her he was harmless.

"May I touch you?" She ran her hands over his chest and across his tightly drawn stomach, only to stop at his navel. She eagerly wanted to touch him, but the ultimate choice was his.

"You need not ask permission of me, My Mistress. All that I am is yours."

Kendall's mouth dropped open at his declaration, but she would wonder over it later. The lure of his body was too strong, especially knowing that she was the only woman ever to touch him in such a manner. Her hands moved to replace his.

Hot marble. He was made of the hottest marble cloaked in the finest of velvets. His eyes dilated as he bit back a groan of pleasure as her warm soft fingers began to explore everything that he was. One finger gently traced a delicate line from the tip to the base and he had to force himself not to run away from this terrifyingly delicious new pleasure.

"So hard, so firm," she murmured as she reached lower with one hand to cup his sac, heavy with his desire, and with the other urged him closer. "I have to taste."

Flame slammed his hands through his own hair as her soft wet mouth closed over the tip of his staff. "Ahh, Kendall!" he managed as the fire in his blood leapt beyond his control. His body began to tremble as he was assaulted with wave upon wave of desire. Sweat sheened his skin and a golden aura surrounded them both as he felt things that even Devo had not spoken of.

"No more, please." Now it was his turn to beg. She slammed hard against his nature as a man and his need for control as he fought to keep from throwing her to the floor and burrowing his hot flesh into her wanting body. Her torturing tongue danced around the head of manhood before her gently sucking mouth began to drive him crazy.

At last, Kendall could stand the pressure in her body no more and pulled away from him. "Now, Flame. Now." she commanded.

In an instant Flame covered her body with his, holding his upper body above her with his corded arms, but instead of slamming home and satisfying both of their urges, he positioned the head of his shaft at he mouth of her overflowing delta.

"May I come inside, My Mistress?" his breath was hot and thick in her ear and his arms began to tremble with the delicious weakness that followed in the wake of such biting pleasure. She arched up, trying to capture more of his heat, but he held her still. "May I enter you Kendall and ease both of our torment?"

"Yes!" The word exploded from her being and he closed his eyes at the desperate hungry sound.

Slowly, he flexed his hips and eased himself inside her about an inch.

"More, oh God, Flame, please" she begged as the feeling of penetration eased the pressure building in her body as it made her hungry for more. But still he took his time savoring each new sensation, his face glowing with discovery along with hers.

"I do not wish to hurt you, My Mistress," he managed though his eyes sparkled with fire and his hair now crackled with visible energy. He meant this joining to deliver extreme pleasure to her and in no way would his goal be compromised.

With strength born of desperation, Kendall wrapped her legs surround Flame's waist and tried to force him inside.

He hissed at her actions as a thunderbolt of power shot from him to the place where they were joined causing her to scream out in ecstasy. Losing his battle for control, Flame flexed his hips and pushed his way into her and shuddered at the feel of her tight hot silken sheath.

Her body wracked with trembling, Kendall gasped at the fullness of him before her body slowly began to accept all that was he inside her.

"Am I hurting you?" He was almost incoherent at the throbbing pleasure of being encased within her. Her walls clenched and wept for him. He took a deep breath and tried to push back the inevitable consummation of the act. "Do I cause you pain, My Mistress?"

Kendall could not speak. Spears of passion gripped her body in its piercing grasp. Her head whipped back and forth on the couch and her body tried to absorb him. She had never reached such heights before, had never been this stretched and full before. She was actually tingling and vibrating at the place where they became one.

"You are killing me with this pleasure," Kendall moaned between great gasps of breath. She could not feel any greater pleasure than this. This had to be the ultimate. And then he moved.

"Uhhh!" Stars exploded in a sea of white light behind her eyes. Tension built on top of sensation until she reached a peak so high, she was afraid to look down, afraid to soar, for she knew that she would never be the same again.

"Let go, Kendall."

She forced her eyes open to see a most amazing sight. Flame was above her, sparks shooting through his hair and filling the room with light, dominate, yet a slave to her needs and his passion. His eyes glowed from the lightning flashes from the storm they created together. It was enough to tip her over the edge.

"Ahh…ahh…Flaaameee!"

Her release pounded through her tossing her body beneath his and granting him leave to experience his own.

It had built up in him for some time as he struggled to submit his body to her ultimate pleasure. Now given free reign, he thrust powerfully into her grasping, giving warmth.

Again her body built, as his savage thrusts became her whole world. Her nails raked trails of sharp sweet fire across his back causing him to growl in pain and pleasure.

Friction caused a buildup of pressure in his sac and an almost tickling burning sensation filled him. He had to burrow deeper inside her body to soothe the burn.

The sounds of his own breath panting in the room caused his head to spin and his blood to thicken. Each of his movements drove him closer and closer to a pinnacle that could only be accessed from within her body. She was the key. He needed more of her.

Grasping her ankles, he positioned her legs over his shoulders and sank in deeper still. He groaned as her slick walls parted and accepted him as he slammed as far as he could go. He threw back his head muffled a sharp cry, his own hair sizzling him every place it brushed against his damp heaving body.

She shrieked as her hands flew up to grasp the arm of the couch. Alarmed, he stilled all movements shocked at the sound that he drew from her throat.

"Don't stop," she whimpered. "Please."

Flame closed his eyes as the sound of her voice, usually strong and in command, pleaded with him. Reassured, he turned his head and tenderly pressed a kiss to the arch of her right foot before he began his motions again.

Bombs exploded in his brain as electric pulses traveled from his surging body to hers. He ground his hips against hers causing his them both to cry out in joy. Quicker and quicker they moved as one until Flame bent over her, bending her supple body, so that he could feed on her sobs and catch her lips in a punishing kiss.

Finally, like lighting strike, his release tore through his body leaving him breathless and weak, carrying her along with him.

"Kendall!" he shouted. Tears ran from his eyes as he gripped her to him. The built up pressure tore through his body leaving him dazed, incapable of speech and totally drained. The golden aura that surrounded them slowly faded and his hair lost the electric flashes that made it glow.

Frozen, Kendall could only whimper as her body throbbed in aftershocks of such a violent release that once again tore through her body.

Finally spent, together they collapsed on the couch, her legs sliding down to cradle his still quivering hips. He roused himself enough to roll from her, causing lingering spasms, no less precious or beautiful, to rack their bodies.

"Don't leave me," she breathed into his ear.

"Never, Kendall." She was asking for more than this moment. He understood.

He rolled them so that she was gently sandwiched between the back of the couch and his warm, damp body. He brushed his tangle silken hair from her face, where it seemed to want to bind her to him. Feeling comfortable and secure, she slept. All through the night he held her close but those gray eyes remained open, his mind lost in thought.

He had to face the danger that threatened his new family and end it once and for all. That was the only way that he would feel worthy of his Kendall and earn a chance to capture her heart.

* * * * *

As the sky began to lighten in the east, Flame rose and eased from his Kendall's arms. She still lay asleep in the couch, so delicate and fragile-looking, that he instantly began to regret his harsh treatment of her.

Sighing deeply to himself, he walked towards the kitchen, intent on finding some dedication to ease what surely had to be sore muscles on her part, when he remembered the hot tub.

It was a simple device, not as efficient as a vaporbath, but just as effective.

Walking out of the back door and onto the wooden floor called a deck, he eyed the large oval shaped tub, a wondering look on his face.

Walking over, he knelt down and he reached in and found the water warm to the touch.

"Why is it a hot tub?" he mused out loud as he ran his hand along the rim, searching for the heat mechanism.

As he searched, his hand accidentally brushed against a trigger that caused the water to bubble and churn.

Jumping back, he eyed the tub dubiously.

What were these humans thinking? Bubbling water was not....

What made the water bubble?

Garnering his nerve, he stepped inside the water and felt the blast of air as it propelled the water.

Suddenly, he was taken back to a time when his father had shown him some new device for the pleasure of women.

"A water spray?" Flame asked, raising his eyebrow in direct imitation of his father.

"It stimulates the clitoral region, my son," Alonzid said as the female who volunteered for this experiment stepped forward.

Shrugging his shoulders and prepared for another lesson, Flame eased out of his baggy tunic and pants, retaining his modestly draped loin cloth, and stepped into the water that lay a few inches deep.

He settled himself comfortably as his father directed and the female made her way into the shallow pit.

At his father's nod, and gaining the Mistress' permission, he gently wrapped his arms around her, supporting her as he took the long tube in one had.

"Where will it be most effective?" Alonzid asked as he checked again to make sure the machine was set up properly.

Flame looked at the tube in his hand, then at the woman, then came to a decision.

While he held the tube, he gently grazed the woman's nipples, bringing them to life as he discovered she enjoyed a light touch.

So delicately, he tugged at her, rolling her hard flesh between his fingers, eliciting a gasp of pure pleasure before he let his hand trail down to the neatly clipped hair of her mound.

"May I spread your legs?" he asked and received an affirmative from the woman and an approving glance from his father.

Easing her legs apart, he touched her clit, noticing she flinched a bit. He eased off and ran his fingers along her pulsing opening. She enjoyed that immensely so he massaged her softly…before he sharply pulled upright, mashing her lower lips against his palm and making her scream out her pleasure.

"Alonzid!" she gasped. "He is as good as the rumors say! He is truly your son!"

Saying nothing, Flame brought the tube into play, pressing the trigger and feeling the vibrating shaft of water that exploded from its tip.

Slowly, he brought the spray teasingly up over her inner thighs making her quiver like a wild thing in his grasp. Teasingly, he circled her, coming closer to her clit even as he shielded her from direct contact with his hand.

Then suddenly he parted his fingers and let the pulsating spray though, granting her contact, listening quietly as her screams began to fill the room.

Would his Kendall like this as much as the other woman? He recalled the scratches she left upon his arms and neck and smiled.

Kendall awoke as a pair of strong arms lifted her *from* the couch.

"Flame? What…?"

"Shh, Kendall! Enjoy what I offer you."

Smiling, she nuzzled into his warm chest, content to allow him to lead this time. Sex with Flame was beginning to mellow her out a bit! She sighed as she heard him open the kitchen screen doors and felt the warmth of the dawning day envelope them.

She found herself being lowered into the hot tub and stifled a giggle. Flame had picked up a few tricks apparently. "What are we doing out here?"

"I am preparing to ease the soreness *from* you limbs, Kendall. I do not wish you sore or stiff."

"That's nice, Flame." She kept her eyes closed; all the better to relish the massage she was sure to get from this glorious man.

He settled himself on a ledge in the tub, placing her in his lap comfortably, the jets at his back.

"Your skin is like silk," he breathed as he rubbed her thighs, spreading them so that the warm waters could reach her ravaged female opening.

"Mmm" she snuggled deeper into his embrace.

"I have injured you in my passion, Kendall. This I did not wish!"

"I'm not complaining, Flame," she said as she reached back to caress his cheek with her hand, loving the feel of his smooth skin. "This is a good ache, a healthy ache."

"But an ache I do not wish you to have." He lowered his hands between her thighs and began to rub her lower lips intimately.

"That is not exactly relaxing," Kendall breathed as her eyes popped open to watch through the bubbling water as Flame caressed her, aroused her, brought back her banked desires for him.

Kendall let her head rest again his shoulders as a low groan filled the steamy air surrounding the tub. She breathed in deeply, loving how the fresh scent was now mixed with the scent of her arousal and of Flame.

She felt herself start to leak her juices and purred as Flame lovingly mingled her essence with the water, soothing where she was sore and bringing her body alive once more.

"Oh Flame! This is so hot!" she gasped as he increased the pressure of his fingers and let his other hand rise up to cup her breasts as his tongue invaded her ear. "Oh don't stop! Give me more!"

"As you desire," he breathed, his heated breath caressing her ear and sending electricity shooting through her neck, a moment before his lips clamped onto the sensitive skin there. "Anything you desire!" He tightened his arms around her body, lifting her, turning her, pressing her body against the shooting jets of water.

"Ohhhh shit!" Kendall gasped as the hot water hit her dead center on her clitoris as Flame held her exposed to his pleasurable torture. "What are you doing?"

"Release, Kendall! It will soothe you."

But then she could say nothing as he adjusted their positioning and the pulsating water hit her clitoris dead on, giving her the direct contact that she needed to send her senses reeling!

Kendall felt the hot sweet caress of the water, felt the hard rough flesh of Flame's hand adding stimulation, and let her senses take over. Wave after wave of heat trailed through her body, tingling her legs, making knees weak.

Her arms flew backwards around his neck, holding on tightly as her back arched into this new stimuli even as her mind screamed that it was too much.

Flame and his solid frame became the center of her world as lights began to explode behind her eyes. Her breath came in raspy bursts, struggling to pull oxygen into her lungs as the cool air caressed her already turgid nipples, bringing her more delight.

"Flame…."

"Release for me," he growled as his hands began to move in tight circles, using the hard tendons of his hands, manipulating her to an explosive end.

Kendall writhed within his grasp, fighting to get nearer, fighting to get away, struggling to find a release of the tension that had grabbed hold of her body and soul. "Please!"

"Then let go!"

Forcefully, Flame slammed one long finger within her wet walls, groaning as they quivered and clenched around his probing finger.

"Yes!" he hissed as he began to thrust inside of her, feeling for the magic button that would send her screaming into climax.

Kendall turned her head to his shoulder and bit down as the coil of tension that grew within her exploded, sending her body into spasms of joy.

The only thing holding her upright was Flame as he supported her. Even as her inner muscles grabbed at his finger, he gentled her with whispered words of praise as he softened his caresses to bring her down off of her climatic high.

"You are so beautiful when you fly apart for me," he purred as she whimpered and went boneless in his arms. She remained catatonic as he lifted her from the tub and carried her into the house. She clutched at him as he dried her body and placed her into the bed that they would share this coming night.

"I would give anything for you, Mistress Kendall," he promised as he ignored his own raging need, and thought of how her release almost triggered his own. "We are petals from the same flower, my Kendall," he breathed, "only you complete me, your pleasure is my own, your happiness paramount in my mind."

Then feeling as if he had lifted a small part of his burden from his shoulders, he placed his erection comfortably against her rear and snuggled in to claim a few hours rest.

Chapter Nine

§ᴏ

The sun shining through the bedroom window woke Kendall. She rose up from layers of slumber to find herself lying in the bed Flame insisted she sleep in after he had recovered from the disintegration of his alteration. Did she do what she thought she did last night? The evidence was right there before her, sore thighs, aching back, weak knees, and parts of her were definitely sore from stretching to accommodate a large presence. But not as sore as things could have been. Thank God for hot tubs!

She sighed as she lay back amid the tangled covers that carried his unforgettable scent. She had never realized that sex could be like that. It was too intense a feeling to be just lust. Even Doctor Dick at his best had never made her feel that way. Maybe Doctor Dick was too good a name for the old boy. Maybe Little Boy Dickey was better!

But thoughts of the good doctor made her think of her sister and the bomb that they dropped on her. Then she realized that it didn't matter to her at all. One tall redheaded man now adequately filled the blank space in her life that she thought Richard could ease.

She smiled and turned to face her lover, only to find an empty space beside her. She sat up, concerned for a moment. What they did wouldn't hurt him, would it? Then she relaxed at the sound of gentle murmuring coming from the kitchen. Flame had risen to take care of his children. He wouldn't run out on her after what they both experienced. Suddenly filled with boundless energy, Kendall sprang from the bed and rushed to the shower. The day was ripe with possibilities.

Kendall padded barefoot into the kitchen wearing a sundress with a long flowing skirt, the color of ripe peaches. Not that she was jealous or anything, but if Caress could work a dress, then so could she.

The light color made her face and skin glow with health and vitality. Her full lips were faintly swollen by last night's passionate kisses and her eyes were deep brown pools of remembered passion that cold easily be aroused again.

Want slammed into Flame's stomach and tightened his resolve to close the last door to his past. This was something he had become sure of since his time with Kendall—he would be free of the threat to his family or would die in the trying.

"Good morning." Kendall dropped a light kiss to each baby who also eyed her entrance into the kitchen with some interest. They seemed to share in the joy that enveloped her like a cloak. The twins exchanged telling glances before returning their gaze to Kendall.

Flame stood at her approach, but she waved him back to his seat. She smiled at the light blush that tinted his face as she walked over to his side.

"Are you feeling well?" she asked, still unsure if she had done him any harm. He looked fit as he sat there in his black jeans and a kelly green T-shirt, but she still didn't know enough about Testrios physiology to be sure.

"I am fine, Mistress," he replied eyeing the curve of her breasts before dragging his eyes up to her face. "I took no harm from the wonderful experience you have introduced me to."

A violent blush stained his cheeks at her not-so-subtle reminder of the past night. Flame had almost expected her to treat him like yesterday's trash, just like Devo said, but he should have known better. His Mistress inquired about his health and honestly treated him like he was something special. He wished he could find a way to tell Devo how wrong he was.

"Can't you call me Kendall, after all that we've been through?" she asked, a little tired of hearing herself addressed formally. As much as she liked the respectful title, she liked the sound of her name as it rolled off of his tongue more. Plus she didn't want to be compared to the women on the world that he left behind.

"Have I earned the right?" he asked.

"More than you'll ever know," she replied earnestly. "I've never met anyone as amazing as you...and look at the babies! They grow so fast. Is that natural?" She was feeling a little uncomfortable with the questions in his gray eyes and was not ready to answer them yet.

"Yes it is natural," he replied catching on to her plan to change the subject and understanding her reasons. He too felt raw with the new emotions that he was experiencing. "I gladly wear the marks produced while carrying my children."

"What marks? I've seen every inch of your body and I never noticed any marks on you." She smiled as his blush blossomed in full force and threatened to rival his hair in sheer color.

"They are there, on my side, Mistr...Kendall." He still seemed a little uncomfortable uttering her given name. At her questioning look, he took a deep breath, pulled up the side of his shirt and pointed to a tiny silver line with some finality. "There it is."

"That's it? Man-oh-man, what did you use for a skin cream? The women here would sell their souls for some of it if that is the extent of your stretch marks!" The tiny line was hardly worth mentioning.

"The cream is a recipe from the Brotherhood. Only we know which combination of ingredients will make it viable. It is one of the many secrets that the Brotherhood uses to ensure its continuing existence."

"What is the Brotherhood exactly, Flame?" Kendall took a seat beside him and patiently waited for an answer. "You've often spoke of it, but never truly explained what it was." Now she was going to hear something good about the people who had sheltered her man. She didn't know them, but she was grateful to them.

"The Brotherhood was once an elite fighting force left over from ancient days when war threatened our existence. If a group had enough money to pay the fees, the Brotherhood would go to the area and crush the oppression."

He thought back to the pictures that covered one of the many secret chambers at the main house of the Brotherhood. Depicted in their carved marble depths were large muscular men yielding large intricately carved swords. Fierce pride and confidence permeated every line of their being. These men were free and they delighted in their freedom.

"They were mercenaries?" What an auspicious beginning for a group of men who now were used as a collection place for the undesirables on a planet. "I thought they were healers?"

"In a way, Kendall. After the dissidence was crushed, they nursed the victims to health. What good is ruling a land where the people are all dead? The early Matriarchs knew that to show kindness was the best way to gain the trust of a conquered people. The Brotherhood provided for that need as well."

"They were a full-service band of warriors for hire. I get it. So why aren't they in power now?"

Flame pauses for a moment to think of the ruin of the old practice fields and the battered and broken swords that littered the old armories. When he first arrived at the great house, he spent hours staring at the empty fields where once great mock battles were fought. The desolate wastelands seemed like a tragic loss to the child that he was and seemed like the voice of the past mocking him as an adult.

"The five ruling houses united to become The Matriarch. The Matriarch felt that the Brotherhood was a threat to their existence. If someone assembled an army and had the funds to hire the Brotherhood, they would almost be a match for the five ruling houses. In their desire to prevent this occurrence, the Brotherhood never stood a chance. The Matriarch held power over the very elements on Testrios. What good are swords against giant windstorms and spears of ice? The earlier Keepers were determined to hold onto their power at any cost, and the price was the original Brotherhood."

Flame recalled tales of futile battles fought against that first body of determined women. He could not help but admire their strategy. Attack where the enemy is most vulnerable. Who could battle when the battlegrounds were slick with ice? How could a solider march when the heat directed at them was so oppressive they could hardly stand?

"The original Brothers were spared because of their healing knowledge, but were forbade upon threat of total destruction to pick up arms ever again. So now we accept all men who are as you say, misfits and in need of healing, and give them a place to live their lives in peace. We also practice some of the old ways in secret."

"The old ways? You guys practice warfare?" The Brothers had a little rebellion going! What would the ruling houses think of that?

"Not warfare itself, strategy and free thinking. Although there are some who would fight for better laws governing men, most are content with their positions in life and would not endanger the Brotherhood."

"You were not content, were you? That's why you are fighting so hard for your family." Kendall had now found something new to respect in the man. Having been raised all his life in a subservient manner, he learned not to accept his position and to strive for something better. She rested her head upon her folded arms as she pictured him as an inspiration for others and that the freedom bug was catching.

"No, Kendall. I was not content to let others decide my fate any longer. I liked choosing my own path. That is why I did what I did this morning." He nodded to the little computer that had so aided him in relocating to this new planet, all traces of contentment leaving his face.

His cold tone and blank expression sent a shiver of fear down her spine and caused her to sit straight up in her chair. What had the man done? Why did she feel like a little black cartoon cloud of darkness was hovering over her head?

"What did you do, Flame?" She had to know how bad their situation was.

"I have sent a homing beacon to the Execution Squad."

"You did what?" Kendall jumped to her feet and disregarded the clash of the falling chair as it hit the floor. How dare he endanger all of their lives without letting her in on his plans? "How could you do that knowing that they will try and kill our babies?"

Flame was shocked by Kendall. Not by her loud outburst, for women had been yelling around him for as long as he could remember. It was the fact that she called Spark and Ember "our babies" that stunned him. He knew that she had feelings for him, but her slip was enlightening. Now he was sure that he had to make them all safe.

His pleasure was obvious and misunderstood by Kendall. Did sex addle his mind? Just as soon as she had gotten used to his quirky habits, he moved himself on the top of her list of annoyances, right up there with screaming women in labor and Caressa. "That's it! We have to get out of here, now!"

Kendall turned to the babies as if undecided which one to pick up and run with first. How could Flame be so stupid as to call then enemy down on them after they had planned his new life?

"Kendall, please sit." He asked in a firm tone. "There are things we must discuss."

Now he decides to face the firing squad, she thought angrily. "No, Flame! We have to leave before they get here!"

Kendall was almost frantic with fear. If they harmed on hair on those babies' heads…

"Sit!"

Stunned into stillness, she slowly turned to see Flame towering over her with fire literally flashing in his eyes and his hair buzzing in the non-existent breeze.

"I know what I have to do. I have to put the past behind me before I can move on to a future, any future. What kind of life can I give Spark and Ember constantly running from the threat of an Execution Squad? What can I offer you while death follows our every move? What kind of man would I be if I did not ensure your safety?"

Kendall looked at the children who seemed to stare at their father in shock at the fact that he actually raised his voice. She couldn't believe it herself.

"What will you do, Flame?"

He had to have a plan. He wouldn't put them all in danger without a plan.

"I will convince them that we are no threat to their power or I will end the threat that they posses permanently."

"You are talking about murder, Flame."

"Only if it comes to that." He was deathly serious and it showed in the firm set of mouth and how he belligerently stuck out that stubborn chin.

"I don't know you, Flame." Kendall turned and left the room.

"What would you have me do, Kendall? How else can I get them to leave my family alone?" Flame's boots clattered on the hardwood floor as he raced after her retreating back and spun her around. His eyes widened as he gripped her upper arms with his hands. He had never touched a woman in this manner in his whole life. What had come over him? What had desperation driven him to do?

"Kendall, I am sorry," he rushed to apologize as he immediately pulled his hands back as if he had touched fire. She eyed him with what he thought was fright, and he paled at the thought.

"What the hell do you think you're doing?" Kendall yelled.

She was far from being scared. She was furious. The stricken look on his face was almost comical. If their situation had not been so grave, she would have laughed.

"I...I...do not know? I want you safe from them. I want my children safe. I do not want to live my life in fear. I want them gone."

Flame was being open and honest in his feelings. He might not know what to do next but he was determined to face his problem head on. "How can I be worthy of you if I do not keep you safe?"

Kendall bit back her anger and annoyance as understanding blossomed with in her. Her eyes began to shine as she threw her arms around Flame. The man was worried about her. No one had ever felt she needed the consideration of worry before. She relished the new experience and the feeling of being cherished. The feelings she was trying to define came gushing from her heart.

"You are more than worthy of me, you idiot. I love you! If you did all of this to prove yourself a man, you had no need to. I don't think I can live without you and I can't stand the idea of them hurting you!"

"You love me?"

Flame had never heard those words before in his life and they gave him a feeling of wonder and a sense of hope. He raised his trembling hands and tenderly cupped her face, his thumbs running lightly over her cheeks.

"I have brought nothing but trouble to your house and you profess to love me? How can you love someone like me?"

"I love you for being you, Flame. You are the most kind and gentle man that I have ever known and yet you would cast aside a lifetime of beliefs to find a way to keep us safe. I love you because you think I need protecting!"

She reached up to wipe away the tears that rolled from his eyes noticing that he did the same to the tears that trailed down her face. "You have taught me so much about dignity and strength, how could I not love you?"

"Kendall!" Flame pulled her to him in a crushing embrace. "I never thought that I would find someone to love me. I love you so much, my heart aches with the feelings." He ran dotted kisses over her face as she laughed with joy.

Kendall felt small and protected, and entirely worthy to love this man. She sighed as he brushed his face back and forth against her head as if savoring each and every contact with her body. Needing to feel his firm, supple lips against hers, she rose to the tips of her toes and gently placed her lips against his.

He groaned at the feel of her mouth against his before returning the favor. Instantly he felt his body react to her kisses as if it was trained just for her. Suddenly, he had to have more of her, had to express his intense emotions physically. He broke the kiss and dropped to his knees. He ran his hands up her warm thighs pulling her skirt up with them. "I have to taste you."

With a rip, the remains of the tiny bikini underwear she wore were cast aside, only to be replaced with his questing tongue and greedy mouth.

Kendall gasped as her fingers latched into his hair as if it was a lifeline. She threw back her head in ecstasy and cried out as he pulled her leg over his shoulder to get even closer to her. Her whole body shook as electric pulses shot from him to the seat of her woman's pleasure, awaking an ultra sensitive spot. Soon he had her braced with her back against a convenient wall and her other leg joined the first over his shoulder.

Kendall cried out at the feeling of weightlessness as Flame supported and balanced her weight. She was soon riding his face and loving every minute of it. Only Flame could devise such a wicked position that she found herself abandoning herself to.

"I can not seem to get enough of you." His hot breath tickled her throbbing flesh as his hands cupped then squeezed her squirming behind and held her still for his possession.

"Please, Flame!" Kendall cried as he began to do some interesting things with his teeth. "I need you in me."

Instead of placing her on the floor, Flame simply fell backwards, supporting her weight so that her knees gently touched the floor, while he still held her suspended over his mouth. Kendall praised his ingenuity, loudly.

When his head emerged from beneath her skirt, his eyes flashed with hot fire, his face wet with her dew, and electric sparks flashed through his hair. She was heading into overdrive and the sight was almost enough to carry Kendall over the top. Instead she turned and groped for his zipper, eager to return a small portion of the pleasure she was receiving. She eased his turgid flesh into her waiting hands.

Flame tossed his head back in a shower of whipping red hair and moaned his pleasure and frustration to the ceiling. He sat back on his knees, bracing his hands on the floor behind him as Kendall rose dominate above him.

"The feelings you give me, Kendall," he moaned.

"You haven't felt anything yet, Keeper." Kendall whispered as her hands snaked up his shirt to caress his hardened nipples and run her nails teasingly across the hard muscles of his chest.

His brain exploded with pleasure as her warm mouth created a damp path down his body and surrounded his turgid flesh.

To Kendall, he tasted like warm sunshine and the essence of man.

"I cannot withstand this pleasure, Kendall," he moaned as she delivered another liquid caress with her fluttering tongue.

He gasped in surprise as she pulled her skirt to her waist and lowered herself over him.

"Guide yourself home, Flame," she commanded as she stiffened her knees and braced her hands on his shoulders. She trembled with impatience as she waited for him to place himself in position.

Flame groaned as he felt the head of his shaft touch the wet portal of her body.

"All this is for you, Flame," she murmured between biting kisses. She contemplated the flavor they made together as he hesitated at her threshold, then decided that he needed an additional invite. "Welcome home."

Flame gave a guttural cry at her words and slammed her down on him. His whole body shook as if struck by lighting and a shockwave of intense heat flowed from him to her, scorching her body with his desire.

"Tight, so tight," his words scorched her ears as his hands moved to lift and brace her rounded thighs as he tunneled deeper into her warmth.

Her hands twisted into his shirt, damp with his sweat, as pleasure caused her head to whip back and her mouth to open in a silent scream. His soft lips moved in to caress her exposed neck as be began the motions that would bring them both to paradise.

"I love you so much," she managed as he picked up his pace of his thrusting hips and his arms enfolded her closer to his heat.

"Kendall, my Mistress, my heart," he all but shouted as he eased her to the floor and covered her with his heaving body.

The abrasive material of his jeans added another element to their hurried mating as it scraped against her tender inner thighs. His hands groped for hers and their fingers tangled then intertwined as passion gripped them tightly. His hips slammed against hers and she arched her body up to catch each punishing thrust, giving as well as receiving. He pulled her hands high above her head, holding her captive to his motions.

"My love!" he cried as she suddenly slammed her hips against his and reached her peak. Shuddering and crying out her joy, she tumbled off into a white-hot utopia, dragging him along with her.

Flame reveled in her uninhibited response and felt a moment of satisfaction before he too was sucked into a steaming vortex of pleasure. He pushed his face into her neck and exhaled his release in one long hiss. Unable to support his own weight, Flame, chest heaving like a bellows, lowered his moist heat against her.

Lying in the hallway, breath heaving with their exertions, Flame slowly rolled off of Kendall and pulled her onto his chest.

"Have I made a mess of everything?" he asked as she burrowed into the safety of his arms. He had thought that he did the right thing by trying to end his problems once and for all with the death squad.

"No." Kendall answered honestly. "They would have caught up with us sooner or later and you were right to try and give yourself an advantage. You did what you had to do. I just don't want to lose you so soon after I've found you, Flame."

"I will not let them separate us, Kendall." He ran a hand caressingly up her back. "I have too much to live for."

"How much time do we have?" she asked, a little frightened of the unknown, but in true Kendall fashion, pushing forward and deciding what to do next.

"A few days at most." Flame had to have something up his sleeve. Why else was he so calm about meeting impending death?

"What's your plan?" she questioned. Now that her initial shock had worn off, she knew that he had to have a good plan. He wouldn't risk their lives on a whim.

"I plan on offering them proof of my destruction so my mother can have undisputed power over the House of Ice."

He now ran his fingers through the tangled mass her hair had become during their love play. Her usual neat bun was a thing of the past.

"What proof is that?" Kendall raised herself on his chest to look down at his beloved handsome face. He gave her one of these devastating slow smiles that never failed to make her knees weak.

"A lock of my hair. Everyone knows that a keeper would die before relinquishing one precious lock. It is a conduit for our energies. That is why no one ever sought to cut the evidence of my energies from my head and spare my house the awkwardness of me having been born with the energies."

"They are supposed to be convinced to leave us alone because you gave them a lock on you hair?" This was his great plan? Kendall's eyes narrowed into small brown slits as she gazed down at her lover.

"Did I forget to mention that the leader of this Execution Squad is my sibling?"

He was serious! Her eyes widened as she realized how serious he really was. "What kind of family did you come from?" This was sheer insanity. His sister was trying to kill him. Where was the family unity in the House of Fire?

"A very ambitious family who will stop at nothing to achieve their goals. My sister might not kill me because of that bond. She felt remorse over what Catla had done. I think she will find my plan reasonable. She will not have the burden of killing her womb mate and my mother will have the power she seeks. I think she will accept my plan."

Flame was serious in his belief that his sister would listen to reason and aid him in his escape from his home planet, but

Kendall wasn't so sure. As she snuggled back into Flame's arms she decided pay extra attention to his sister when she and her cohorts came to visit. One could never be too careful when dealing with a woman scorned.

Chapter Ten

ɞ

"Rise and shine, My Mistress! Is it not a beautiful day?"

"Argh!" Some idiot yanked the covers from over Kendall's head, exposing her to the harmful rays of the punishing sun! Cold morning air wafted over her comfortably sleep-warmed skin. Immediately her body, seeking protection from the dangerous morning daylight, curled up into a fetal position as her arms raced to cover and protect her head.

"We must leave today, My Mistress! I have packed our things and your morning meal awaits!"

One bloodshot, sleep-reddened eye cracked open and peeped through the shelter of her arms. It had to be a nightmare! Some longhaired, red-headed fool was smiling down at her, cheerfully inviting in the hazards of early morning sunshine to the sanctity of her bedroom.

"What time is it?" the inhuman voice croaked as it eyed the harbinger of cold air and sunshine.

"It is way past the crack of dawn, My Kendall! Crack of dawn!" the devil threw back his head with laughter. "I heard that on your listening device and I think that it is an apt description."

"I didn't hear dawn crack!" the pitiful creature that was Kendall growled, anger growing in its somewhat feminine voice.

"Didn't hear dawn crack!" the red-headed buffoon cackled with glee. "You have made a joke, Kendall. I have never known a woman to possess a sense of humor!"

Something inside Kendall cracked…like the dawn.

"You meat-head!" she roared as she flipped her naked body over onto her back. "We don't have to leave the cabin until noon!"

Flame's eyes widened as he watched the changeling that was once the love of his life. It had the same voice as his Mistress, the same beautiful eyes, and the same delightfully rounded body! It was a body that he now knew quite well. But this thing did not possess the sweet nature of his Kendall. The creature now struggled to sit up and swing its legs over the side of the bed.

"I have made..." he began only to be cut off.

"Shh."

"But Kendall, I...."

"Shh." This time with a finger placed over its lips for emphasis.

"Kendall, I have...."

"Quiet you!" she growled, turning to glare at the man with red-rimmed eyes. "You kept me up half the night making love, not that I'm complaining, but then you wake me at this ungodly hour when we don't have to leave here until later on this day! You just shh!"

Flame blinked in surprise, then nodded once. "As you wish, My Mistress." He spoke in a low dejected voice, void of all earlier delight and Kendall felt guilt pushing out her earlier annoyance.

Shoulders slightly slumped; Flame turned at started to leave the room. There was such a hurt aura surrounding him that Kendall instantly felt contrite about yelling at him. After all he was only trying to help.

"Don't go, Flame," she let out with a heavy sigh. "I'm sorry that I yelled. It's just that I'm not used to all this nocturnal activity and you surprised me this morning."

He stopped at her words and looked over his shoulder at her, shooting her a hurt look. He looked absolutely adorable in a white T-shirt and his blue jeans. And that look was a heartbreaker.

"Come here," she smiled sweetly at him before rolling onto her side and motioning him forward with one finger.

He didn't need to be asked twice. In a flash, Flame dropped his wounded look and was on the bed beside Kendall pulling her naked self into his arms, and taking her mouth in a gentle kiss.

"Are you mad at me?" he asked, even though he knew she was not. It was fun to tease his mistress.

"No, I'm not mad," Kendall said between the light kisses she peppered across his chin. "I can never stay mad at you when you do the sad puppy dog eyes."

Flame did not know what exactly that meant, but he would remember "The Look." It served to get him out of hot water with his Mistress.

"I have prepared food for you to break your fast. The convection ovens used here are not very big, but they operate on the same principle as the solar-powered ovens on Testrios. I have prepared you muffins for you breakfast, along with fresh fruit and coffee. I have sampled several cups of it and have found that I like the stimulating effect it has on my body."

Kendall took one look into his bright eyes and suddenly knew the reason for the early morning wake-up call. Flame, her adorable alien, was on a caffeine-induced high.

"No more coffee for you, big guy," she murmured. "I'm going to take a shower and then when I wake up, we'll talk about you and your new coffee addiction."

Flame grinned as he reclined on the bed and watched her bare backside as it swayed across the room. And to think that he never noticed that portion of the female anatomy before.

After her shower, Flame insisted that she sit on the now stripped bed and let him brush her hair. "Any man worthy of his house would do this every morning for his life-mate. It is required of him, to show his willingness to perform even the meanest task for her pleasure."

Kendall let her head fall back on her neck as Flame gently detangled her freshly-washed hair with gentle strokes of his hairbrush. He paused for a moment to add fragrant oil to her hair that instantly softened the dark strands and added a brilliant shine.

When Kendall saw her hair in the mirror that Flame had produced and held up for her inspection, she was amazed at the condition of her short mane.

"What is that oil you used in my hair, Flame? It's never looked this good before!"

"I have pleased you, Kendall?" he asked, pretty sure that she would answer in the affirmative.

"I am more than pleased, Flame." Kendall was amazed as she shook her head and watched her usually unmanageable hair flow softly around her face. "It hasn't looked this good since I first had it cut! What did you put in it?"

"Meertat oil," he replied as he watched her feminine reaction to the minor cosmetic.

"Meertat oil?" Kendall asked. "What is a Meertat?"

"The closest comparison I can come up with, My Mistress, is one of your Earth Skunks."

The pleased look on Kendall's face melted in a heartbeat to one of utter disgust. "Skunk?" she croaked out.

"Yes, My Kendall. The malodorous smell is processed out and fragrant herbs are added to help give luster and shine to any woman's hair." He sounded like a commercial for a new hair product as he smilingly told her of the oil and it's properties.

"You put skunk oil in my hair?" she all but shrieked as she raised and lowered her hands to and from her hair. Her eyes widened so much, that Flame was afraid that they would pop right out of their sockets.

"Meertat oil," he corrected as he watched her act...well, a little insane over the simple oil in he had brushed into her hair.

Finally, Kendall turned disbelieving eyes to his content face. The knucklehead acted as if he had done her a favor.

"Don't ever help me with my hair again unless I give you the hair products to use."

"But you liked your hair, My Mistress," Flame almost stammered in his confusion.

Meertat oil was highly prized by the women of Testrios. Often it was sought out by any member of the Brotherhood and bartered for fresh supplies since only the Brothers knew the secrets of turning the distastefully smelling oil into a wonderfully scented hair tonic.

"I liked it before I knew what that...that...stuff that you put in my hair was!"

"Meertat oil is highly prized, My Mistress, and I thought that you would enjoy its lasting effects."

Once again Flame wore the wounded puppy dog look and Kendall felt contrite and guilty. Damn that soulful look!

"I am not from Testrios, Flame." Kendall spoke softly to soothe his wounded ego. He was trying to show his feelings for her in the only way that he knew how.

"I know this, My Kendall, but I thought that you too would enjoy a little pampering."

Now she really felt like pond scum. "I enjoyed it, Flame, I really did, but I guess I'm not used to Testrios hair preparations. I apologize if I hurt your feelings, but the skunk oil was a bit much. Try and understand my point of view. How would you feel if I put...uh, one of Ember's dirty diapers on your face and told you that it was good for the skin?"

Flame's face at once screwed up into a mask of revulsion as he eyed his mistress. "That is disgusting, Mistress! Why in the name of the Matriarch would I do that?"

"That's exactly how I feel about skunks and by comparison, meertats."

Kendall knew that she had proved her point when Flame's face cleared and a thoughtful expression settled onto his handsome visage.

"I think I understand now, My Mistress. What I find commonplace you will probably find outrageous, and what I think is strange on this planet will probably be normal."

"You've got it, big guy!" Kendall crowed as she again felt her hair, brush against her face and strove not to cringe.

Flame noticed her reaction and did the only thing that a true man would do. "Will you allow me to wash you hair, My Kendall?" he asked, wishing to help ease her discomfort.

"No, I don't think so," Kendall stated after a moment of deep thought. "I guess if you can try and get used to Earth things, I can try out a few Testrios items. Just tell me what you are doing next time, before you do it. Agreed?"

"Agreed, My Kendall." Flame was happy that his Mistress was possessed of such a deep understanding of human nature and that she was willing to open her mind to new things.

"Now, let's take my skunk oil do, and go get that breakfast that you have so thoughtfully prepared. What kind of muffins did you make?"

"I made the muffins from this wonderful substance called scrapple!"

"Scrapple muffins?" Kendall croaked. That sounded disgusting.

"Yes, My Mistress. And it is of Earth so you will not find any difficulties in eating them. I have made you two dozen to eat with these small fruits called prunes. They are truly the staples of the gods."

Flame never understood the tears that filled his Mistress's eyes as he served up her meal of hot scrapple muffins, pitted prunes with grape jelly, and the thick black coffee that took over seven tablespoons of coffee grounds to make. But because he wanted to make sure she stayed healthy, he sat and watched her consume almost every bite.

This is for my mother, she thought. Who compromised and ate pancakes made of corn meal and pickled sausages and orange yogurt eggs for her breakfasts! Thanks Mom, she groaned, for teaching me compromise. Now I know why there were so many antacids in the house! God, I must love this man!

Moments after the last bite was downed, Kendall raced for the bathroom, to the delight of the grinning red-haired. They looked into each other's gray eyes as if to say, "Thank goodness for soy baby formula."

Flame eyed his offspring for a moment, before he shrugged his shoulders and left the room to begin packing the minivan.

Yes, thank goodness for formula, the babies seemed to confirm as a slightly green Kendall returned from the bathroom and shakily poured herself a tall glass of water. Grownup food seemed to be an acquired taste.

"I want to drive," Flame declared later as they fastened the children into their seats.

"I don't think so, Flame." Kendall ran her hands over yet another pair of jeans, cream ones this time, and eyed the disappointed look that replaced the one of joy that filled Flame's eyes.

"Just to the end of the timberline?" he pleaded.

"No."

After their breakfast fiasco, Kendall and Flame had begun packing the minivan for the trip home. Flame had worn an expectant expression on his face all morning and Kendall had expected a question like that to pop up.

"But I can operate the combustion engine on this vehicle, Kendall. Please?" he asked shooting her the puppy dog eyes.

Both of the babies in the back seemed to look on in amusement at the interaction between their father and their adopted mother.

"No."

"I can fly a space ship, Kendall. I flew it hundreds of light years to reach this planet. How hard can it be to drive this primitive vehicle?"

Primitive! I'll show him primitive, she thought before she looked into his expectant eyes. She felt like she was kicking a puppy! I know I'm going to regret this, Kendall thought as she handed the keys over to Flame.

Like an eager child, Flame latched onto the keys, and like most men instantly began to get possessive about the controls.

"Gas, brake, gear shift..." he rattled off each part of the car so quickly and accurately, that even Kendall was impressed.

"How did you learn all of that?" she asked satisfied that he knew the basics. She climbed into the passenger seat and locked her safety belt into place.

"I read the manual while I was preparing your breakfast," was his distracted reply as he adjusted the seat to fit his tall frame. "I had hoped that you would allow me this opportunity."

"Can you start it?" she asked.

Flame shot her a disgusted look before turning the key in the ignition and smoothly starting the car. In that universal way that all men have, he told her that she asked a stupid question with one sarcastic look.

"Damn man," Kendall mumbled at being the recipient of that particular look. "A few days of freedom seem to have gone to your head."

Flame grinned sheepishly before turning to look down at the dashboard in embarrassment. She was right. A few days of freedom and he was starting to act like a House Mistress. Reminding himself to censor his actions and treat his Kendall with all due respect, he took his foot off of the brake and eased the car forward. And they were off!

He did it! He was driving this earth transport! He was so elated that he cried out to Kendall, "I have mastered this vehicle, My Mistress! Soon I shall know everything required to see properly to your welfare!"

They were moving, but at about two miles per hour. If they traveled at this rate, they should be home by the time the children entered elementary school!

"Sure…yeah, right." Kendall mumbled after watching the trees pass in slow motion. "Oh, great provider," she intoned. "We have been driving for a few minutes and we haven't even left the front yard. Use the accelerator."

Flame felt a bit foolish, but did as she asked and the car shot forward like a bullet.

"The Brake!" she screamed as what was left of her unusual breakfast threatened to exit her body the same way the bulk of it had earlier. "Use the damned brake!"

So he did. He stomped on the brake pedal and slammed the car to a tooth-rattling halt.

Kendall grunted as she was slammed forward, caught by her safety belt and slammed back into her seat with the force of a cannon blast.

"I have stopped, just as you have commanded, My Mistress," Flame cheerfully chirped from the driver's side. "Do I not have great control over this vehicle?"

Before she could wait for her brain to settle back into it's proper place, Kendall was again jolted as Flame began accelerating once more. This time she felt all of her skin try to leave her skeleton behind as they roared down the dirt path that led to the main interstate, I-95. The babies seemed to encourage their fathers' new need for speed from the back seat. Kendall was too busy praying with her eyes tightly closed to pay much attention to the twins.

They soon came to a traffic signal.

"Red means stop and green means go." Flame recited as they approached the nearly empty intersection.

As they were approaching the standing green light, Kendall saw that it was turning yellow. Now I can reclaim the steering wheel from that mad man, she thought as they approached the intersection.

But then she noticed that they were not slowing down. Actually, they were starting to move faster.

"Uh, Flame?" she questioned as they came closer and closer to the traffic light. "You do realize what the yellow light is for?"

"Yes, My Mistress. Yellow means to go faster!"

With that, he slammed his foot on the gas and they shot forward. The roar of the engine was surpassed only by Kendall's shriek of fright as she tried to cover her head with her flaying arms and again slammed her eyes shut. But amazingly enough, they were safely passed the light and Flame was slowing the car.

"Where did you learn to drive, you numb-skull! You could have gotten us all killed!" Kendall nearly screamed as she saw that they were alive and that he had slowed the car down to a tolerable seventy-five miles per hour. "Are you trying to kill all of us?"

Stunned by her behavior, Flame pulled the car over to the shoulder of the road and let it coast to a stop. "I learned by listening to a very intelligent Earthman on one of your communications devices. I think that his name was Jeff Gordon."

"He is a professional automobile racer, Flame." Kendall's chest heaved with her efforts to keep under control. "He gets paid to race like that on a closed track! You don't drive on the highway like a Nascar racer!" She was shouting and feeling the urge to overcome her physical restraint, she balled up her fist and socked him right on his rock hard bicep.

"Damn!" she yelled as her fist came into contact with his muscular arm. She felt like she had just hit a brick wall.

"You can hurt yourself, My Kendall, by hitting me when I am not prepared. If you wished to pummel me for some error, you should let me know so that I might loosen the muscle first." He was all contrite expression and subservient attitude.

"Green is go, red is stop and yellow is go slow, prepare to stop!" He even took the fun out of aggravated assault, she groused as he gave her a sunny look of understanding.

"Oh, I see now, My Kendall. Thank you for correcting my error."

Again she felt annoyed by his way of making her feel guilty. She felt like a child who needed to be taught control so as not to hit her playmates. "I apologize for punching you, Flame. That wasn't necessary and it was mean-spirited." She looked up at him, regret on her face and waited for him to tell her that she was no better than the women that he had escaped from on Testrios.

Flame had understood that her frustration needed an outlet and was truthfully unfazed by her attack. He had scratches that made more of an impact. But the fact that she was willing to humble herself and apologize to him made him feel like a true house leader. Only a person concerned for his welfare and feelings would have done so.

"There is no need to apologize, My Kendall. You did not harm me in any way." He smiled at her and gave her a little shot of the puppy dog eyes. "May I continue driving now that you have corrected my skills?"

Flame was no fool. He knew that Kendall was ready to take the keys and ban him from driving for life. He also knew that she was feeling guilty and would want to make up for what she was sure to feel was a lack of control on her part. Allowing him to drive would ease her conscience and let Flame have some fun while learning all about Earth customs. It was a win-win situation.

Kendall cringed inside, but looking at his sorrowful face, she decided to let him continue to drive. He had his own bank account and could easily afford any speeding tickets he got! If the police took him away…well, she could take the children home and he could get a first hand look at the American judicial system. It was a win-win situation.

"The speed limit is sixty-five, Flame," was all that she said as she sat back and let him start the car.

Flame eased the car onto the road, vowing to follow all of the signs posted on the road.

Driving was easy.

Kendall reached over and turned on the radio, only to hear George Michael singing his heart out about freedom. They both thought that the song was appropriate as they continued on down the road. Freedom indeed.

* * * * *

Flame was doing so well with his driving, that Kendall let him continue to drive them until the children cried to be fed and changed. By that time, Flame with the help of Kendall had memorized just about all of the traffic rules that she could recall as well as the do's and don'ts. After that first horrendous start, he was now driving like he had been operating a vehicle for years.

"You are a great driver, Flame." Kendall complimented as she took charge of Spark. After a few days of baby care, she changed diapers like a pro, hardly ever flinching at any of the smelly surprises she found inside.

Flame flushed with pleasure over her comments as he watched his little girl savage the latex nipple of her bottle like she had not been fed in weeks.

The sun was shining, the birds were singing, and Flame had never felt this good in his whole life. He openly smiled at his small family. He would fight the whole Matriarch to keep them safe.

He looked at Kendall and delighted over her antics with Spark. She was blowing raspberries again on his little tummy causing him to giggle and kick his chubby legs.

His hair was still mostly a red-gold color, but the silver streaks were becoming more prominent. Ember's soft red hair was liberally streaked with the silver and again he thought about what it meant. Their natural mother was Keeper of the Snow, so did that mean that the twins had inherited the power of the House of Ice?

Thoughts like that turned his attention again to the approaching death squad. His computer would alert them to when they entered the Earth's atmosphere, but until then, he planned to live each day like it was his last.

"I'll drive the rest of the way, Flame." Kendall had burped the baby while Flame was lost in thought and now was securing the sleepy baby into his seat. "Driving is hard when you are not used to doing it."

Flame nodded his agreement before raising his daughter to his shoulder. "I love you, My Kendall," he stated with simple sincerity.

His words, so unexpected, caused her heart to burst with joy. He had to be thinking about his sister, she thought, but the fact that he would take time out of his dark musings to reassure her left her feeling important. It was also important that he knew that she understood his feelings and returned them.

"As I love you, My Flame." She spoke clearly while looking directly into his eyes. "You are the only one for me."

Flame closed his eyes at her declaration, then looked up into her beautiful shining brown eyes. "You are my life, my air, the fire in my soul."

Kendall's eyes filled with tears of happiness at his words. He was so different from all that she had come to know about men and she cherished him above all others. "Lets go home, big guy, so that I can show you just how much I need you."

157

Ember was placed into her car seat and they drove away, leaving the mountains behind. In the back seat, Ember and Spark exchanged looks of contentment before nodding off to sleep.

Chapter Eleven

ॐ

"What will you do at this job that you call work?"

Kendall grunted as she tried to lift one of her suitcases from the floor of the minivan. She glared at Flame as he easily hefted her other case as well as shouldering his duffel bag. Why did the man have to be so strong? She glanced as his bottom as he straightened and turned to walk towards the house. Why did he have such a gorgeous tush?

They had unstrapped the sleeping children and placed them in one of the two spare bedrooms that Kendall's house possessed. She had thought to use them as an office and a guestroom, but now she saw them painting the identical rooms pink and blue, for her baby girl and her baby boy.

As they unload the minivan, Kendall began to explain the concept of working for a living. The trip home from the small cabin seemed to fly by quicker than their trip to the mountains. Kendall still could not believe all that had changed in her life during the past five days.

"At work, I help deliver babies." Kendall said with a grin as she slammed the door to the van closed.

"I usually don't deliver them on my couch at home, but the principle is the same. At a hospital, the health care professionals get paid for caring for the sick, infirm, and…well…pregnant women. Men here on Earth don't get in that condition. You'd better be glad that I found you, buddy. If someone else had found you, you'd be an episode on the X-Files by now."

"X-Files?" Flame cocked his head to the side as he tried to puzzle through the strange meaning of her words.

Kendall rolled her eyes heavenward and grabbed his hand. "Come on, Flame. Let's go inside and I will explain all about television."

Once inside, Kendall stopped and looked around her living room. How could everything look so much the same when she felt so changed?

Flame seemed to understand a little of what she was feeling, because he dropped the bags at the entrance to the living room and pulled her close to snuggle into his chest. He brushed the top of her head with his chin as he surveyed the room where his new life and Kendall's new adventures had begun.

"You owe me a new couch," she said at last. "I don't care how you got the old one clean, I don't want that couch to bring back memories of your first visit with me." She grinned up at him, brushing a lock of his vibrant hair from her face.

"I will provide anything that you desire, My Kendall." Flame snuggled her closer to him by draping a possessive arm across her chest. His Kendall felt so good pressed close to him.

"And, I don't want to cook more than I have to." If it were this easy to get things out of the man, she would be hard-pressed not to take advantage of him. Kendall turned a brilliant smile up to her man.

Flame grinned down at his beautiful Tarcas-brown Kendall, his deep gray eyes showing his pleasure in her teasing. He would do whatever it to took to keep her safe and happy.

"I know where your kitchen unit is, My Kendall. Why do you not take a rest and I will prepare your meal."

"No, thank you, Flame," she replied as she pulled out of his arms, memories of his breakfast still imbedded within her mind and causing her stomach to do the samba. "I need to go shopping because we need to restock the kitchen. We have no fresh food in the house."

"I'll go, My Kendall. You need to rest."

Kendall paused on her way to the front door to turn and look at him standing in her living room with the bulk of their luggage spread out about his feet.

Suddenly, she couldn't catch her breath. The room seemed to spin and she felt a little weak in the knees. This was happening all too fast!

"I think I need a little time for myself, Flame." Her voice was a bit shaky though she tried to hide it.

"What is wrong, My Mistress?" Concerned, Flame began to walk towards her. Her sudden pallor worried him. If she was ill, he could find a way to help. Maybe this hospital of hers would be the place to take her.

"Nothing, Flame," she replied as she backed up to the door and fumbled with the knob. Unable to see what she was doing, she turned and tried to wrench the door open.

Suddenly she had two children and a man to shop for, to worry about, and to care about. There would be changes in her life and in her in her house! Midnight feedings, diaper changes, toilet training, dating... it was all too much. She had to get away!

And what about his sister and her squad of hired goons coming here to kill him? Would her life ever be normal again?

The warm press of his hands against her shoulders helped calm her somewhat as she pressed her head to the cool surface of the wooden door.

"I understand, Kendall," came Flame's gentle assurance. "I have invaded your life and taken a large part of it in such a short time."

He dropped a kiss to the top of her head and gave her shoulders a reassuring squeeze. "So many new things must be difficult to deal with."

"You are not difficult to deal with," was her muffled reply. It was a bit hard talking when your face was plastered against a front door.

"It is a difficult situation, My Mistress. We have overwhelmed you with our problems and I understand your desire to be alone. As a young man, I often felt the burden of my existence and sought the solitude of my own company to put my life into perspective. I begin to think that you need to do the same, my proud, brave Kendall."

"I don't feel brave," she responded in a shaky voice. "I feel...I don't know what I feel. I know that I love you, but...I just don't know."

"Then go and sort out your feelings, My Mistress. I will be here waiting for you and loving you. You are ever in my heart, My Kendall."

He pressed another kiss to the top of her head and stepped back, allowing her freedom.

Kendall eased the door open and slowly stepped out into the early evening air. She had some thinking to do, just to put her new life into perspective and grocery shopping would give her the time she needed to do just that. Firm decisive action was what was needed. The old Kendall reasserted herself and combined with the new Kendall, the one without inner self-doubts....Watch out world!

Holding her head high, she gamely strode to her minivan determined to put her thoughts in some semblance of order, or die trying.

Flame mournfully watched as Kendall drove off in her vehicle. He had changed so many things in her life in such a short time, that he felt a little guilty, okay...a lot guilty.

He realized that she never thought to have children or a family and suddenly over the time span of a few days, she had both. He knew that she loved him, but was love enough?

The soft wail of his son drew his attention back to the present. He could tell Ember's demanding cry from Spark's quiet sobs of need almost as well as his Kendall could. Then Ember's voice joined her brother's and the solo became a duet. He put aside his musings for later. His children needed to be changed and fed. He turned and walked up the stairs to see to his son.

Flame had Ember nodding off in her cube in one of Kendall's spare bedrooms and Spark bouncing on his shoulder when there was a knock at the door. Expecting to see Kendall, he eagerly raced down the stairs and opened the door only to have a weepy-eyed female hurl herself at him.

Instinctively stepping back to protect his child, he neatly avoided having the woman land on him. The loud thump of her hitting the floor caused him to look down to see who this woman was. Obviously she was not of Testrios with all the crying and sobbing that she was doing, but something about her seemed familiar.

"Caressa?" he questioned with an arched eyebrow as the woman raised her tear- streaked face.

"Oh, Flame!" she cried as she pulled herself to her knees. "I thought you were Kendall. I want my sister!" Fresh tears streamed down her swollen face.

Flame was at a loss. Kendall crying nearly broke his heart and left him feeling like a helpless fool; this woman's caterwauling merely made his head hurt.

Still patting Spark on the back, he continued to look down at the woman, waiting for some inspiration to strike and tell him what to do about her. He knew that Kendall did not want to see this particular woman any time soon, but she was her sister. Did he have the right to make her leave the premises?

"Aren't you going to help me up? You're the one who made me fall in the first place!" she sobbed pressing the heels of her palms into her eyes and pulling herself to her knees.

When Kendall did that, his heart melted and he wanted to press her close to his heart to alleviate some of her pain. When this woman did it, it looked…well…childish.

"I believe you threw yourself at the first object you saw, Mist…Caressa, and I removed Spark from the danger that you presented. My first duty is to my son. I will help you if you but allow me a moment to see to his needs."

Then Flame really began to like Earth. If this had happened on Testrios, he would have been severely reprimanded for not finding a way to see to Spark and to this woman at the same time. Here, she was wrong and he could point that fact out to her without fear of reprisal. Yes, he was really beginning to enjoy being an Earthling.

"I can get up without your help!" came her petulant reply as Caressa pulled herself to her feet with an air of injured dignity. "You men are all alike anyway. When you get what you want, you all act like spoiled children."

Flame shook his head in confusion. Who said that he wanted something from her and that he wanted her to behave like this? Who was acting the spoiled child?

"That is ironic, Caressa, since it is you who was lying on the floor in tears."

Flame felt that it was only right to point that fact out to her. He watched as the heat of embarrassment caused her face to redden and nicely match her bloodshot eyes.

"If you would like to step inside, I will see to your comfort until Kendall returns home."

Gathering together the tatters of her pride, Caressa threw her head back and quietly strode into house as Flame stepped aside and waved her in with a sweeping motion of one broad palm.

She strode over to the couch and with great drama, flung herself down upon it in a tangle of floral printed skirts, throwing arm over her face in a show of feminine helplessness.

"Something troubles you, Caressa?"

"Flame," she asked in a soft voice, peering over her arm, "You understand men, right?"

Feeling unease trickle down his spine, he slowly nodded.

"Then can you please tell me why Richard is such an ass?" Her voice broke on his name and tears began to leak out of her eyes once more.

He had many reasons why he thought that man to be an "ass", but felt that her question was rhetorical. Wishing that he were anywhere else on this planet than with this particular woman, Flame looked down at his son, only to have his son stare back with sleepy eyes. His expression seemed to say, "You're on your own with this one, Pop."

"What has he done to make you feel so, Mist…Caressa?" He had to get used to addressing women by their given names, he thought.

That was the opening that Caressa was waiting for. In an instant she was sitting up, adjusting her long floral skirt around her legs, and patting the sofa cushion beside her. "Come sit here, you darling man, and I will tell you. I have never been so hurt in all my life!"

Uneasily, Flame lowered himself onto the sofa beside this strange woman. Already his mind was on what Devo had said about women seeking the next best thing when they slacked their thirst on an unsuspecting man. This woman had proved herself unworthy of trust once by mating with her sister's chosen man, but his earlier training demanded that he at least hear what her distress was all about.

"Well," she reached one hand towards his leg, only to suddenly have a startled-looking baby blocking her path.

Flame was unashamedly using his son like a human shield. The baby opened his eyes and eyed his father with annoyance before settling down into his new position and thrusting one chubby fist into his little rosebud mouth.

Pulling her hand back and looking a bit confused, Caressa continued with her story.

"That man said that I was nothing like Kendall, that I was next to worthless! Is it my fault that a career in modeling leaves little time for medical school?"

The tears were starting to flow freely down her face now, and Flame was at a loss as to what to do. He sat there and stared at her wondering if he should hand her the box of disposable paper cloths called tissues, that Kendall kept on the "coffee" table.

The table was not made from that wonderful elixir, so why was it named after the early morning beverage? He shook his head at yet another fascinating oddity that he'd discovered on Earth. But then his focus returned, to the weeping woman on the couch.

"Were you trained in the healing arts?" he asked politely.

"Nooo!" she wailed.

"Then why would he say such a thing?" If she had no training in a skill, why would she possess knowledge of it? Richard was a lot more idiotic than he looked. Again Flame wondered what Kendall had ever seen in the half-man.

"Because I didn't know what a massive myo-cardio infarction was!" She dropped her face wailing as if she was mortally wounded by his words.

Flame continued to stare, confused by the woman and Spark began to look as if he wanted to join her in a good sympathy cry.

Slowly piecing together her words, he came up with the definition, a great cessation of the cardio muscle, the heart. In layman's terms, a heart attack.

"Why would he wish to speak with you of a heart attack?" His honest question unleashed a new wave of tears causing his eyes to widen with anxiety.

"Even you know what that is!" she sobbed. "Maybe Richard was right! I am worthless!"

Not knowing what else to do, Flame groped one-handed for the box of tissues and thrust them at her. All of this crying was sorely testing his patience and beginning to make him nervous. She ripped at least three of the small soft papers from the box and buried her face in the mass of white.

Earth women, he decided after a moment of watching her blubber and wail, were a strange species. Spark looked up at him as if requesting that he put an end to this nonsense before all the noise gave him a headache too. Flame could easily understand his son's problem. Already his temples had begun to pound at the horrendous racket she was making.

"Caressa?" Then, "Caressa!"

He had to almost yell to be heard over the sounds of her sniveling. Spark jumped and gave his father an evil look, as evil as a newborn can achieve, and began sucking furiously on his fist.

At the sound of her name being called at a near yell, Caressa quieted somewhat and looked at the man who had made no move to comfort her as another man would have. Most of her display was calculated to get some sympathy from this man, but it seemed he was immune to most of her feminine wiles.

"What are your strong points. What do you have training in?"

That shut her up. Richard had really hurt her with his thoughtless words, but the possibility that there was a grain of truth in them had scared her witless. His question was one she had pondered before leaving Richard's apartment in a huff and heading for sanctuary in her sister's home.

"Training? What are you talking about? I'm a model! I'm trained to look good in every situation and present the people I represent and myself with decorum. I speak French and Italian and I know the difference between a fake diamond and the real thing. I can tell a Bob Mackie and a Donna Karen original from a cheap knock-off. So please tell me, what are my strong points are good for?"

"Maybe teaching others what you know?" Flame's logic was sound. If modeling required such skills, would not other models benefit from her experience?

167

His words stunned Caressa into total silence. "But Richard said that I was a worthless clothes hanger and that anyone with half a brain could model."

His words had amazed her, but they'd planted a small seed of an idea and a glimmer of hope.

"If anyone could model, would not the world be overrun by them? As I understand it, models are in great demand." That was one of the bits of miscellaneous information his computer had picked up about this planet. Everyone seemed enamored of great beauty.

Although Caressa could be considered most pleasing to the eye, he found that he preferred the honest beautiful face of his Kendall. Her beauty was natural, as lovely as the mountain sunsets that they had watched together, and as stimulating as the raw sounds of need that came from her throat as they expressed their love physically.

Thinking of her looking so confused and needing time to herself caused him to sigh with great sadness. As much as he hated to acknowledge it, he could understand Caressa's problem. He, too felt like a worthless burden to someone he loved.

"You're right, Flame!" Caressa got a determined gleam in her green-brown eyes that caused him to forget about his own problems for a time and again focus on her.

"Properly trained models are hard to find, that's what put me in such high demand. Anyone can look good in clothes, it takes someone special to make the public think that they too can achieve style and elegance with ease."

What had he started? Flame looked nervously at Caressa as she bounced excitedly on the couch like a small woodland creature Kendall had called a bunny rabbit.

Taking him completely by surprise, she leaned over Spark and kissed Flame full on the lips.

Flame leapt completely off of the sofa, jerking Spark into total alertness in his attempt to get away from the grinning woman. Spark let out a frightened shriek and eyed the woman who caused his sleeping problems with contempt.

"What do you do, Mistress?" he nearly roared as he pulled his startled child to his chest for a comforting hug. He eyed her over his son's head with suspicion.

"I'm going to open a school for models, Flame; complete with an agency to promote them. I'll be Maryland's answer to Ford's!" She crowed the name of what he had learned was a famous modeling agency as if it were the enemy waiting to be vanquished.

"We need to celebrate!" Her eyes ran across the room as if looking for a worthy target to become the recipient of her jubilation on.

Her words had him backing out of the room and towards the stairs and the safety of the bedroom above where his daughter slept. She would not try and use his body for her "celebration" if his children were present, would she?

Totally ignoring his panicked reaction, Caressa sprang from the couch and raced to the kitchen, causing Flame to calm a little. He looked down at his son and hugged him closer. It was hard being a man, as his son would surely discover as he grew to full adulthood.

"Ah-ha!" came Caressa's muffled voice from deep in the kitchen.

Curiosity winning out over caution, Flame eased his way to the back of the house and tentatively peered into the large room.

Bathed in the light of the waning sun, Caressa stood triumphant, brandishing a carton of something frozen and two spoons.

"Kendall is never out of Triple Chocolate Cherry Ecstasy!" she crowed as she looked at a clock mounted opposite the refrigerator. "Oh, look at the time!" she cried before racing back to the living room and motioning Flame to follow.

"It's time for my favorite talk show! You've solved all my problems Flame, and did it in record time. How can I thank you?"

Flame looked confused as the woman walked over to a large wooden armoire, he thought that was the word for it, and swung the double doors open. Inside sat a large display window and a score of strange boxes with lights and dials. It was some sort of communication center, he realized. He moved in for a closer look, only to have Caressa latch on to his arm.

All those warnings Devo had skillfully implanted in his mind came screaming to his recall, and he thought that he was going to have a fight on his hands. His body would respond to no woman other than his Kendall, and he in no way found this clinging desperate woman sexually attractive.

Before he could open his mouth to form a protest, she all but pushed him onto the sofa and slapped a spoon into his empty hand.

"We can't watch The Dave Killerman Show without ice-cream!" she declared instantly easing his fears and piquing his interest.

"The Dave Killerman Show?" he questioned as he took a firm grip on the spoon.

"You don't get him in Ireland?" she asked as she dipped the spoon into the sinfully rich frozen confection.

She slowly, and with hands trembling in ecstasy, placed the spoon in her mouth and closed her full lips over it. Eyes closed, she slowly pulled it out moaning in obvious delight.

"He has the best show around," she continued, oblivious to the fact that he stared at her in wide-eyed amazement.

He recognized the sounds as those a woman might make while in the throes of heightened sexual awareness, but he had not touched this woman in any way! Was it this "ice cream" that caused such a reaction? He had to investigate.

Adjusting his calmed son into better position in the crook of his arm, he dipped his spoon into the ice-cold mixture finding it a bit firm and hard to scoop. Caressa tilted the carton in his direction as she began to expand on the wonders of talk television.

"This is a good one," she said as she patiently waited for him to dig out a spoonful of the frozen treat. He acted as if he had never seen ice cream in his life. "It's about couples who suffer because of mental abuse from their mates because of their bondage lifestyles."

Spark's little head lifted at that, but no one paid him any attention. Caressa was humming the opening theme music to the show and Flame was eyeing the stuff on his spoon with a contemplative look. The red-headed infant's full attention seemed to be riveted on what was happening on the screen.

Flame carefully placed the spoon into his mouth, ready to pull it and the strange substance on it out at a moment's notice, and his eyes widened in amazement before he too closed his eyes and moaned in delight.

A wonderful flavor exploded on his tongue. The firm texture of the ice cream melted into a creamy mass filled with the robust flavor of deep chocolate tempered by the sweetness of fresh cherries, offset by the tiny chunks of bitter dark and semi-sweet chocolate pieces. He had never tasted anything so soul inspiring, except maybe for Kendall. Finally, he fully understood the sounds that the woman was making.

This stuff was as good as sex! Well almost.

"A man who savors his chocolate!" Caressa nodded in approval. He made sounds of unbelievable enjoyment and Caressa approved even more. If a man savored his food like her sister's red-hared giant, he could savor...well...other things as well.

Kendall was right, she decided right then and there. She had saved her sister from making a mistake with Richard and now Kendall had found this wonderfully expressive man who was obviously worthy of her. He never even made one move to stare at her spectacular legs, and in her not so humble opinion, they were spectacular.

Then Flame's eyes were caught by the spectacle on the screen. A man had a woman tied onto a makeshift bed and was demonstrating the correct way to administer discipline without causing harm. Mute, he watched every move the man made while Flame absently dug into the carton Caressa still held. What was he doing with that paddle? Women allowed this to happen? Could the women also discipline the men in this fashion?

Flame was in for an education.

Chapter Twelve

ဆ

The sound of muffled sobs drove Kendall to throw open her front door.

"Who is hurt?" she cried racing down the short hallway with Richard on her heels.

While she had been determinedly stalking down the aisle of her neighborhood grocery store, power shopping, she came to a sudden epiphany between the carrots and the lettuce in the vegetable aisle.

She watched as a couple with two kids argued about whose responsibility it was to watch over their children while the father went off to play golf.

The tired-looking mother argued that she needed a break from the children and the father declared that he couldn't miss his tee time. "I have important clients coming, you know," he cried.

The children in question looked miserably at each other as they held hands and slowly walked behind their bickering parents.

True, everything was moving so fast in her life, she had never known such a full range of emotions, but that wasn't bad at all. Never had she felt a love so powerful that the very mention of his name made her heart weep with joy. Never had she been so thoroughly and completely loved or cherished like she was something special. Flame had brought her heart's every desire, to be needed and wanted equally. He'd even brought her children! She couldn't love Ember and Spark more if they had come from her own body. Who could ask for anything more?

Flame was patient and understanding, and would soon be self-supporting. She knew Flame would ensure that he carried his own weight. He considered it all part of protecting his Mistress from all harm. Even more essential, he proved that he could be counted on. He'd never put his needs above hers or the children's like the argumentative red-faced father that stormed down the aisles. He'd consider it unmanly.

She hated the thought of him sitting alone and confused in the house, waiting on pins and needles for her to return and assure him of her love. She was one lucky woman to have found him on her front lawn, and she couldn't wait to rush home and tell him so.

But as she pulled up in front of her house, she was met by a sheepish looking Richard wearing his trademark brown suite.

"What do you want, Dickey-Boy?" she asked as she climbed from the driver's seat and opened the side door. She was anxious to get to Flame and make up for scaring him the way she had.

"I know you don't want to see me right now, Kendall." He worriedly ran his hands through his hair, ignoring his new nick-name. "But this is an emergency. Have you seen Caressa?"

"Have I seen my sister? What's wrong Richard? Did you two have your first lover's spat?" Kendall had groceries to unload and a man who needed some good loving. She didn't have time for Richard and Caressa or their problems.

"This is serious, Kendall. I was stressed after afternoon rounds and said some really hurtful things to Caressa and now she's run off."

Kendall snorted as she hefted her two grocery bags from the floor of the minivan, and slammed the door shut with the swing of one hip.

"Caressa is a big girl, Richard." She turned to the good doctor as she pointed out that obvious fact. "Give her some time to cool off and then she'll go on home, like a good little girl."

She turned and started up her walkway, smiling as she saw that her MoonFlowers had opened their milky white petals for the soft kiss of the moonlight. The heady fragrance of the blossoms touched a cord within her heart. She had been enjoying the scent of these very blossoms when she had first found her auburn-hared spaceman on her front lawn. She would always associate the smell with Flame.

"But she doesn't know anyone else in Baltimore!" Richard's plaintive voice drew her back to the present. The man could never take a hint. He was matching her step for step as she walked to her front door, paying no attention to the beautiful miracle of the MoonFlowers and their unique scent. "The only place she could run is to you."

"Listen to me, Richard." Kendall finally groused out as they stopped at her front door. "I have not, nor do I want to see my sister now. Go home! She's probably there waiting for you now."

She handed one of the bags to Richard as she inserted the key into the lock. If he was going to stand around pestering her, he could at least make himself useful.

That's when they both heard the sobs coming from inside the house. Ignoring Richard, Kendall thrust the door open and raced to the source of the heart-wrenching cries. Richard, hearing Caressa's distinctive wailing sound rushed after her.

As she raced down the hall, the thought of Flame in any pain was enough to make her murder the person responsible. Had the Execution Squad located him? Had the government learned of his existence? She was mad with worry, desperate to find out what was wrong with him.

Dropping her bag unheeded to the floor, she was confronted by a sight that almost stopped her heart.

Flame, her Flame, was slouched low on the couch as he sobbed his eyes out into a tissue. Beside him sat Caressa, red-faced and crying openly, her eyes fixed to the television screen. On her sister's lap sat a riveted Spark, also staring in wonder at the screen, watching a woman in a leather corset cling to a man who lay chained to a chair on a studio stage.

"Do not believe her deceitful words," Flame cried out to the TV. "She will only abuse you again when she feels your resolve to leave has lessened."

"You tell him, Flame!" Caressa cried in complete agreement, blotting her eyes and tenderly running her fingers through Spark's hair. "She doesn't love you like you deserve to be loved!"

The baby seemed entranced by all of the leather and exposed skin on the screen.

"All right!" Kendall bellowed causing everyone to look in her direction. Even Spark turned away from the action on the stage to fix his large gray eyes on her.

"What the hell is going on in here? Why are you darkening my doorway so soon, Caressa, when I told you that I did not want to see your face around here? Why is Flame crying and what have you got my baby watching? Look at him! Are you trying to turn him into a sex fiend?"

She stood in the doorway; arms akimbo, firing off questions faster than the crying duo on the couch could answer. Then she spotted the carton of her most favorite ice cream, sitting empty on the coffee table with two dirty spoons.

"You ate my ice cream!" she bellowed. "You two have a lot of explaining to do! Starting with why my son is watching this…this…trash and why my ice cream is gone!"

"I think we all deserve an explanation!" Richard bellowed from behind Kendall causing Caressa to eye him with disgust and Flame with something akin to extreme hatred as the waterworks abruptly dried up.

Spark seemed to blink in anticipation of the bloodletting to come, and perked up as much as an infant needing sleep could. Something was happening with the grown-ups and he had a front row seat.

"Oh, Dallie!" Caressa cried as she passed Spark to his father. "You have a real treasure in Flame." She sprang up from the couch and ran with arms outstretched to her sister, totally ignoring Richard.

Kendall stood frozen as Caressa embraced her.

"Flame helped me figure out what I want to do with the rest of my life." Caressa gave her immobile sister a little shake and pulled her unresisting form into the living room.

Automatically, Kendall reached for Spark and the baby gave a crow of delight as he saw his mama. A still-sniffing Flame rose to his feet as he handed the baby to Kendall and motioned for her to take a seat.

Of all the things she had expected to see when she charged through the house, this scenario was, in a few words, not one of them. She cradled Spark in her arms and waited for the explanations to begin.

In full melodramatic mode, Caressa executed a quick turn and clapped her hands twice in front of her. "I'm going to open a modeling agency!"

"You're what?" Richard stepped into the room, looking a bit flummoxed by her words. "You can't do that!"

His words had Kendall and Flame eyeing him in shocked anger. Caressa wasn't the smartest thing to ever walk the face of the Earth, Kendall knew, but no one had the right to disparage another person's dream. Flame had come up with the perfect business opportunity for her sister.

Flame was angered by the lack of respect shown to the odd woman. Yes, she had hurt her sister with her unthinking actions, but she still was a woman and deserving of respect. Before anyone could say anything in her defense, Caressa surprised them all yet again.

"What makes you think that I can't do this, Richard?" she questioned with eyes narrowed in anger. All the jubilation on her face was wiped clear by his words. "Just because I didn't attend Harvard Medical School doesn't mean that I don't have a decent education!"

Kendall silently applauded her sister while Flame looked a little amazed himself. It seemed that Kendall's sister was not all, as they said on the TV show, fluff. She, like her sister, had a backbone, when she cared to remember it was there and how to use it.

She stalked right up to Richard and jabbed a finger into his chest, wrinkling his perfectly pressed suite. "I'm not a worthless ornament to parade about on your arm. Flame showed me that I have strong points and value all of my own! I can do anything I put my mind to, with or without you!"

Richard turned a thunderous look to Flame, who in turn gave him a small knowing smile. "This is all your fault you...you...home-wrecker!"

"Don't speak to him that way!" Instantly both Kendall and Caressa were yelling at Richard. Flame paid him no notice.

Richard stared in shock at his beautiful, biddable Caressa. She had never raised her voice to him before and now she was defending another man. "How many women do you need, buddy?" Richard all but growled at Flame.

"I think that it's time we went home and talk about a few things, Richard." Caressa spoke to him like Flame had spoken to her earlier, the way a parent would controlling the tantrum of a child.

"But..." Richard tried to defend himself, but Caressa laid one finger against his lips to shut his mouth.

"I think that it's time to go home, Richard," she repeated firmly.

Richard looked around the room and then gave Caressa a small nod. "At home then, my dear."

Caressa walked over to Kendall and knelt before her sister. "I know that you didn't want to see me for a while."

"Still don't." Kendall ruefully muttered to her sister with a small smile. It was true she didn't want to be around Caressa, but she still loved her and was happy that she was standing up to Richard.

"But I'm grateful to you for allowing Flame to help me." She continued as if she didn't hear Kendall's comment.

"As if I had a choice," Kendall muttered.

"I know you wouldn't have turned me away, Kendall. You may be angry with me right now, but I'm the only family you've got and you love me." She bent down and gave Spark a little kiss on his forehead before gracefully bouncing from her place on floor. "That one is going to be a heartbreaker," she predicted. She then set her sights on Flame.

"I don't know what I would have done without you." She and stopped in front of the blushing man. Looking up, she gave him a confident smile. "You helped me find my worth with a few words. I will never forget it and will always be grateful." She reached up, pulled his face down to her level and planted a soft kiss against his cheek.

Richard frowned, tapping his foot impatiently as he flipped back the sleeve of his suite jacked to peer in an obvious gesture at his watch.

Flame glanced at Kendall to gage her reaction to the small kiss. On Testrios, he would have been blamed for enticing the other woman to such a display of openly touching another woman's property, and quickly punished by his Mistress. He waited to see what Kendall's reaction would be.

Far from being angry, Kendall smiled at Flame's concerned expression. Flame knew then that Kendall trusted him man fully. She had reason to. Why would he want her sister when he had a woman that could melt his bones in bed and who loved him to distraction? He wanted only Kendall. She accepted all of his faults and still loved him. Only her tarcus-brown eyes could flash and make him weak in the knees and only her words could infuse his spirit with strength and need. No other woman's touch meant nothing to him. Kendall was his all.

"You've got yourself a fine man here." Caressa turned to her sister as she made her pronouncement.

"The very best." Kendall agreed as she gazed into Flame's smoldering eyes.

Spark, sensing that there would be no bloodshed, had finally given in to his growing body's needs and had fallen asleep. Kendall rose to her feet and headed for the baby's bedroom, wanting to get him tucked into bed.

As she passed Richard, she murmured, "You had better treat her right or I will sic my Irish Wolfhound on you." She nodded towards Flame who stood and watched his Mistress converse with the half-man, a deep scowl darkening his features. "And his bite is definitely worse than his bark!"

"You both know the way out, I trust?" she added as she ascended the stairs with the sleeping baby cradled in her arms.

Caressa took Richard by his hand and began to lead him to the front door. "I'll need office space, Richard, to make a go of my agency. I'm thinking of calling it Crystal Faces. Isn't that catchy?" She kept up a steady stream of conversation as she and Richard exited the house. "Something with lots of windows. I look best in natural light."

The door closed softly behind their retreating figures and Flame shook his head. Never had he met two more difficult people. Of course Caressa had introduced him to the wonders of ice cream and talk shows, but she was still a unique individual.

By the time Kendall had returned from placing Spark into his cube in his room, Flame had retrieved the grocery bags and was staring in confusion at some of the contents. "What is Redi-Whip?" he asked as he examined the small can of whipped topping.

An instant blush heated Kendall's face and she refused to meet his eyes. That can represented a little fantasy she had while strolling past her grocer's freezer. It involved the now eaten ice cream, cherries, the whipped topping of course, and a few unique containers. "Never mind about that!"

Before he could question her further, his black bag stashed in the living room began to emit a piercing sound.

"What's that noise?" Kendall asked, all thoughts of her fantasy forced out of her head by the loud squeal.

Flame's face paled as he placed the can on the counter. He retrieved his bag and the little black computer that was making the awful sound. "It is the early warning device I programmed into the computer, Mistress. It is making this sound because the Execution Squad has entered Earth's gravitational pull."

Kendall groped for a chair. "How much time?" she forced through her frozen throat.

"Maybe two days time, My Kendall, possibly three."

He spoke with a shaky yet determined voice before taking the chair across from her. He flipped open the small device and began speaking into it with that strange flowing language.

He paused at her questioning look to explain. "I am giving the coordinates to the location where they can find me. I am sending them several miles away from here to a wooded area beyond your lake. You and the children should be safe here while I deal with my sibling and the soldiers that she has brought with her."

"Oh God, Flame!" Kendall gasped out as she reached her trembling hand across the table for his. "I'm so frightened."

And then, as if her show of fear weakened her, she released his hand and rose unsteadily to her feet. With a strangled sound of confused fear and hope, she faced the bank of windows that overlooked the lake.

After crossing her arms in a protective gesture, she stared at the beauty of the moonlight's reflection off of the still lake waters.

Could their time, their loving time, come to a close so quickly? Frustrated anguish settled deep within the pit of her stomach and almost caused her to be physically ill. Loving someone was hard, but the possibility of losing that person...well, that was almost intolerable.

Just as she was ready to give into her urge to cry and scream like a baby, Flame came up behind her and enveloped her in his warm embrace, pulling her back to settle against his hard chest.

"How can I live if something happens to you, Flame?" she choked out as she lost her battle with her tears and sagged against his great strength. "How can I go on without you?"

"Shh, My Kendall," he soothed as he rocked her back and forth, as if she were a small child in need of comfort. "I will come back to you, no matter what."

"We have a family to raise and a business to build." Her voice broke as all the fear and anguish building up inside of her broke free in a muffled sob.

Instantly, Flame spun her around and pulled her into his warm hard body, tucking her head underneath his chin. The feel of him was a comforting anchor in the storm, as her world spun out of control.

"I never wanted my love to bring you such pain!" He cried out as if mortally wounded by her tears. "I wish I had stayed away from you."

"Never say that!" Kendall near shouted. "Never even think it!"

Kendall lifted one trembling hand to caress his beloved face. Her tearstained eyes bored deeply into his. "I don't regret loving you. You brought sunshine into my life. I'd still be lost without you, Flame. Lost and alone!"

Tears welled up and ran down his masculine face, enhancing his beauty and showing her how deeply he cared about her. He bracketed her face, shiny and shaking with the force of her emotions, and began to visually memorize each and every feature.

"You are my air," he whispered between small sipping kisses, tasting of her tears. Each salty tear held the essence of her spirit and was shed for the love of him. He savored the salty sweet taste of each one.

"You are the most important part of me, you are my strength," he continued. "Without you, my existence is meaningless."

Kendall let out a small wailing cry as she pulled her face from his hands and burrowed as close as she could get to him. The pain that they shared was unbelievable, but it was bittersweet for each would bear this pain a thousand times over to experience the sweetness of their love.

"We have to pack a lifetime into the days that we have left," Kendall decided as she sobbed into his chest.

"A lifetime," he agreed as a warm golden glow began to circle the two star-crossed lovers. His emotions were expressing his love more eloquently than his words.

Together, they stood and watched the small waves build and ebb with the tide. There was no further need for words.

Chapter Thirteen

ঔ

"Look at that smile, Flame," Kendall exclaimed she blew raspberries on the squirming baby's belly. "I think Spark is going to look just like you." It took some doing for Spark seemed a little taciturn, like his father, but when you got him smiling, he just couldn't seem to stop himself.

Kendall and Flame both sat on the floor in the living room playing with Ember and Spark after the two children had their baths. Flame seemed determined to spend as much time as he could with his babies, just in case the unthinkable happened.

"I think that Ember is going to be a man-killer when she grows up," Kendall added, reaching over to stroke the little girl's red-streaked hair. "But in a good way," she added as she watched his eyes widen in shock! Be careful with idiom, she reminded himself. At least until he saw more of that Killerman show.

Flame contemplated the sight of his Kendall and the unconditional love she poured out to both Ember and Spark. The sight of this woman, his woman, mothering his children reminded him of all the things that he had missed while growing up on Testrios.

While he had a mother, the powerful house leader spent very little time in the presence of her disappointment of a son. As a result, he had never known a tender touch or a warm embrace from Tessla. Did she even have the right to claim to be his mother? What made a mother anyway? He had the distant kind of motherly attention, and now he craved more for his children.

"I think that if something happens to me you would be a great mother for Ember and Spark." Flame stopped his playful dressing of Ember to seriously look at Kendall. "If something should happen to me, I will ensure your safety and that of my children. Will you be a mother to them on this world?"

Kendall sat up and away from the squirming baby and eyed his father. Flame was dressed in another pair of blue jeans and a white T-shirt that matched her own, but the common clothing did nothing to disguise the uncommonness of his being.

After their emotional outpouring the other night, Flame carried Kendall in to bed and they just held each other close. Kendall lay spoon position with Flame, and savored the feel of his hair-roughened body snuggled so closely to hers as if she would never know that sensation again. She categorized little things about his body in her memory, the way his breathing pattern seemed to always match hers, that the softest skin on his body was just behind his ankles, and how his body heat always carried his scent and totally warmed her body from the inside out.

Flame stroked her soft skin as if his very hands would remember the feel of her. He inhaled her special scent and buried his face into her thick black hair. He memorized the feel of her warm breath against his chest as well as the feel of her soft toes trailing down his legs, before she settled her foot on top on his. He found joy in all of her gestures and movements, and was again thankful that he had found the other half of his being.

Just the physical act of touching bare flesh to bare flesh fed their spirits and gave solace to both of their weary and troubled souls.

Flame had awakened Kendall at dawn so that they could watch the sun explode the dark night over the lake with its colorful entrance, and usher in a new day.

"Have you ever beheld such beauty?" Kendall whispered, almost afraid to destroy the majesty and magic of the moment with the coarse sound of her voice.

They stood on the deck at the rear of her house naked and wrapped only in a shared blanket to protect them from the chill air of the early morning. Together they leaned against the wooden railing and watched the glorious hues of red, gold, and pink meld together to chase away the darkness and become dawn.

"Never," Flame softly replied as he watched the colors of the new day wash gently over her face, highlighting her features in a way that made her seem more beautiful and exotic to his loving eyes.

He pulled her naked body closer to his warmth and relished the feel of her firm body, her heat, and her special smell trapped in the confines of the soft warm blanket with him.

"There is no one like you," he murmured as he bent his head and began to nibble and kiss at the side of her neck.

Kendall threw her head back and moaned out loud her enjoyment of his gentle caresses. His teeth seemed to instinctively find her every erogenous zone on her neck and bathe them with his inner fire and heat. Her arms reached back and pulled his head closer to her, so that he would not miss a single one.

As the blanket slid down with their motions, his hands reached around to cup and mold her soft breasts with firm unyielding hands. Instantly her nipples hardened into sharp points of desire that begged for his loving touch.

A hard knot of tension tightened in Kendall's stomach as her body clenched with excitement. The banked fires of her passion exploded into life, fanned by her tender handling of her lover.

"I need you, right now!" she demanded on a groan as one of his clever hands traced a path down her gently rounded tummy to the thatch of dark wet hair that shielded her desire.

"Flame!" she cried out as his knowing fingers found her cleft and sought out the small pearl of her pleasure. He stroked and teased her with a steady dizzying pressure, driving her higher into the arms of passion.

His hair whipped around them, awakened by the morning breeze and his own ardor, caressing and singeing her nerve endings and wrapping her in its living fire. A soft golden glow surrounded both of them as she felt his manhood rise against the sensitive skin of her bottom.

The beauty of his beloved's face bathed in the colors of the new day only heightened the deep sensual feeling that he experienced in her presence. He wanted to see that same face explode in desire as he brought about her completion.

He pressed and rotated the palm of his hand against her wet heat and brought her to another level so painfully high that she had to grip the wooden railing to keep from toppling right off of the dock.

Her low groan of pleasure caused a slow build up of delicious pressure in his stiff manhood and fire to spread a slow burn over his nether regions. He felt not the chill of the new day, nor the urgency of their present situation; all he felt was the throbbing need for this woman, his true lifemate, and the joy she could bring with her seductive body and her tender loving heart.

"I have to come to you now, my Kendall," Flame moaned as this body's needs took precedence over all other thoughts racing through his mind. "I need to be one with you."

"Yes, Flame. Please now!"

Hearing her inflamed words caused a low roar to mount in his ears and his body to arch uncontrollably against her warm skin. Sliding his fingers, still wet with her desire, up to her waist, he lifted and drew her hips back, closer towards him. He lowered his mouth to her shoulder and delicately nipped the soft skin there as he pressed his strong chest against her back to cause her to bend over the railing. It was her hands that reached back and guided his invading love staff to her quivering cleft.

Flame fought the urge to thrust unrestrained into her hot welcoming sheath, but instead rested the ruby crested head of his magnificence against her wet slit and began to slide himself against her, creating a breathtaking friction that set her senses ablaze.

"Please," Kendall whispered, as her body clenched in want of what he was with holding from her, teasing her with, making her need.

"You are mine, Kendall," Flame fairly growled as spears of passion radiated from where they strained against each other, making his head spin and his body to perspire. "You were meant for me."

Before she could form an answer, Flame reared back, and without his usual gentleness, slammed himself home.

Kendall's body arched back at the lighting strikes she felt as his full thrust slammed into her. Her body fought to adjust it self to his large size by clenching and quivering around his hard length. Animal sounds of pleasure and pain mixed and mingled in her throat as rose up on her toes and pushed closer to his heat, her body accepting all that was he.

Flame closed his eyes as her body took in the full measure of him. Never had he felt this full before, never this wild. He had to fight back the animal instinct to drive himself into her until he spilled his seed deep within her and marked her as his. He laid his head against her trembling back and fought to control the urges racing through his body.

"What you do to me." He whispered as his body once again began to override his mind as his hips began to move.

With almost painful slowness, Flame pulled his entire length from her body, leaving only the very tip of him inside to taunt and tease her. Her breathing suspended in anticipation of his next powerful jolt, but again he surprised her by lingering at her opening.

"Tell me!" he growled.

"Flame?" she squeaked.

"Tell me!" he demanded.

The feeling of him just penetrating her, just lying there was threatening to drive Kendall insane with her need. What did he want from her? She braced her hands on the railing and tried to shove him deep inside her again, where he belonged, but his strong hands forced to stay in that position, dominated and cherished at the same time.

"Tell me!" he demanded again, both hands, now shaking with his fight for control, tightly gripping her waist. "Please, I have to hear it from your sweet lips, my Heart."

Finally, understanding blossomed in her head. She knew what Flame needed to hear from her.

"I love you!" she cried and shrieked it and with a loud groan, he again slammed himself inside of her, finally home.

It was a wild and tumultuous mating. Like a stallion in heat, Flame reared back his head and pumped inside her with unrestrained joy. Her cries of pleasure were only matched by his shouts of passion as they both very vocally expressed their delight.

Kendall forced her body back against him, desperate to feel him deep inside while Flame fought to hold on long enough to drive her to climax.

While thrusting powerfully into Kendall's heat, Flame eased one hand down her taut stomach and let his fingers softly part the flesh and seek out her tiny nubbin of pleasure.

Kendall let out a small shriek as his clever fingers began to manipulate her hot wet flesh. She arched her heat into his hand as her nails dug gouges into the wood of the railing. It was too much, it wasn't enough, and it was undeniably...Flame.

"I love you, Kendall," he groaned, losing himself in her reactions and with his final thrust, they both exploded with extreme carnal bliss, shouting their joy to the heavens, as the golden aura surrounding them exploded over the lake along with the first rays of the sun.

Kendall felt a curious moisture on her back as she fought to keep to her feet and regain her breath. Never had the beauty of a morning affected her like this. She felt Flame's strong body and warmth surround her as they both struggled to regain their composure.

"Flame," she managed to speak through her rough voice as he slowly disengaged himself from her snug sheath.

She turned to face her lover and the moisture on her back was explained. Tears of rapture filled his eyes and rolled down his face.

Instantly, Kendall felt a quiver of alarm shoot through her love worn body. Before she could question him, he laid a gentle finger against her lips.

"Such beauty never existed for me until you come into my life, My Kendall," he said. "I now know that I can face anything this life has fated for me, because I have experienced your love."

Kendall reached out and bracketed his face with her hands, before pulling his mouth down to hers for an all-consuming kiss. No further words were needed. They both understood.

When the sun was well on its journey across the sky, the love-sated couple entered the house, showered, and dedicated the rest of the morning to family style fun with their children.

After a nature hike to the lake behind the house where Flame learned that it was prudent to feed the geese if you did not want to be nipped in displeasure, and hours of tickles and hugs to make the children laugh, they made their way back to the house.

Night had fallen by the time that they finished their evening meal and now both Kendall and Flame took joy in the simple pleasure of feeding and bathing their children.

They laughed through a wild bath in the kitchen where more water wound up on the floor or the happy parents than in the little plastic tubs where the twins splashed and played.

Finally Kendall and Flame now sat on the living room floor preparing Ember and Spark for bed.

"Kendall?" his deep voice questioned gently.

"You are expecting to return to me," she said at last, pulled back to the present by the sound of his voice.

Losing the man of her dreams just when she found him made her a little sick at heart. The pain of those dark thoughts was enough to cause her breath to stop and her eyes to water.

"I will do everything that is within my power to return to you, My Heart, but if things do not proceed as I have planned, I will ensure that you are not bothered by my family in their quest for power."

Unable to bear the pain in his eyes, Kendall looked down and saw silvery drops of tears on Spark's face. Automatically she hefted him to her shoulder to comfort him. It took her a moment to realize that the tears were coming from her own eyes.

"Kendall?" Flame's voice was touched with worry as he eyes the crying woman who held his son.

"I'll guard them with my life, Flame." She buried her nose into the soft fluff of bright red hair on Spark's head. "Please, just come back home to me."

Uncomfortable with exposing her feelings even to Flame, she rose and walked into the bedroom where Spark and Ember's cubes sat. "I love you, little one. I love your sister too, but that man out there is my life. I'll keep an eye on him for all three of us." Spark's little gray eyes seemed to fill with anguished understanding and he observed his Mommy's grief.

Kendall quietly walked the baby murmuring comforting things for him to hear, but she didn't know if she did it to comfort the baby or herself.

Sensing that she needed a few minutes alone, Flame finished dressing Ember and paced the living room with her, agonizing over his decision to confront the Execution Squad.

"I must face them, my little heart, for if I do not, we will never live in peace."

He pressed little kisses to her silver-streaked red hair.

"If I can not stop them, you and your womb mate will be safe from my family. I swear it!"

Ember's usually bright and playful gray eyes were now filled with fear as she observed her father. Sensing that the children knew of the danger to come, Flame made an extra effort to comfort his little girl. The thought of never seeing his children's precious faces cut as deep as the though of never seeing his Mistress again. Flame truly loved his children and would see to it that no matter what happened; they would be reared here on Earth with Kendall's loving influence.

Soon Ember's large gray eyes closed and she nodded off into sleep. Flame carried her to the bedroom where Kendall sat looking at Spark through the clear material of the cube.

"He's going to be something special if he is anything like his father," she whispered as she watched him place Ember into her cube.

"Will you come with me, My Mistress?" he asked as he turned to face her. "I would perform a special rite with you, if you would allow it."

The fire that leapt into his eyes told her that this would be no simple ceremony. She nodded and placed her right hand into his. He pulled her to her feet, clicked off the bedroom light, and guided her to the master bedroom and into the master bath.

Keeping in touch with the rest of Kendall's ultra feminine bedroom, her personal bathroom was filled with decadence and luxury.

Her large white sunken bathtub was the size of a small Jacuzzi and dominated the large room. Beautiful hot house flowers flourished on the low shelf that surrounded the tub and in hanging pots placed around the room. The floor was carpeted in a cream color that perfectly matched her ceiling.

Hand painted borders depicted couples in several different positions and in different stages of orgasmic ecstasy. The beautiful gilt figures were taken straight from the walls of a Pasha's harem, and recreated in miniature to match the mood of her sultan's bedchamber. The walls were painted to resemble the columns in a harem bath. On the wall opposite the tub, a beautiful ever-blooming garden of rare roses and eastern flowers was painted. On the center of that wall rested a heavily padded fainting couch upholstered in the dominant cream and gold colors of the room. Kendall had spared no expense when designing her own private sanctuary. The master bathroom reflected her inner spirit and she had found hours of comfort there.

Flame began by placing candles around the shelf surrounding her tub.

"Where did you find them?" she asked gesturing to the soft white tallow tea candles in their small glass cups.

"They were in a storage area in the kitchen. Do you mind? We need tapers for the ceremony, but these small candles will do." She shook her head and he proceeded to fill the tub with warm water.

The heat generated by the splashing water soon filled the room with steam. When he tossed in a handful of powder from a pouch sitting on her lounge, the room began to fill with an exotic scent. Flame's image in her eyes to soften and blur and the now fragrant steam began the job of relaxing her tense muscles.

With a wave of his hand, he lit the candles as he walked towards Kendall.

"When a woman is life-mated," he began with a sexy low voice, "it is the duty of her mate to prepare her for their first night as lovers."

Kendall gulped and nodded. This was serious if he was bringing up tradition.

"I would like to prepare you, My Kendall, for it is an extension of my love and desire for you. I would show you my feelings every way that is possible for me to do so."

The "in case he did not return" was not spoken but easily understood by both.

"Will you allow me to undress you?" he asked with a small grin. He had now figured out that his words inflamed her senses as well as his touch and he would use both to heighten her enjoyment of their coupling.

"Yes." She spoke softly and her voice carried shivers down his spine.

He dropped to his knees before her moved his hands to the snap of her jeans, she preferred to go barefoot in her house so did not have to bother with shoes. The sound of the snap caused her breathing and heartbeat to accelerate. He eased her zipper down and smoothed the denims from her body. She braced her hands on his shoulders to step out of the mass of material, and received a mild shock where her skin made contact with his.

At her gasp, he looked up at her through those sinfully long eyelashes, and she began to melt inside. "My emotions, My Kendall." He spoke to her as he ran his hands over her bare legs. "Do you mind the sensation?"

"God, no!" was her quick reply. "If anything, it adds a new element to our joining, something that is yours and mine alone."

He nodded and proceeded to ease her shirt off her body leaving her standing in her underwear. She shivered, but not with cold. The room's heat combined with Flame's hot glances were doing a good enough job of keeping her warm.

"Do I get to undress you?" she asked as he slowly rose to his feet, inhaling her very essence as he stood.

"No," he replied distractedly. He stood back to watch her body shimmer in the soft glow of the candles and rising steam. She was a goddess. That she waited for his touch awed him.

"Why not?" she questioned. "No" was a word that rarely came out of his mouth, especially when directed at her.

"Because it is faster this way, My Kendall." In a matter of moments he striped out of his shirt and jeans, and stood before her proudly naked and unashamed.

Again the sight of Flame in his natural state almost brought tears to her eyes. All that golden skin was hers. All of that long flowing hair was hers. His manhood, growing before her eyes accented softly with that auburn hair was hers. All that he was belonged to her and she was damn proud and excited to have the privilege. Already his body was taking on that deep golden aura, his mating glow, and the sight almost brought her to her knees.

Flame was having a hard time fighting for his usual control; a common occurrence since he had first made love to his Kendall. Every time he came near this woman his body acted with a will of its own. Her beauty astounded him and the courage she held when faced with dealing with the unknown humbled him. His heart raced as he took a step closer to her. He wanted to drown himself in her scent and bathe in her essence. He wanted to burrow so deep inside her that the outside world would disappear, just cease to exist for the both of them. He needed her like he needed…air. She was a basic element to his survival and he would gladly give all to make sure she was happy and content.

Remembering his duty, he turned and shut off the water before approaching Kendall and removing the last two barriers that stood in the way of her naked flesh, another lacy bra and a scandalous bit of material that covered her bottom and shielded her womanhood from him.

After testing the temperature of the water, he lifted and laid her within the tub's depths, her head cushioned on a soft bath pillow.

"Aren't you going to join me in here?" she asked when Flame suddenly stopped all movement. "It's big enough for two."

Flame nodded, but his eyes were glued to her bare breasts.

"What?" she finally asked. Something had shocked her lover and she wanted to know what had caught his attention.

"They float!" his said more to himself, but Kendall heard him anyway and felt her face redden.

Pulling himself away from his discovery, he shook his head as if to clear it of all thought, then stepped into the warm water and sighed as the heat began to penetrate his pores.

He eased her long legs apart with gentle hands and knelt between them, fighting to keep his attention focused on his duties and not on the curling thatch of dark hair that protected her feminine secrets.

He grabbed a nearby bath cloth and dampened it with the water that held them in its warm embrace. Tenderly he washed her face, pausing every few minutes to lean over and deliver small sipping kisses to her lips and her neck. Kendall smiled at him and ran a dripping wet finger over the bridge of his nose.

"Why isn't the water evaporating?" she asked for his skin felt as if it was on fire. His body was fever-hot and that turned her on.

"Because I an exerting supreme control over myself, My Mistress. If I were to let go of my emotions, I would scorch you with all of this heat."

That sounded pretty good to Kendall, so she decided to see how high she could fan the flames.

She grabbed the soap from a nearby dish and slowly began to twirl the bar until a rich lather exploded into her hands. "Stand up, Flame."

He eyed her wearily as if he knew some extreme torture was about to follow, but stood anyway as his bath cloth plopped unheeded back into the water. He could deny his Kendall nothing.

Water slouched over the edge of the tub as Kendall stood and began to run slick soapy fingers over his hard chest.

"I am supposed to bathe you, Mistress," he gritted out between clenched teeth. The touch of her fingers was causing his body to vibrate. He closed his eyes in an attempt to regain some control.

"This is Earth," was her reply, "and I can do anything I damn well please."

Flame moaned as her small soapy hands ran across his shoulders and into the sensitive undersides of his arms. His body began to shake as her clever little hands ran down his tight stomach and across his thighs, rubbing and massaging.

"Turn around," was her next order and he was so helpless in the grip of her passion, his passion, their passion that he could do nothing but comply.

The combination of her small soft hands working their magic on his body and the heated humidity in the room caused his head to swim. He had to clench his fists to keep from turning and driving himself into her, right up against the wall.

Kendall reached up on the tips of her toes to wrap her arms around his chest. Flame let out a groan as the hard tips of her nipples dug into his back. He actually growled when her quick fingers eased over his sides to cup and caress his bottom.

"You have nice firm buns, Flame." Her hot moist breath caressed and tickled the sensitive insides of his ear and he had to brace his hands against the wall as the full force of his desire slammed into him.

Finally her soft little hands ran around to his front and softly stroked his hot hard flesh. His knees almost gave out, as she gently cupped what was tender and firmly stroked the steel that what was not. He soon found his hand joining hers and showing her exactly which strokes he liked the best.

Kendall thrilled at the feel of his hand guiding hers as they both pleasured his body. It was a heady experience, feeling his soapy male flesh slip and slide with ease through the grip of their combined fingers.

"When we have time" she murmured, "I want to watch you touch yourself for my pleasure, Flame. I want to watch you and learn all about what you like the best."

The images that statement conjured up! Losing more of his precious control, Flame turned to grab Kendall, only to have her slip right through his soapy arms and land on her knees in front of him. Her slick body with its firm softness sliding against him caused him to imagine what it felt being inside her warm giving sheath. But then he looked down and saw what she was about to do.

"Kendall, don't," he cried out just before her warm mouth encased him.

Kendall had never felt more excited in her life. There was something to be said for taking control. Although he never realized it, Flame had held the ultimate control during all of their sexual escapades, and she wanted a little of that control back. Power was indeed a heady thing, and she wanted a chance to thoroughly explore hers.

"You are so beautiful here," she whispered as she teased and licked at his rock hard flesh.

Flame struggled to keep himself in check as Kendall sought to…to…he did not know what she sought. What she was doing was causing his body to tingle and his brain to turn to mush. His head fell back against the tile wall as he reveled in the tingling flashes of heat that raced through out his body. He could feel pressure building and building and he feared that his body would explode, but he did not care. He was losing himself in the glorious sensations that she was producing in him, for him, and he loved her even more.

Of their own accord, his hands tangled in her soft hair as his head slid from side to side on the cool tile of the wall. Then she began to hum.

"You taste delicious, Flame. Like fire and heat and all my man."

"Kendall, I'm going to…" he began.

"Explode," she whispered as she continued minister to him with her self- appointed task.

"Kendall!" he cried as his sac tightened and his bones began to vibrate. Flashes of light and fire filled the air and the water surrounding them began to bubble and steam.

"Ahh!" he shouted as his release tore trough his rigid body, slamming his head back against the wall and causing him to release Kendall and slam his hands through his own wildly whipping hair.

The glass cups which held the tea candles exploded and for a moment fire shot from the shattered wax coated glass towards the ceiling with a loud whooshing sound before quickly burning its self out. The water stopped rolling around in the tub and the steam, scented with the herbs that he had added to the water, began to rise and fill the room. Then Flame slipped down the wall, all the strength leaving his legs and turning his body into a mass of quivering nerves.

"What you do to me, My Kendall!" he gasped when he began to recover his voice. He looked up at the grinning woman who stood smug above him and let out a deep sigh of contentment.

"I just gave you a reason to make sure nothing happens to you." She said this with a superior look and an arched brow.

Her body was on fire from his reactions and she hoped he was up to finishing what he had originally started. "You taste like all of my tomorrows, Flame."

In a sudden blur of movement, Flame stood and began to drag Kendall from the tub of water. It seems that it didn't take Testrios men a long time to recover, for Flame was again ready for her.

"I will give you a reason to long for my return!" he cried as he carried her wet body to the bedroom.

"Do not wake the children," he cautioned as he tossed her onto the bed, headless of her down comforter, and began to lap up the droplets of water that dotted her squirming body.

Kendall twisted under the assault of his rough tongue bath and held back a cry of joy as his lips fastened to her turgid nipple. She nearly screamed as his oh-so-hot hands massaged and stroked her damp skin. Down they traveled until they tangled in the wet hair that sheltered her femininity.

All thoughts of gaining her permission flew out the window as Flame felt her wet heat part under his adoring touch. Her tiny pleasure pearl exploded from its hidden hood and with great reverence he gently stroked and toyed with it.

His mouth traced a volatile trail over her body only to replace his hands at her mons. He felt his energy pour into her in ever-widening waves as he tasted and tormented his love. Nothing was good as loving his Kendall, he thought as he flickering tongue over her.

Kendall bit down on her lower lip as her body jerked uncontrollably. She stuffed her fist in her mouth to stifle her cries as his fingers, damp with her dew; crawled up her body to tease and pull at her painfully aroused nipples.

"Flame," she moaned and he deftly he turned her onto her stomach and began to nip and nibble at the small of her back.

"Oh Flame, please," she moaned. With trembling hands, he pulled her to her knees. Large hands caressed and pulled at her breasts and nipples wringing a muffled cry from her dry lips. Her hands flew back to tangle in his hair. His vibrating body glowed dimly in the dark room. He pulled her closer to the heat that he generated and she relished the feel of his hardened manhood against her back and his aura of heat surrounding her.

"If I had a mirror above this bed, Kendall, I would place it in front of us so that you could see how beautiful you are to me." His whispered words brought tears to her eyes.

"No." she whispered in reply looking over her shoulder at him. "How beautiful we are together."

Then she muffled a cry against his neck, for he chose that moment to slowly press the tip of his swollen cock inside of her. He gripped her hips to hold her in place as he slowly began to part her throbbing heat. She arched her body closer to him and felt she felt herself absorb more of his largeness into her very being.

"I love you," she whimpered as he began to move.

"I want to make this last forever," he responded, but knew that it would not, for she began to thrash and shake beneath his controlling hands. Quickly he pushed her down until her hands braced her body, in an effort to still her wild movements.

Needing to feel more of him, she lowered her upper body until her hardened nipples grazed the covers on the bed and her hips were lifted higher. This allowed him to slide deeper inside of her, deeper than he had ever been before.

"Oh yes, My Kendall!" he moaned at the tight wet feel of her fully caressing his length.

For a moment Flame gave into his primitive animal instincts and began to pummel her depths, with Kendall urging him on with little gasps and whimpers of pleasure.

When the bed began to protest such wild movements, he pulled away from her, despite her protests, to change their position. He came down on top her, holding his great weight off of her with strong yet trembling arms.

"I want to see your eyes when you breach the gates of paradise," he whispered as he slowly slid inside of her and began a vigorous swirling circling motion with his hips.

"Flame!" Kendall cried as her legs clamped around his waist. "Yes, oh damn it! Yes!"

They both groaned together at the feel of her enthusiastic welcome, while bolts of electricity danced across their moist skin, transferring joy and excitement back and forth between the two of them.

"Kendall," Flame spoke with his ragged desire-roughened voice, "I'm going to explode inside of you now."

His heated words were enough to tip her over the edge and into orgasmic bliss. Her reactions combined with the feel of her clenching inner muscles were too much for him to bear.

"Kendall!" he cried as he felt his hot release shoot from his body in throbbing bursts.

Together they reached a peak of unparalleled pleasure and together they slid to the other side of paradise, muffling shouts of joy against each other's love-dampened mouths.

Flame eased to his side, lifting his weight off of a grinning Kendall, and gently brushed the strands of his hair off of her face and body. She shuddered at the feel of that warm silk caressing her over-sensitized flesh and curled into her Flame.

Flame pulled her warm body, limp with pleasure, closer to his sated one and began to stroke and caresses her back. He was her willing slave and protector. He would protect her from all, even from his own self if necessary.

Kendall sighed in contentment and lay her hand on Flame's still heaving chest. Power was indeed a heady, intoxicating thing. Flame's lovemaking was fantastic and fiery, but that was only one aspect of their relationship. Here was her true soulmate. Whatever she lacked, he more than made up for, and the same could be said of him. They balanced out each other. She felt the peace that came from their physical and mental joining, and it fed her hungry soul. How she loved this man!

If tomorrow went as smoothly as today, tomorrow would be one of the best days of her life.

Chapter Fourteen

ಬಿ

It was an exercise in hell. Only the devil himself could have orchestrated the events of the next few days. There she was, snuggled safe and warm in the arms of the sexiest man she had ever known, when she felt something hard and cold press against the back of her head.

Waving a weary arm to brush the annoyance away, she pushed against it only to slam into something considerably bigger than the fly or the gnat she was dreaming about.

With a wince of pain, she cracked one eye open to see what the annoyance was. Looking up, she saw a trio of grim-faced women standing in her bedroom, one with a very serious looking weapon in her hands.

"So, my sibling has found a very cozy nest to land in," sneered the woman who appeared to be in charge.

She was tall, much taller than Kendall's five-feet-nine inches, and carried an unmistakable likeness to the man sleeping beside her. Even her accent, a combination of a Russian lilt, melodious French, with the slow delivery of Italian, was the same.

"You're the sister," Kendall managed, both eyes popping open in surprise.

"Sibling. The only sisters that I lay claim to are the women of Testrios."

Tossing long raven-black hair behind her, the stern-voiced leader lowered her weapon and eyed Kendall with Flame's piercing gray eyes. Kendall suddenly felt like a new species of bug under a microscope.

The woman's commanding voice caused Flame to awaken and sit straight up beside Kendall in the crumpled bed sheets. Tossing a steely-eyed look of shocked anger at the women in the room, he eased Kendall slightly behind his naked back before speaking to the woman who was his sibling.

"Mistress Teeta." He nodded his head slightly to her, causing his unbound hair to slide over his bare shoulders and chest.

The other two women murmured in approval of the broad expanse of muscle that contrasted sharply with his auburn waist-length hair.

"At least you have not forgotten all of your training, Flame," his sibling quipped as she turned to view the ultra-feminine room and all of its luxurious trappings. "I expect that you have hidden the bratlings around here somewhere."

Incensed, Kendall narrowed her brown eyes at the heartless woman who looked so much like her lover. "They are your niece and nephew," she groused, pushing aside Flame's protective gesture and proudly facing the women again.

Although she had never been more frightened in her life, Kendall refused to let this…this…woman intimidate her. So in true Kendall fashion, she took decisive action and stood her ground. These female creatures would not cow her.

"It speaks," Teeta murmured as the two women in the background laughed openly at Kendall's brave stand. Turning, she again narrowed her eyes at Kendall, as if she were solely responsible for her having to track her brother to this backwater planet.

"How did you find our exact location, Teeta? I thought you would be waiting in the forest where I programmed the coordinates to lead you."

Desperate to draw attention away from Kendall, Flame insolently spoke to Teeta, drawing her ire once more towards him. Teeta's wrath was something that he did not wish his gentle Mistress to have to endure. There was no telling what she would do to what she considered an inferior alien.

For a moment Teeta's eyes flared with a violent anger. In two steps she reached Flame's side. No one was prepared for the vicious backhand that she delivered to him, especially Kendall who now glared in mounting anger at the tall, dark hared-woman.

Flame's face turned with the force of Teeta's blow, sending his hair flying around his head to fall covering his face. For a moment, it waved with a life of its own, before settling down around his shoulders.

"Flame!" Kendall cried reaching for him, but he gently brushed her hands aside and slowly raised his face to meet his sister's gaze. Blood trickled down the corner of his mouth but he refused to wipe it away. Instead, he steadily watched his sibling with no expression showing on his face.

"Do not ever speak to me in such a disrespectful tone again, Flame. I will beat the arrogance out of you with great pleasure, if you try that again." Teeta was angered, but unlike her womb-mate, she let everyone read the displeasure on her face. She knew she was the one with the power here and there was no need for her to hide her emotions, especially from her troublesome sibling or his alien lover.

"I have taken worse blows, Mistress," he replied, both happy and relieved to have Teeta's attention solely on him once more. Teeta's greatest strength or weakness, depending on how one perceived it, was her unpredictability. She was capable of destroying Kendall right there with no provocation other than she saw his Mistress's words as an insult.

"Rise and face me, Flame," she demanded stepping back from the bed. At her command, the two giggling women behind her quieted, eagerly looking forward in anticipation of a peep show.

Flame, as usual, did not disappoint.

Even though he blushed almost as red as his hair, he stood and tossed the blankets that covered him to the bed, exposing his perfect body to the hungry gaze of the women in the room. The two women went very still, and then one was heard to whisper to the other, "Catla did not sample this one? I knew that she was strange, but to pass on a specimen such as this?"

"That is enough!" It was time for Kendall to take swift decisive action. Tossing aside her blankets, she rose proudly and strode in all of her naked glory to the foot of the bed. She quickly pulled fresh clothing from Flame's bag and handed him the first pair of pants that she grabbed, the leather-like ones that he brought with him from Testrios.

She knew how much his compliance with his sister's orders cost him after his new-found freedom. She was sure that these women were trying to strip him of the one thing that made up the essential Flame: his quiet dignity.

"Get dressed," she spoke gently to him before turning in all her bare skin to confront these intruders in her house and her new life. In her best no-nonsense voice reserved for know-it-all doctors and fainting husbands in the delivery rooms, she commanded, "Leave this room immediately."

When no one moved she drew herself up to her full height and bellowed, "Am I not Mistress and leader of this house? Have your mothers taught you no manners? Leave this room at once!" It seemed a little authoritative action was in order.

After a moment of thought, Teeta nodded and motioned to her women to leave the room. "We shall await you in your great room, Mistress."

"I'll be damned," Kendall breathed in amazement. "It worked." She watched as the trio of women turned on their heels with the precision a drill team and exited the room in single file, Teeta in the lead.

Turning to a Flame who had just finished tightening the zip cords on his pants and was pulling on a shirt retrieved from his bag, she cried, "You have to get out of here now. Take the children and run! They won't listen to reason. Where are the children?"

Kendall had hoped that Teeta would not notice their absence and began to search through the house looking for them. She knew that Flame had not anticipated the squad's early arrival and that he had no time to hide their precious children.

A fully-clothed Flame walked over to the bathroom door with Kendall dogging his every step, and cracked it open a bit. Inside the two babies slept in their cubes undisturbed by the ruckus in the next room.

When Flame had attended their late night feeding, he must have moved them to the bathroom just in case something like this happened.

"I will not leave you, Kendall." He looked deep into her eyes and she knew from the determination shining there that he would end this situation today, no matter what the cost.

He clasped her shoulders and pulled her to him in a brief embrace. "I will stand and fight for you, My Kendall, for our new life together. If I seek to escape, they will hold you responsible and destroy you before seeking the children and myself. I will not risk losing you or my children to them. You are all dear to my heart and as essential to my well-being as the blood that runs in my veins."

"Flame," Kendall cried, the force of her feelings overwhelming her. She grasped handfuls of his luxurious hair in her fists as if she wanted to memorize the texture of the thing that made him so sought after to begin with.

"I will find a way to make all of you safe," he murmured as he gently rocked her in the warm cradle of his arms. His racing heart beat in time with hers as they sought comfort in each other.

"We, Flame. I won't let you go through this alone." Pulling herself together with some effort, she gathered her raw emotions and raced to dress. "I will hurry and make myself presentable, Keeper. It's not polite to keep our guests waiting."

"Will you do one thing for me, My Mistress?" Flame turned her to face him and handed her a pair of scissors. "Will you cut the lock of hair from my head?"

Kendall fought back the tears that welled up in her eyes as she motioned him to sit at the bottom of the bed. She pulled his head forward to rest against her stomach and gently, wit the lightest of touches, pulled the whole mass of his hair forward. She bit back a sob as she selected one long lock from his nape. With a prayer that his plan worked, she snipped through it.

Flame gasped as if in pain and clutched her tightly for a moment as if the shock of losing that little piece of himself was too much for him to bear.

Kendall felt as if she held an uncontrollable blaze in her hand as the lock of red hair writhed within her grasp then lay still.

Flame tossed back his hair and pulled her face down to his for several small kisses. "Thank you," he whispered with each kiss.

She hoped that that one small bit of Flame's energy was enough to satisfy his power-hungry witch of a sister waiting in her living room. Again she closed her eyes and uttered a small prayer to make his plan successful. But above all else, she prayed for his safety.

* * * * *

"Why can we not enjoy the man before we kill him, Teeta?" one of the whining women, Grilla, demanded. She was one of many devoted House of Ice followers trying to make a good impression on the future leader of their great house.

"It makes no difference that he is no longer pure. I want to see how he performs. After all, he received early training from Alonzid and every one knows that the men he teaches are among the most skilled in the bed sports."

"May I remind you two that that is my sibling you are lusting after."

Grilla had the audacity to look a little shamefaced.

"Need I also remind you that we have a mission to complete with all due haste?"

Killing her sibling was her set mission, eliminating him and his offspring. She had never really liked him much, but seeing what he had gone through at Catla's hands had somehow made her a little more sympathetic toward his death.

She sighed heavily and leaned against a window that faced the flowerbeds that graced the front of this small house. This place reminded her of the history pictures that she had been forced to study as a child, pictures of Testrios before the war that had separated the planet and created the five continents. Now her duty was to take her awkward sibling out into all that lush greenery, brightly colored flowers and tall trees and splatter his molecules along the landscape. She hated history.

She turned as the short female that Flame was fornicating with descended the staircase and entered the room. Instantly, she motioned for the two women to re-enter the upstairs bedroom and prevent her sibling from joining in on their conversation. Turning to face the woman, the mistress of this house, she wondered what to expect and how to treat one such as she. She decided to give her a little respect. After all, she might be from a backwards culture, but she was a woman.

"So you are the sister?" Kendall noted that the two women prevented Flame from leaving the upstairs bedroom, but said nothing about it. They would not harm him unless they had direct orders from this woman standing there smugly before her.

She compared Teeta's shiny black jumpsuit made of that leather material that Flame's pants were made of, and tried not to feel underdressed in her jeans and long -sleeved flannel shirt.

"Sibling," Teeta automatically corrected this woman yet again. She reminded herself that she must have patience when dealing with these Earth creatures. After all, they were not considered very bright.

"And your mission is to kill your...sibling." That was said with enough venom to raise one of Teeta's black brows.

"Speak not of what you think that you know, Mistress."

"I know that that man has been through tortures rarely seen in any nightmare." She took an aggressive step forward. "I know that that man was a victim until he escaped that slave pit that you call a home. I know for a fact he could have incinerated you and your cronies in a blink of an eye, yet he chose not to."

"Think you I care?" came the bored reply.

Kendall paced the room in extreme agitation. How could she reach this woman? She seemed set on autopilot and her destination was the destruction of her own brother.

"Are you jealous?" Kendall queried with a sly look in her eyes.

"Zealous?" she questioned, purposely mishearing Kendall.

"No. Filled with destructive envy. Filled with an unholy desire to punish your...sibling," the word was sneered, "for a quirk of nature and fate that he held no control over."

Teeta's eyes narrowed into dangerous slits as she viewed this Earth woman. It seemed that she had underestimated the intelligence of this opponent.

"It seems that my sibling has gained a worthy protector in this provincial planet. How...amusing."

"It makes no difference what you call it, Teeta, or how amused you are. It's still cold-blooded murder."

Teeta turned away from that piercing brown gaze to again stare out at the colorful array of flowers. Leave it to Flame to find a champion for his cause.

"I am bound by my duty," she finally replied, staring out of the window, focusing on nothing. "If it were up to me, I would forget that he was ever born."

"Are you so useless?" Kendall demanded as she walked over to the dark-hared woman. "Have you no skills other than being Tessla's daughter, future ruler of the House of Fire? Have you no other position other than being the one that nature cheated? Was it your dark hair that led you to believe that you were not woman enough to inherit your rightful place as the next ruler?"

"You know not of what you speak!" Enraged, Teeta turned to face her tormentor. "You will never know the shame of not being enough, not being the best, of feeling less than an unimportant male! My useless sibling, damn him, should never have been given my gifts, my heritage!"

"Then take a piece of it and go home!" Kendall held out the quivering lock of hair. "Tell everyone that Flame is dead. Your mother will stop seeking him out if that is what you tell her. Bribe your soldiers or swear them to secrecy. If you have any love for Flame, please do him this favor." Kendall's impassioned plea brought tears to her own eyes for she knew that the future of her small family lay within the hands of this woman.

Teeta eyed the lock of hair and them began to laugh. Gesturing wildly she continued, "Do you think that I hold any love in my heart for that abomination? I never loved him! I never cared what happened to him. I was glad when he was

211

sent to the Brotherhood, but it was not enough! It was I who drew Catla's attention to him! I wanted him gone!"

"Have you no guilt or shame?" Kendall hissed. All hopes that she had of trying to understand this woman's pain evaporated into thin air. "Do you know what that monster put him through?"

"Oh, I have guilt, Mistress. I was there. I remember seeing what my anger had done to him. I guess that the old sayings are true. You can feel your womb-mate's pain. I felt his pain, Mistress. So I fixed it so that he would be in pain no longer."

Kendall's mouth dropped open as she realized what Teeta was telling her. "You killed her? You killed Catla?"

"As you can see, I am no stranger to murder. No matter how I feel about my sibling, he is of the House of Fire. I could not let her shame a member of my house."

Kendall stood there, stunned by what Teeta had revealed. Was this woman insane?

"I had it all planned out: With that simpering fool Catla dead, I could run the House of Ice in any way that I saw fit, in my mother's name of course. Then when my mother's life was extinguished, I would rule it all, both of the greatest houses on our planet. So yes, I gladly dropped the poison in Catla's cup. I was doing Flame a favor really. He was on his deathbed and could not be blamed, so it was the perfect plan. Perfect until he became pregnant and destroyed everything that I had worked so hard to build."

Teeta turned towards the window again,

"The pregnancy was not his fault." Kendall felt compelled to add. "That was Catla's doing."

"True, that sin belongs to Catla."

"Then why kill your sibling and his offspring? Ember and Spark can be raised here on Earth and will have no interest in your quest for power."

"Is that what he named the girl child? Ember? That was to have been my name if I had been born with the energies. The

Family always chooses an appropriate name in hopes that their generation would be blessed with a child with the energies." Then she added, "The children are no longer an issue. That was said to make him run. Flame has a habit of destroying all of my best-laid plans. Did you know that the Matriarch was considering letting Flame have a say in his daughter's upbringing? I guess that is information you would not know. Not even Flame had any idea that my mother supported the idea that he should have influence over the girl-child. If I allowed that to happen she would never be my little adoring puppet. She would never be just a figurehead if Flame were to teach her to question everything about our way of life, as he does. So you see, Mistress, The House of Fire does not want Flame dead. I do."

Chapter Fifteen

સ

"Flame!"

Kendall turned and dashed up the stairs, two at a time, to the bedroom, beating Teeta there by seconds. Slamming open the door, she found him sagging between the two women of the Execution Squad, one woman pulling a small dart out of his chest. The reason was abundantly clear. A wall of flame was slowly dissipating from in front of the bathroom door. Flame was protecting his children without harming the two women. He still felt bound by the laws of his of his society.

"Teeta killed Catla!" she screamed before she was tackled from behind.

"Heed not this woman!" Teeta screamed, before a solid right hook caught her in the jaw.

Rolling around on the floor, the two combatants took no notice that the two women had eased Flame to the ground and were now staring at each other in confusion.

"Only Teeta wants him dead!" Kendall screamed before Teeta slammed her to the ground.

Teeta was bigger, but Kendall had had one week of ups and downs that lead up to this hell. She had a shitload of frustrations and anger to draw from, and she had a target for an outlet.

With a scream that would serve the ancient warriors well, Kendall broke the woman's grip and turned to face her. Target spotted and locked in!

Kendall slammed both of her palms down on Teeta's ears causing her to shriek with pain and grab at her head. Rising to her feet, she delivered a kick to her jaw and watched as she collapsed to the floor. Thank goodness for Tai Bo!

Turning to the stunned women who watched their fallen leader in confusion, she declared, "He is to be set free immediately. The Matriarch did not decree that he was to be put to death."

Haughty as a princess in her ripped T-shirt and jeans, she walked over to Flame, and dropped to her knees in front of him.

"You are free," she declared as she brushed his hair back from his face sweaty brow.

He lifted his head, a look of wonder in his drug-hazed eyes before they widened and he opened his mouth to shout.

A sharp pain exploded in the back of her head and everything went black.

The sound of an engine brought her back to consciousness. She tried to sit up but gave a low moan of pain instead.

"Flame?" she forced the words past her dry lips.

"Shh, My Mistress, I am here," came his reply before a soft touch caressed her face.

"Where is here?" she again tried to sit up but a flash of pain in her skull convinced her that maybe she should stay right where she was.

"In the back of your ground transport. The children are here and we are safe for now."

"Who is driving?" she asked wondering if they were going to die by at the hands of the Execution Squad, or because of a fatal wreck.

"Teeta," was his curt response as if he was more aggrieved by a woman driver than by being captured and drugged by a death squad.

"Teeta can drive an Earth vehicle?" Kendall was a little awed by the woman's...tenacity.

"She has read the owner's manual," he replied in a droll voice that was so unlike her Flame.

"How did they find us?" she asked. She knew that the coordinates he gave them would have led them far away from the house.

"They used a sophisticated tracking device that is attracted to heat," he explained.

"You mean infrared?" she asked and tried not to laugh at his disgruntled look. Despite the fact that Flame obviously respected her intelligence, he was still a bit of an intellectual snob.

"We have some great leaps in technology since the wheel," she couldn't help but add.

"Yes. With all of the heat that we were generating, we made an easy target to find." He watched as a blush added color to her pale cheeks.

"Yeah," she added at last, her blush under control. "I think we set the mattress on fire." She smiled at the color that highlighted his cheeks.

"What were you saying before Teeta hit you on the head and rendered you unconscious? They will tell me nothing." He motioned to the two women who eyed their tête-à-tête with suspicious eyes that watched every move they made lest they try to escape.

She could hear confusion in his voice and knew that the drug that he had been given was wearing off.

"Your family, your mother, doesn't want you dead," she whispered. "Teeta does. With you out of the way, she can rule through Ember and have control over both houses when your mother dies. She even killed Catla so she could rule when you were sent back home to the House of Fire. With no clear heir, your mother would have allowed her governance over the House of Ice. I think that Catla knew of your sister's plans and that would explain why she had you impregnated so soon after your mating and why she would risk drawing the anger of your mother's house. She was desperate to keep women of her bloodline in power. These poor fools following your sister don't know it, but she will probably kill them too. No one can know what she has done here if she wishes to rule unchallenged. Any witnesses will be too much of a risk to her plans."

"Silence back there, or I will silence you myself," came the surly voice of the other woman beside Grilla.

"Sure," Kendall taunted. "I want to be alive to see the punishment you get for killing the father of the future leader of the House of Ice. That is, if you live long enough to see your home world again." The last was said almost at a shout.

There was absolute silence in the van. Both women looked at each other as if something had become quite clear. Grilla nodded to her companion and began to eye their fearless leader with a look filled with awareness and quite a bit of cunning.

"You will not have to worry about being a witness to any event." Teeta's voice sounded smug and sure. "As soon as we get to the area where I have chosen to leave our ship, you, that man, and those accursed children will all die. Laser burns will be easy to disguise in the charred wreckage of this vehicle after I push it off of a precipice. You will all be victims of a tragic accident."

"What proof do you offer as to the death of the future ruler of the House of Ice, Mistress Teeta?" Flame now taunted after seeing the reactions of his sibling's minions. "With no bodies to take back for burial, how will you prove that we are dead? With witnesses that may or may not be alive to testify?"

"Shut him up!" Teeta screeched at Grilla who now wore a thoughtful expression on her face.

Before he could plant more seeds of doubt, the van pulled to a stop.

"Why not kill us at the house, Mistress Teeta? Or do you plan on killing your accomplices while they are occupied with causing our deaths? Maybe it will be a large group of people who die in this vehicle this day. I think that they will be easy enough to overpower while they carry out your orders for the death of my Mistress, the children and I."

Flame had caught on to Kendall's earlier attempt to sow the seeds of distrust among the small group. It was a sound plan his Heart had come up with, an excellent strategy. His Kendall was a warrior in her own right.

"More impertinence, Flame? You may close your mouth, sibling. I will rule the House of Ice as my own no matter what you say. You are the powerless one here." Then to the women, "Bring those two, but leave the children behind. We can deal with them later after we give their loving father exactly what he deserves."

The side doors were slammed open and Kendall was dragged from the van as Grilla's unnamed companion grasped her arm in a punishing grip and yanked her from the car. Kendall bit back a moan as pain and nausea vied for dominance of her body. By taking several deep breaths, she was able to fight down both reactions and steady herself outside the van. Her escort gave her a moment to reorient herself before forcing her to step away from the vehicle.

Grilla hurried Flame's exit along by prodding him in the back with the tip of her weapon. Flame only had a chance to longingly eye his children before he was pushed out of the van and onto the grassy knoll that Teeta had selected for the site of their sudden demise.

Once everyone had been herded from the van, Teeta ordered the women to draw their weapons as she drew hers and caught her sibling within her sights.

"Your proof is in your lock of hair, Flame. I will tell Mother that you were running from us with this Earth creature." She looked derisively at Kendall. "And that you had a little accident. They can easily come back here and substantiate my claims. Everyone knows that a Keeper must be dead before anyone could remove a lock of hair. After all, it is a major source of your energies."

She held up his hair, which still throbbed with his life force and smiled. "I grow tired of this shameful business. Let us put it to an end."

She motioned to her accomplices to raise their weapons as she raised hers. All three of the women's weapons were now trained on the unarmed victims.

Immediately Flame took a protective position in front of Kendall. His head raced with the thoughts of what he might have to do.

"Leave her out of this, my sibling. I am the one that you want dead. Leave her to raise my children here on Earth. No one need ever know that they survived."

Behind him, Kendall's heart was being painfully ripped right out of her chest. He loved them enough to sacrifice pride and his very life for them. Never before had she heard him beg for anything and now he was pleading with the one person who had no reason to hate him.

"Please, My Womb-mate!"

At his impassioned words, Teeta's arm began to shake, and slowly the barrel of the weapon began to lower.

Tears welled up in her eyes as Teeta again felt the anguish of her twin. Damning the bond formed between the twins while they shared the same womb, Teeta strengthened her resolve and focused on her goals.

"I will rule!" she cried out just before a silent blue light hit her in the chest lifting her off of her feet and throwing her several yards back.

"I think that you have also just suffered from a little accident, my dear Teeta." Grilla slowly trained her weapon on Flame and away from the woman lying in a crumpled heap on the ground.

"You and your Earth woman made a valid point, Flame. Teeta never showed us our orders, and if she indeed killed

Catla, the Matriarch could hold us all responsible. Catla was no fool. She knew Teeta was going to make an attempt on her life, so she had Flame impregnated in the event that she actually succeeded. She would have done the same thing if she were placed in Catla's position." This was said as she gestured to the still- smoking body of her fallen leader.

"Still, you must die, Flame. One day, for your daughter's sake, you might decide to take a trip back to our homeworld and expose us to gain your child's power and place within the House of Ice. We cannot allow that to happen, Flame, for you see, we will be the heroines of the House of Ice. We will return your daughter to her grateful family after we tell them that we had to kill the power-hungry Teeta. We will tell them that she managed to kill Catla as well as all of you before we could stop her, that her mind had been warped and corrupted with the need for power. I wish that we could help you, but we have our own positions to think of, Flame. I'm sure you will understand."

She nodded to the other woman to keep her sights on Flame. "And I will enjoy watching your pain as I kill the earthwoman first. She is an annoyance and needs to be dealt with as soon as possible."

She pointed the weapon at a startled Kendall whose headache and nausea grew to dizzying proportions. She knew that she was staring death in the face, so to speak, and that she would never see her Flame or her precious babies again. She closed her eyes and braced herself for her trip to the afterlife.

"No!" Flame felt all the ties to the laws that bound him to such women evaporate as the power in him begged to be set free.

His primitive need to protect drowned out all training that had been bred into him since childhood. The energies rose steadily throughout his body as his eyes glowed from within with the unholy light of power that demanded release. His flame red hair stood out on end as a violent trembling shook the ground. The air around them became still in anticipation, as the Keeper of the Flame unleashed his awesome deadly power.

Kendall looked to Flame at the sound of his loud objection, and felt her world tilt on its axis. The gentle soft-spoken man she knew was no more, replaced by the human fire torch that stood protectively in front of her. She could feel his power, so familiar to her after all the passionate love making that they shared, vibrate throughout his body in full force. She could feel a dry heat, almost comforting in its warmth and terrifying in its intensity, seep into her pores and envelop her trembling body. What had these foolish women unleashed?

A small dome of white light circled Flame. Kendall, who had fallen to her knees, stared in amazement at the sight of Flame in all his glory. Her startled eyes could not adjust to the brilliant white that surrounded them. She covered her face with her hands just as Grilla began firing her weapon.

Screaming, Grilla shot wildly at the freighting apparition that seemed to grow right before her very eyes. The beams from her weapon struck, without causing visible damage. In fact, it looked as though the swirling light absorbed the energy of the blast. She was now facing the wrath of a true Keeper.

Raising both hands palms outward, a white-hot blast of fire exploded from Flame's hands. It sought out then surrounded its target. It enveloped Grilla, illuminating her skeleton and causing her to rear up onto her toes as destructive energy flowed through her body. Her eyes widened until they looked as if they would pop from her head and her mouth opened convulsively. The powerful blast of energy disintegrated Grilla to ash before her panicked scream could escape her throat.

Next he turned his sights on her accomplice, who begun firing just as wildly at the now energized shield that Flame had created just as Grilla had.

Seeing that she had garnered his attention, the other woman took two steps back before turning to run towards the van. The children would make the perfect hostages for dealing with what appeared to be a very powerful madman. She took two running steps towards the minivan, before she too was hit with an identical beam. The force of the blow lifted her at least three feet into the air and exploded her into ash. Then even the ash disintegrated under the powerful force of the concentrated beam of fire.

Raising both hands above him, Flame released a primal scream as he forced the power back under his control. Both of his hands, hands that had just unleashed the power of fire in death, slammed through and fisted in his unbound hair, as if it to settle down as his energy slowly began to abate.

Slowly it receded and the moving barrier that protected them shrank and divided becoming invisible. Flashes of orange, blue, and white flame circled around his arms and legs, hungrily as if waiting for a chance to break free from their controlling master. The ground around them lay dark and scorched as his hair settled down around him like a red silken cloak. He once again mastered his power and called the energies home to rest within him. Slowly the flames seemed to sink into his body as he lowered his arms by degrees and turned to face Kendall.

She had always had an idea of just what Flame was capable of but never had she thought to see the devastating full force of his power set free. Dazed, she could only look up at Flame as he turned to face her. While her first instinct was to run, the tears streaming down his grief-stricken face reminded her that this awesome being was essentially just a man.

He was a man who had just broken all the rules that he had lived by for so long, that they had become a cloak of honor to him. Here was a man who had gone against everything he believed in, everything that he had been taught was right, in order to save his family.

"Flame?"

Without a hint of uncertainty, she raised her arms to him and he immediately pulled her to her feet and engulfed her in a crushing embrace. She felt the tormented shudders that racked his body and sought to offer a little comfort to his spirit. He had killed today, and for a peaceful man like Flame, a man who would rather avoid danger instead of searching for it, this was a difficult thing to accept.

"I can never go home." His ragged voice rasped in her soft hair as he pulled her tighter. "Not even for Ember can I go back to Testrios, not after this. I have gone against my father's teachings and can no longer be considered one with the House of Fire."

Kendall had no words to express the deep regret that she felt. She also had to fight back a glimmer of selfish happiness. If he could never return home, then he would not leave her.

"This is your home, baby," Kendall softly murmured in Flame's ear. She'd always wanted a man that would fight for her, that would protect her at all costs, and she had finally found him.

She rained kisses, soft comforting kisses, across his face and finally his trembling mouth. She sipped each tear as if they were a precious elixir, and indeed they were. A man with a great conscience shed them, for acts he had committed to keep their small family safe and secure.

Teeta groaned from her prone position on the ground and decided that she was not dead. She was in too much pain to be in that blissfully solemn condition. Her personal body shielding had protected her from serious injury, but could not spare her the minor problems that cropped up when hit with a laser cannon. She probably had a few broken ribs, but she would survive.

She had never quite trusted her House of Ice cronies, and was now glad that she wore the protective armor beneath her uniform. She lain on the ground and watched her would-be assassins become smoldering Testrios ash piles with great amusement. Then she watched as her sibling embraced the argumentative woman of Earth.

Teeta had managed to hold onto her weapon when she was hit by the blast and now had Flame easily within her sights. She raised the gun, trembling deep within her shaky arms, but she could not bring herself to pull the trigger.

The body armor had saved her from fatal wounds, but it was her sibling who had, however unintentionally, saved her life. She plopped back to the ground with a small self-depreciating snicker.

After taking a moment to compose herself, Teeta rose painfully to her feet and brushed the bits of loose green earth grass from her legs and back. She tucked away a stray lock of hair behind her ear and then turned to make her way to the area where she had camouflaged her ship.

"Teeta!"

She turned as Flame called her name. "You address me so discourteously, Flame?" Her imperious tone rang out over the eerily silent field.

"What do you intend to do, My Sibling?"

"I would have killed them all, Flame. I would have killed Grilla and her accomplice and I would have brought your children back to Testrios. I would have ruled in Ember's name. It was never my intention to kill your offspring. After all, they are blood."

"By the time Ember had reached her adulthood, she would have gladly killed our own mother had I asked it of her. She would be completely under my power. Your son, Flame, he would have been raised as a proper Testrios male and then mated off to another Great House to bring me more power. I was going to present him to the House of Water and then, my dear sibling, I would have had more power than any other woman alive. The future of Testrios would be shaped in my glorious image! Nothing and no one could have stood in my way. I would have been a goddess."

She tossed her black hair behind her as prideful as a cat, then turned to Kendall.

"I would have taken great pleasure in your demise, woman of Earth. You have brought me nothing but trouble."

"The feeling is mutual, woman of Testrios," Kendall replied standing tall beside her only true love.

She had felt his shoulders tighten with tension at Teeta's cutting words and knew even though the woman had caused great pain to him, Flame was more hurt by her plans for her imagined future with his children. She was no better than a modern day slaver, although it seemed that these practices were quite common on Testrios.

"You are fortunate, my sibling," Teeta replied in all honesty, observing the look of love on Kendall's face. No one had ever looked at her like that in her whole life, and she doubted that anyone would now. Bah! Let others bask in the sickening sweet sentiment of love, she wanted the looks of awe and fear that power brought.

"Stay here with her, Flame. And remember, if you return, I will take great pleasure in killing you."

"And my children?" he asked. He would harm even his sibling if it meant keeping his children safe and away from that planet.

"They are dead."

At the flaring of his eyes and his aggressive stance, she laughed and added, "You were all dead when I found you. It seems that the grudge against the House of Ice runs deep and our unknown assailant had struck again, despite our sire's best efforts to prevent it. Mother knew who gave you your escape ship, Flame. It was she who told our sire of the Execution Squad and that they were after you.

"It seems I was a little too late in arriving here to protect all of you, losing both of my soldiers in the process. I will still present your lock of hair, Flame, as proof." Then almost as an afterthought, "You need retraining in respecting a Mistress as a proper Testrios male."

"But he is already a most proper man, Teeta. For me." Kendall bristled at the woman. No one made disparaging remarks about her man without expecting a big fight.

With an almost-respectful nod in Kendall's, direction, Teeta turned and limped away, disappearing into the trees. A moment later a low rumbling was heard, then a nearly invisible ship shot straight up, off into the sky.

"It's over." Relief tinted Flame's voice as he looked at his brave mistress beside him, but she had already turned her back to him and was racing for the van.

"I want my babies!" she cried as she leapt into the van to check on the infants waiting quietly inside. Slowly, Flame followed.

He paused to look over the field and vowed that he would try to put the past in the past where it belonged. He had saved his family and that was all that mattered, except for maybe Kendall's reaction to him now. Would she love him now that she had truly seen the effects of his strange energies, and seen the monster that he had become?

"Come on, Daddy!" she cried as he dragged his feet, slowing down his walk to the minivan.

"Mistress, I must speak with you." He spoke in a calm, low voice to show the seriousness of his thoughts.

"If you are worried about that little fire-throwing exhibition, don't be. I already know that you won't French fry me if you get angry. So stop worrying about it."

"But do I not frighten you?" he asked. "Do you trust enough in my love to protect you from even me?"

Flame's voice had risen with his uncertainty as he stood, arms akimbo, at the side door to the van.

Kendall looked up from where she was closely examining the now awake children. Both were alert and seemed none the worse for wear after their ordeal. It was their father who seemed to need reassurance.

"Flame, do you not know that you are truly the keeper of my heart?"

His eyes flashed red for a moment at her simple statement of love before he could get his emotions under control, then he began to smile that slow sexy smile.

"Don't you know that my home is wherever you choose to be? Don't you know that you will always have a home with me?" Her brown eyes flashed at him from under her dark lashes as she returned his smile with a lusty grin of her own.

She understood his uncertainty and with a few words knew how to alleviate all of his fears. Though she would probably have nightmares about the whole affair, she knew that she would always find strength and safety within Flame's loving arms.

Flame opened his arms wide and embraced the warm bundle of feminine flesh that was his Mistress, his love, his Kendall. He'd finally found a place where he belonged, where he was accepted, where he was safe. Wherever Kendall was was his home. Life with his Kendall would be a continuing learning experience. Look at all the changes that she had made in his life thus far. He now had a flower-strewn house, a potential business, safety for his children, driving, her crazy sister, daytime television, and triple chocolate cherry ecstasy ice cream! His life had changed so much and in such a short span of time.

And it was good!

Chapter Sixteen

§

The click of heels against the hard marble floor of the Great Hall caused a hushed silence to fill the crowded room. Large pillars of rare Tarcus stones graced the entrance of the long room while fountains of cool bubbling water separated each massive brown column.

Muscular male servants rushed through the throng of women who had arrived since word of Tessa's return had spread.

Dressed in loose ankle-length tunics and flowing pants of white, the golden-skinned, dark-haired men carried golden trays of cool refreshing drinks to the guests sitting at the long tables that flanked a large silk draped throne situated in the center of the room. Behind the throne sat a large golden brassier where a perpetual conflagration blazed at all times, proving the power of the ancestor who'd first lit the fire there as this house was created.

This was the most powerful house to ever exist and the woman who ruled it governed it with an iron fist.

Tessla sat on her throne dressed in her red and gold sarong-styled dress and watched her dark-haired daughter approach. With her long brown hair styled in an elaborate twist on top of her head, the golden- skinned woman looked beautiful and strong, a fit leader for a powerful house.

Behind Tessla, dressed in his elaborate red and white tunic and pants, she could feel the tension radiate from Alonzid as his large charcoal gray eyes took in the sight of the child he had carried within his body for twelve long months. Even though not an expression crossed his handsome face and there was no pressure from the hand that gently clasped hers, she knew that he agonized over the fate of his only son, Flame.

She glanced over her shoulder with her knowing golden eyes and examined her life-mate. Earlier this evening, he had once again proved why he was a master of the sensuous arts. She recalled the play of his long dark, silky hair against her naked body and had to fight to bring herself back to the present. She turned from the unusual and arousing sight of her Alonzid in his ceremonial clothes and brought herself back to the business at hand.

As Teeta reached the front of the room, all of the servants snapped to attention and as one, bowed low and respectfully to the daughter of the house. Several of the men, although remaining in their proper positions, looked around anxiously to see if the man, one of their ranks who was being honored, followed his sister. But Mistress Teeta stood alone.

"What news have you brought me, daughter?" Tessla's royal voice, deep and commanding, rang out clear true and commanding in the quieted hall. She felt tension further tighten in Alonzid and felt him strive for control.

"I bring sad news, My Mother," was her formal response.

"Tell us all of how you fared, My Daughter." Tessla's voice had tightened subtly and Alonzid, remembering his duty, put aside his own nagging questions and gently squeezed his life-mate's hand. Tessla did not like her wishes being thwarted by anyone, including her wayward son or her daughter and heir.

"I was sent too late to retrieve my womb mate, the man named Flame." Teeta managed to add the correct amount of remorse for this situation.

A shocked gasp filled the room at her words. Flame was gone? Impossible! He was this generation's Keeper of the Flame! There had to be some good explanation for this.

Alonzid felt the jolt of his daughter's words and the room began to spin. Only with the greatest of control was he able to withstand the urge to pounce on his daughter and demand answers from her to all of the questions that flooded his mind.

Tessla reclaimed command of the room by lifting up her left hand. Again all eyes were on the powerful ruler of the House of Fire.

"Tell me, My Daughter. Do we go to war with this primitive planet over the death of my son?"

Again there was an amazed silence. War with a whole planet over the demise of one male? Then again, some people concluded, the powerful ruler could not let this insult go unpunished. Flame was the son of not any Great House...he was Keeper to the House of Fire.

"No, My Mother. Flame was racing away from the assassins when they managed to destroy the land vehicle that he had acquired."

"How did..." Alonzid broke off his impassioned question and knelt on one knee to apologize to his life-mate.

His outburst bewildered many. Alonzid was the supreme example of Testrios manhood and it was unlike him, even in the face of this tragedy, to forget himself.

Tessla nodded her acceptance of Alonzid's apology. She felt proud that he had lasted this long before attempting to get his own questions answered. Foremost in his mind had to be a question about how the assassins found his much-loved son on the small blue planet.

"How was it that the assassins found your womb-mate, Teeta?" she asked as Alonzid resumed his proper position behind her. She knew that this is what her life-mate wanted to know and she would have his question answered. It was a small comfort to the man who had so loved his son that he placed his own life in jeopardy trying to protect him, and she would give him the answers he sought.

"I believe he was attempting to send us a plea for assistance, My Mother. You may check my flight computer to find the actual coordinates that he sent to me. I believe that the assassins intercepted his message and it led them straight to his position."

Alonzid studied his daughter. No one could read her body language better then he, and he sensed some inaccuracy in her story. Her features were ever so slightly tightened and she stood in a slightly defensive manner, as if she expected her words to be doubted. Still underneath that, was a small glimmer of…triumph?

Teeta tensed under her sire's scrutiny. The ever-astute Alonzid could easily ruin all of her plans with his suspicious and observant nature.

Ever since walking into this familiar hall she had been bombarded with feelings of inadequacy. She should feel proud that one day all of this greatness, all of this power would be hers, but instead she felt like a little girl, fighting for approval from her stern perfectionist mother. She felt her self-doubts spring to the surface and struggled not to let them escape her control.

Not this time! Throughout her life she had been besieged with stories of her unusual brother, and how his very existence would change the beliefs of her people and alter their way of life. No one spoke of her great accomplishments, of her skills in logic and strategy or about how she was undefeated and unsurpassed in warrior skills both ancient and new. All anyone could ever speak of was her useless and strange womb-mate.

But not today, for this day Teeta would have her glory. She would be triumphant as all of her careful planning came to fruition. She pulled out her final telling proof, filling the hall with stark quiet.

"Flame lingered for a few moments, My Mother. Long enough to sever this lock of hair from his own head."

With true showmanship, Teeta whipped out the writhing twining lock of auburn hair.

There was dead silence in the room. Tessla felt waves of grief ripple through her life-mate, even though his outward appearance remained calm. The only evidence of his great pain was a single tear, hastily wiped away, that escaped despite his iron will.

Teeta forced a sad look on her face even though inside she cackled with glee. She hung her head in feigned sadness as she continued her story.

"Flame had detected the assassin's ship, My Mother, almost as soon as we tracked him to his location, but we were too late to offer much assistance. I lost both members of my crew in the ensuing battle to drive them away from my sibling and the wreckage of his vehicle. With his dying breath, Flame pleaded with me to return his children home, to your protection, Mother, before he severed this lock of hair as proof of his death. I believe he wanted to return to the benevolent care and protection offered at the hands of your house, My Mother."

"And what of my son's children, Teeta. Where are they?" The children had been the main issue all along. They were of both the House of Fire and the House of Ice and possessed great power by virtue of their heritage alone.

"In accordance with your wishes, Mother, the female was named Ember and the male, Spark. Both were born with red hair and possessing the energies of a Keeper."

There was an amazed outcry at her announcement. Three generations who possessed the energies alive at the same time! What power the House of Fire possessed!

"So where are these little Keepers, Teeta?" Tessla wanted the issue of her wayward son here, where she could protect them until they were of a useful age. No one must have the power to use these children against her or her house.

"They sustained too much damage in the fight, My Mother, and expired shortly after their sire's life force escaped his body."

Teeta had to fight hard not to laugh at that point, knowing that both children could never be used to usurp her power. Let her mother and sire bemoan their loss. Teeta relished their absence and that of their precious Flame!

Alonzid studied his daughter's face. She was hiding something. Then it struck him. All of the inconsistencies in his daughter's tale, previously hidden by his guilt and anguish, came together to tell him something remarkable.

"Where are their bodies?" Tessla was aware of something happening with her life-mate, but dismissed his sudden tension as a reaction to his grief. She would deal with him later. Right now she wanted proof of the children's destruction so that she could lay her own doubts to rest.

This was the tricky part, Teeta thought as her quick mind came up with a way to explain the lack of the children's bodies.

"Their bodies are gone, destroyed as the assassins returned for another attack. Their hatred of the House of Ice runs deep Mother. I barely escaped with my life and the proof that Flame had perished. They wanted even this small piece of his energies as a trophy and only because of my body armor was my life spared so that I might return this to you, Mother." Teeta gestured to the singed whole blasted into her uniform by the deceitful Grilla and silently thanked the dead woman for her small treacherous deed. It seemed that she was good for something after all.

Everyone in the room gawked at the burnt hole, almost unnoticeable against the deep black of Teeta's uniform, but proof of a near fatal blast lay right before their eyes.

Teeta felt her heartrate speed up as her mother eyed her stained and damaged uniform. She knew that if she had stopped and had her injuries checked and took the time to wash before this meeting, her plan would have failed. As it was, she let a small sliver of true pain cross her face before quickly hiding it behind a mask of indifference. She was in great pain from the blast; she suspected broken ribs, but now used the pain to collaborate her story.

"Are you hurt, My Daughter?" Tessla was instantly concerned for her heir. If something should befall Teeta, there was no telling what would happen in the ensuing battle for control of her dynasty.

"I will live, Mother. I wanted to personally deliver this news to you and place Flame's final tribute to you in your hands."

As much as she would have loved to make it sound like Flame had died cowering like the lowest of desert worms, that would not be believed after the courage he displayed in dealing with Catla. While she had the pleasure of seeing her sibling dead in the eyes of their people, she did not have the satisfaction of seeing his reputation torn and lying in shreds beneath her feet. It was a bitter pill to swallow, but the taste of ultimate power would wipe out any sour taste from her mouth. Besides, there could be no blot on the honor of the House of Fire. After all, she would one day rule this house as well as the House of Ice.

She allowed her steps to falter a little as she walked closer to the great woman seated in front of her. In true ceremonial form, she dropped to her knees in front of her, dropped her chin to her chest in a display of proper grief and offered up the lock of hair in both of her opened palms.

"A final tribute to the male of your line who was born a true Keeper, My Mother." She fought to hold back giggles of delight as her mother slowly grasped the lock of auburn hair and bade her daughter to rise.

Teeta took the traditional place, at her mother's left, and ignored the looks Alonzid was giving her. Her sire would be harder to fool, and because he had her mother's ear, she had to be meticulous in the way that she presented herself. He would be watching her closely, searching for anything that she knew and did not tell of his precious son.

Tessla had no choice but to accept her daughter's word. With the proof she had been presented, she had no choice but to make the announcement of her son's death and the demise of his offspring.

Sharp as ever, Tessla noticed her daughter's reaction to the death of her womb-mate, but kept any worries she felt to herself. If there were something going on with her daughter, she would handle it her way and in her own time. As for now, her people needed reassurances that their position in life would not change, and that a leader for the House of Ice, now under her jurisdiction, would be named, least all out war develop in a quest for power.

"Hear me, My People." Tessla spoke as she stood, releasing her life-mate's hand and the room calmed once again. Their leader would know what to do.

"We have been delivered a punishing blow by the fates, the loss of The Keeper of the Flame and his children who also possessed his energies." There was sad murmuring and whispers, but Tessla calmed them by raising her hands in a "be still" motion.

"But the power of our Great House will not be affected by our loss. This is proof that my son lived," she held up the twisting lock of hair, "that my son fought, that my son died in an attempt to keep his house, the House of Fire, safe and protected. His death will not go in vain or unpunished. No one challenges the House of Fire and lives!"

The people began to nod in agreement with their leader. Flame had proven his bravery and courage by withstanding what Catla had done to him, his cunning by escaping the assassins originally, and his loyalty by contacting his sister to get his children and future heirs to safety. The House of Fire produced an excellent caliber of male and they would seek revenge for the unnecessary destruction on one of their own!

"My daughter," Tessla continued, "will now lead the House of Ice and a special taskforce to find these assassins and eliminate them will be formed by her! They carried their vendetta too far when they touched a member of my family in their quest to Destroy the House of Ice! Justice will be ours and death to all who oppose us!"

Her words were met with a roaring cheer. The women demanded recompense for the damage done to their Great House. No one who dared to dishonor the House of Fire and lived! The Matriarch would ban together to seek out and destroy the parties responsible. No one flaunted the peace bringing rules of the Matriarch and lived!

In the midst of their cheering, Tessla turned and motioned to her life-mate that it was time to leave. She had movements to plan and strategies to employ, but first she would see to Alonzid. All of this talk of the death of his son had to be painful for him and she would try to alleviate his sadness. Truthfully, although Tessla had cared for her son, she'd never really developed a bond for the strange male her egg had produced. She felt more for his missing daughter Ember, but understood Alonzid's pain. If her daughter had been senselessly murdered, she would burn with a need for revenge greater than the desire she felt for it now.

Death to the assassins.

The true assassin strove to control her laughter as she watched her mother exit the room. How quickly her plan came to fruition. She almost felt pity for those who would oppose her, for they could easily be marked as a part of the conspiracy to destroy the power of the House of Ice. Maybe she could do away with the Brotherhood too! They were the ones who had taught that simpering fool, Flame, to think independently from the rest of the male cattle.

Having so much power within her grasp was enough to stir desires within her body that she believed long dead. She pointed to an attractive brown-haired servant with a particularly massive chest carrying a cool pitcher of water and motioned him to stand before her.

"Attend me," she snapped and motioned him to follow her from the noise and excitement of the women in the room to her own private quarters.

"Power is an arousing thing," she spoke softly to the handsome male and he nodded his agreement.

Having served in this house his whole life, he had heard stories about Mistress Teeta and her depravities. He braced himself and followed the bewitchingly beautiful woman from the room. He knew he would have to use all of the skills he possessed to satisfy this one and it still might not be enough. He pitied the men of the House of Ice. When this ravenous monster with its deceptively beautiful face descended upon their ranks, all would be made to suffer. No matter how depraved Mistress Catla had been, she was no match for the extremely intelligent and twisted mind of Mistress Teeta.

* * * * *

In their private sleeping chamber, Tessla stripped off her dress to lie down unashamedly naked across the white silk of her bed. Tessla detested clothing of any kind against her golden skin and refused to wear garments in the comforts of her private chamber. She motioned to her life-mate to do the same.

Poor Alonzid. He had been struggling to hold back something ever since he saw that lock of red hair twisting in Teeta's hands. She now watched him pad barefoot across the white marbled floor to retrieve her clothes before he began to remove his own.

"Something troubles you, My Pet?" she asked as he pulled his tunic from his body to reveal his wide muscular chest, toasted the color of sand from exposure to the Fire continent's punishing sun.

Dark-haired Alonzid was originally of the House of Wind, chosen by Tessla's mother to ensure continued good relations between the two houses. Even though his straight hair stood out amongst the wavy-haired people of this continent, he was accepted as one of them and often emulated by the younger men of the house. His keen intelligence and the quick way he processed information made him a vital asset to Tessla. If she had missed anything during the audience with her daughter, Alonzid was sure to pick up on it.

"Yes, My Mistress." He spoke quietly as he approached her bed, still wearing his low slung ceremonial pants. The only thing that kept them from falling to his ankles was the small drawstring that fastened below his navel and held the light material around the small span of his hips.

Alonzid was blessed with the body of a god and the knowledge of how to use it to his advantage.

"Well, what is troubling you, My Pet?" Tessla asked as her fingers found and toyed with the knot that held the drawstring taunt.

Alonzid didn't appear to be affected by the crippling sorrow that had consumed him back in the great hall. In fact he seemed to be holding some great and pleasing secret. He was not the type of man to expunge his grief in the sex act, so for him to deliberately approach her in a way that was sure to enflame her senses meant that she had missed something important. Her life toy was celebrating something and she knew that it had to something to do with Flame.

His pants dropped to his ankles as a grin spread across his handsome face. "That lock of hair, My Mistress."

"What troubles you about my son's final tribute to his mother and leader? I found it most appropriate."

She grasped his hands and pulled him down beside her on the bed. She knew that he would tell her of his thoughts, but she could have a little fun while he found the words to express himself.

"It moves, My Mistress. It vibrates with his life's energy." He bit back a groan of pleasure as her delicate hands began to tickle over his stomach. A true leader, Tessla knew how to get directly to the point of any topic and her hands were now focusing in on what she desired from him.

"I can see that, My Pet," she replied as she peppered kisses down the thin trail of hair that lead to his throbbing manhood. "It moves with the energy of a Keeper even now, locked up in the vault to protect it from those who would attempt to destroy the final power of the Keeper."

"Yes, My Mistress," he gasped as her hot mouth closed over the tip of his hardness. His agile fingers quickly and gently undid the pins that held her great mass of brown hair in its elaborate style.

"But if my son's life force had left his body, would not all of the energies he possessed on this plane dissipate? My son is dead, yet his hair resonates with life."

That brought Tessla's head up in a flash. "What do you say, Alonzid? Is Flame alive?"

"Upon this, I can only speculate, My Mistress, though I believe there is a good chance that my son survives and is well."

Instantly the ramifications of that thought coursed through Tessla. If Flame was still alive, that meant her daughter had lied, or that he had somehow tricked her into believing him dead.

"This requires great thought, My Pet." Tessla lay back amongst the tangled sheets of her bed, all thought of slaking her lust gone. If her daughter and heir had lied to her this would mean that she was party to a deception that would give her great power and influence while manipulating her own mother to achieve it. If she had been fooled by her sibling, it would mean that she had missed some important details and was not quite ready for control of a great house.

"I shall have to watch and wait carefully, My Pet. If there is deceit and deception developing in my house, I will put a stop to it before it causes any damage. If my daughter is participating in it, she will be handled personally by me. No one must think that there is any division of power from within my house. That, My Dear, would cause a civil war that I do not wish to see. I cannot have my people fighting amongst themselves for scraps of power. That would surely take us back to the old days before the Matriarch gained power and we would lose all that we have gained. We must appear united to Testrios. I will not have my house lose face."

I will have my son and his offspring safe, Alonzid thought to himself as he began to massage the tension from his Mistress's forehead. "We will watch together, My Mistress."

Alonzid would protect those he cared for at any cost. His daughter Teeta would bear watching.

Epilogue

හ

The small family sat on the hillside in the late August sunshine sharing a blanket and a picnic basket filled with treats, specially prepared by their loving father. The tall auburn-hared man sat in front of a smaller version of himself. His son had a shocking shade of red-gold hair and a few solid silver streaks that ran down the side of his hairline. Those platinum locks blended with his fiery red hair that was contained in a neat tail near its ends with a small leather thong. The boy loved anything made out of leather, but required most of his leather things to be brown.

The solemn faced little boy looked up in concentration at his father as he nodded at what the big man had to say. The miniature replica of the man shot a telling glance at his sister and they both rolled their eyes as if what the man said was funny.

Beside them sat a little girl filled with uncommon beauty and hair the basic shade of her brother's. She turned to the woman who sat behind her and giggled at something the brown-haired woman, her mother, said. The girl's unusual hair was streaked liberally with silver strands that only added to her beauty, and tied back in a loose ponytail almost identical to her brother's, except for the curly ringlets that framed her face.

The brown-eyed mother shushed the girl as her brother's hands began to dance in the air. His red-gold hair stood up on end and swirled around his small body as his eyes flared brilliant red. After a moment of straining, a small rose appeared in the air before him.

The boy smiled as it glimmered and turned in the afternoon sun, in shades of red and gold. He turned his proud little face to his father and was met with a brilliant smile in return.

With a sly glance at his mother, the boy focused in again on the rose and watched as it began to melt and then expand. With a small flash of white light that showed shaky control of the energy, the boy closed his eyes, gritted his teeth and forced the energies back into his command. As he did, the melted rose began to glimmer and stretch. When he opened his eyes again, a small milky white MoonFlower shimmered before him.

He smiled at his mother's gasp of amazement and grinned up at his father, showing off his new control of the talent.

With a giggle, the little girl reached over and touched the bloom of fire and almost instantly, it crystallized into a solid crystal Moonflower. The little boy reached out and plucked it from mid-air as his sister's hair settled around her shoulders.

The father shook his head and looked up as if searching for strength, before he too broke out into a devastatingly sexy grin of his own.

The little boy presented the crystallized flower to his mother and giggled when she smothered his face with little kisses. His giggle was so enchanting that soon everyone on the blanket was laughing with him.

"What does that mean, Flame?" Kendall asked as she included her mischievously grinning daughter in the affectionate embraces and smooches.

"It means that I am in for a whole lot of training," he replied. He spoke as if he was resigned to do some task which he had no idea how to complete.

"I think that they may both carry the energies from the House of Ice as well as the House of Fire. Catla was Keeper of the Snow, My Kendall, and it seems that within the streaks in the children's hair may be her energies emerging combined with the energies of my family's line. We will have to wait and see what develops as they grow, My Kendall. I will have to do more research into the House of Ice. The computer disks are stored with the other Testrios items at the warehouse." Flame referred to the main building of his business, Flash and Flame Pyrotechnics.

The business was starting to become a rousing success as more people caught on to the colorful combination of fireworks and laser lights. Many wondered why the combination hadn't been tried before. But no one knew it was a little extra "magic" that helped create such wonderful displays of sound and light.

Kendall's face immediately creased into a deep frown at his words. Would her children ever be allowed to lead normal lives?

Flame pulled his wife...he liked that word, into his arms and kissed her until she stopped frowning and a sensual light lit her beautiful eyes. And she accused him of being a worrywart! Kendall had taken over the job as the uneasy one in the family and often had to be teased out of deep contemplative moods. So much for her take charge, act first and ask questions later attitude. It had all began soon after they were married.

Kendall had finally gotten her fine wedding with all of the trimmings. Of course her color scheme was red and white, and the wedding took place in her beloved garden where they had first met. Some didn't understand why the couple waited almost until sundown to speak their vows, but the smell of the MoonFlowers added a nice romantic touch to the ceremony.

The children, grinning adorably at the small crowd of well wishers in matching old-fashioned umbrella strollers, seemed almost smug as their parents spoke of undying love and loyalty. They were truly content and seemed to relish the moment as much as their mother and father.

Caressa, the bride's sister, sat and wailed her way throughout the whole ceremony, causing several men present to offer her handkerchiefs and consoling hugs. Her scowling husband said nothing as his beautiful and pregnant wife basked in all of the attention she was receiving. He still couldn't believe that she wanted to start a business of her own! He glared at the groom from his seat as if his wife's new independent streak was entirely Flame's fault.

The twins looked at their parents and then at each other and grinned as if they were privy to secrets that no one else knew.

"Flame?" her voice pulled him back to the present. "Will they come looking for my babies?"

"We are dead in their eyes, My Kendall." Flame softly reassured her as he looked over at his happy children. Ember was tugging a lock of Sparks bright hair and giggling at the faces that he made at her while trying to match his father's stoic dignity.

Spark tried hard to emulate his father's calm demeanor, but his own out-going personality always seemed to emerge no matter how hard the boy tried to stifle it. This amused Kendall to no end. Spark was too much of a free spirit to ever be as conservative as his father and Flame knew it.

Ember, on the other hand, was a little princess in personality as well as in lineage. She delivered imperial commands and expected them to be followed. She was not a cruel or selfish child, she just wanted things her way. She was also a constant source of amusement to Kendall, who often had to explain that just because someone else had an opinion that differed from hers, it was not necessarily wrong.

Ember was a fun-loving child who often brightened up a room with her mere presence. But like her father, she was highly observant and able to make quick decisions and stick to them. And on top of all that, she absolutely adored her brother and would follow him anywhere. Spark often felt the same way; he was her silent protector.

As Flame held his beautiful Mistress in his arms and observed his wonderful children, he decided that they were the true keepers. There was no greater energy in existence more powerful than the love he felt for them. Each one...Kendall, Ember, and Spark held a large piece of his heart. In truth, they were the keepers of his very soul.

Blazing heat of fire, came to the earth one night.
Chased from afar, it settled down with pain.
One man, one life, one unholy plight.
Would her life, ever again, be the same?

He begged for her help, to save his life.
Never knowing if she would turn away.
Her existence filled with despair, with strife.
Knowing somehow, he'd love her, he'd stay.

Though their time was short, their struggle much clearer,
They'd lead each other through the trying hours.
Reflecting, and reflected, two matched mirrors
Ecstasy combined, their merged bodies, unbridled powers.

Complete, whole, their love intertwined,
They are shackled, chained; yet freedom they find.

- Katherine Schlem

Why an electronic book?

We live in the Information Age—an exciting time in the history of human civilization, in which technology rules supreme and continues to progress in leaps and bounds every minute of every day. For a multitude of reasons, more and more avid literary fans are opting to purchase e-books instead of paper books. The question from those not yet initiated into the world of electronic reading is simply: *Why?*

1. *Price.* An electronic title at Ellora's Cave Publishing and Cerridwen Press runs anywhere from 40% to 75% less than the cover price of the exact same title in paperback format. Why? Basic mathematics and cost. It is less expensive to publish an e-book (no paper and printing, no warehousing and shipping) than it is to publish a paperback, so the savings are passed along to the consumer.

2. *Space.* Running out of room in your house for your books? That is one worry you will never have with electronic books. For a low one-time cost, you can purchase a handheld device specifically designed for e-reading. Many e-readers have large, convenient screens for viewing. Better yet, hundreds of titles can be stored within your new library—on a single microchip. There are a variety of e-readers from different manufacturers. You can also read e-books on your PC or laptop computer. (Please note that Ellora's Cave does not endorse any specific brands.

You can check our websites at www.ellorascave.com or www.cerridwenpress.com for information we make available to new consumers.)

3. *Mobility.* Because your new e-library consists of only a microchip within a small, easily transportable e-reader, your entire cache of books can be taken with you wherever you go.

4. ***Personal Viewing Preferences.*** Are the words you are currently reading too small? Too large? Too… ANNOYING? Paperback books cannot be modified according to personal preferences, but e-books can.

5. ***Instant Gratification.*** Is it the middle of the night and all the bookstores near you are closed? Are you tired of waiting days, sometimes weeks, for bookstores to ship the novels you bought? Ellora's Cave Publishing sells instantaneous downloads twenty-four hours a day, seven days a week, every day of the year. Our webstore is never closed. Our e-book delivery system is 100% automated, meaning your order is filled as soon as you pay for it.

Those are a few of the top reasons why electronic books are replacing paperbacks for many avid readers.

As always, Ellora's Cave and Cerridwen Press welcome your questions and comments. We invite you to email us at Comments@ellorascave.com or write to us directly at Ellora's Cave Publishing Inc., 1056 Home Avenue, Akron, OH 44310-3502.

COMING TO A BOOKSTORE NEAR YOU!

ELLORA'S CAVE

Bestselling Authors Tour

UPDATES AVAILABLE AT

WWW.ELLORASCAVE.COM

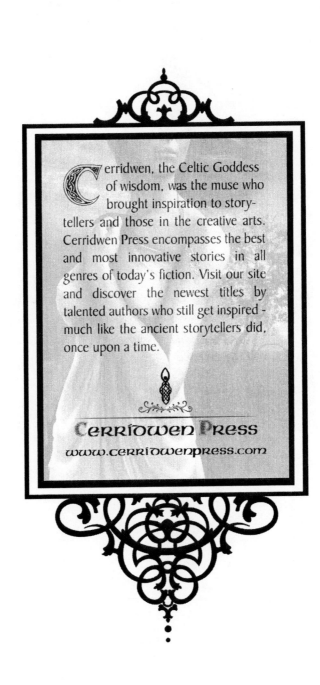

Cerridwen, the Celtic Goddess of wisdom, was the muse who brought inspiration to storytellers and those in the creative arts. Cerridwen Press encompasses the best and most innovative stories in all genres of today's fiction. Visit our site and discover the newest titles by talented authors who still get inspired - much like the ancient storytellers did, once upon a time.

Cerridwen Press

www.cerridwenpress.com

Discover for yourself why readers can't get enough
of the multiple award-winning publisher

Ellora's Cave.

Whether you prefer e-books or paperbacks,

be sure to visit EC on the web at
www.ellorascave.com

for an erotic reading experience that will leave you
breathless.